Floo

Phoeb

gasp ..., On stop, stop. It's too much . . . I shall die, I shall . . .'

Louisa smiled, smug that she had accomplished what she set out to do. Phoebe thrashed so hard she almost dislodged Louisa and she sank her teeth into Louisa's shoulder to muffle her cries, but Louisa held tight, determined not to lose the pressure of Phoebe's leg between her own.

'Oh God,' Phoebe murmured. 'What did you *do*?'

'Didn't you like it?'

'Oh yes. I loved it. But is that how? I thought . . . well . . . I thought it was something different.'

'Different?' asked Louisa, wanting to laugh. 'With a cock or something? I haven't got one, darling.'

'No, I know,' Phoebe said, her breathing still heavy. Her skin was hot and damp all over. 'I thought . . . I dreamed, it was different.'

'How?'

Phoebe disengaged herself and sat up in the bed. 'I'll show you,' she said, determinedly and she pushed Louisa onto the bed on her back. Louisa suddenly realised what it was the girl was doing and although she couldn't believe it she was not about to stop her when she felt the tickle of breath ruffling her pubic hair.

By the same author:

Mixed Signals
Make You a Man

Flood
Anna Clare

BLACK LACE

Black Lace books contain sexual fantasies.
In real life, always practise safe sex.

First published in 2007 by
Black Lace
Thames Wharf Studios
Rainville Road
London W6 9HA

www.black-lace-books.com

Typeset by SetSystems Ltd, Saffron Walden, Essex

Printed and bound by Mackays of Chatham PLC

ISBN 978 0 352 34094 8

1

The tides were deceptively predictable, or so Phoebe thought. For the whole of her life she had seen how the waters of the Thames rose and fell in time with the seasons and sometimes she thought they obeyed the rising of the moon like clockwork, like the hours kept reliably by the timepieces in her father's small upstairs drawing room.

Perhaps it wasn't the case, because while the clocks were reliable, the tides could be as anarchic as the time switch placed inside Phoebe's own female body. It took a heavy rain or a high wave to strike the estuary and the already damp edges of the city would become so water-logged that the poor came draggling from the borough of Lambeth clutching their possessions like the refugees of a biblical flood.

The waters rose and the clocks continued ticking out the seconds, chiming the quarters of the hour so loudly that Phoebe had come to dread the cacophony to the point where she longed secretly to take a mallet to her father's treasures and watch them spew guts of spring and cog all over the carpet. She didn't dare, of course. She was forbidden to touch them. Whether it was just his monomaniacal obsession with the things or because the business of maintaining a carefully calibrated piece of machinery was deemed too complex a job for the skittish mind and hands of a woman, her father wound each and every one himself. Sometimes her brother Philip was forced to observe, but Phoebe herself was not permitted to even clean them.

She hated them. They reflected her father's determination that order was at the soul of civilisation. From her perch in the attic window seat, Phoebe could see for herself that he was wrong. On this unusually clear night after the rain had washed all the filth from the air and brought it down on the heads of Londoners, she could see how high the waters had risen. If a simple thing like a river could burst its banks and throw London – the heart of the Empire and the most civilised city in the world – into chaos, then her father was plainly mistaken.

Phoebe had the attic bedroom in keeping with her status as an unmarried girl. She was not particularly learned, so her father had failed to dispose of her by making a governess of her and not poor enough to be sent away to work as a maid. She was neither rich nor beautiful, thus deflecting potential husbands, so she kept the house and imagined herself shrinking slowly into pale-lipped spinsterhood – Miss Flood, the unmarried sister, the eternal maiden aunt.

She preferred to hide in her attic – two floors up from the merciless bongs and chimes of the wretched clocks, so that the racket sounded distant enough to be almost charming. She had space to set out her sewing machine and for a shelf containing her pattern books and the aged, well-thumbed volumes of fairy tales that her mother had read to her when she was very small, before she had died giving birth to Philip. She could lose herself in her sewing and her books, but only to a point. She could never lose track of time with those clocks two floors below her, and she resented their intrusion when they chimed a quarter to seven.

A quarter to seven meant supper and it never did any good to be late, so she unwound herself from the window seat, shook out her skirts and went downstairs to the dining room. Her father was already sat waiting at the head of the table, peering at his watch as if there weren't fifteen minutes until the meal was served.

'Have you seen your brother?' he asked.

'No, Papa. It *is* only a quarter to seven.'

They sank into silence until a little before ten to seven when Dora entered the dining room. 'Beg pardon, Mr Flood, sir, but there's a gentleman downstairs at the shop door.'

Phoebe's father blinked in bemusement. 'A gentleman?'

'Foreign gentleman, sir. Looks like a sailor of some sort.'

'The shop is closed, Dora. Tell him that.'

'I did, sir, but he was most insistent. Says he has a rare and precious timepiece what might merit your attention, sir.'

Phoebe watched with some amusement as her father was torn between the two things dearest to him – the keeping of correct time on the one hand and the acquisition of unusual new clocks on the other. 'Tell him to wait until after supper,' he said.

'Why don't you ask him to come up?' Phoebe suggested, emboldened by her father's dislocation. 'That Irish stew will stretch to everyone, won't it, Dora?'

'Yes, miss. I made plenty,' said Dora, although she looked wary, as if knowing what her master's reaction would be.

'A foreign sailor!' exclaimed Mr Flood. 'And you want to invite him to supper, Phoebe?'

'I think it would be rude not to,' said Phoebe, enjoying herself. 'If you're prepared to make him wait while we eat we should offer him a cup of tea at the least. Anything else would be ... well ... unchristian.' She

3

smiled when she said it, needling her father with the last word. He liked his Bible, almost as much as he loved his clocks.

'It's one thing putting money into the collection plate,' said her father. 'Feeding foreign sailors in one's own home is quite another.'

'It all goes to feeding the poor, Father – which we're told is a virtue.'

'"Blessed are the poor",' quoted Mr Flood. '"For theirs is the Kingdom of Heaven".'

Phoebe felt her temper rise. 'Blessed must be the poor who *aren't* having the beatitudes reeled off to console them,' she said, irreverently. She took such joy in her father's shocked expression that she made up her mind to leave the table and attend to their guest. She would be the cog who refused to make the house turn like clockwork and some wicked part of her wanted to see what happened when she did. She was keeping her own time, because it was that time of the month again.

There are systems in place, her father told her. Systems and structures to feed the poor and the needy. There are charitable foundations – those fruits of progress. This is the nineteenth century – we don't have to dish out alms for every beggar who comes knocking at our door as if it were the Middle Ages. Money in the collection plate is enough.

'For you,' Phoebe said, rising from her chair and revelling in her unfeminine failure to acquiesce. 'You'll excuse me, Father. I'll dine in the kitchen tonight, I think.'

As she went downstairs she heard her brother entering the dining room and asking what was going on, but she didn't stay to listen to the conversation. She felt too pleased with herself for bucking the tyranny of time if only for a brief moment. The clocks chimed seven and dinner was not yet served; a disruption of the natural order of things that would surely cause the universe to collapse in on itself judging by the importance her father attached to punctuality.

The universe failed to collapse in on itself. The only thing that was any different about the house was the man sitting at the kitchen table. He stood up and ducked in a stiff half-bow when Phoebe entered the room, his battered straw hat clutched in his hands. His possessions were in a couple of largish bundles beside the kitchen door, wrapped in damp canvas. He looked so cold and wet that he might have been washed up to the back door by the floodwaters.

He had a short jacket and a red neckerchief about his throat and his skin was deeply weathered and darkly tanned. It was hard to pin an age on him, since although his face was dark and lined by the sun, his eyes were bright, brown and had a mischievous glitter in them that Phoebe was sure had gone out of her own eyes when she was only a child of maybe thirteen.

'Dear lady,' he said, his accent heavy and indefinable. 'Thank you for seeing me. I hope that I have not ... ah ... inconvenienced you?'

'Not at all,' Phoebe said. 'We were just about to have supper. Perhaps you'd care to join Dora and I, Mr ...' She left it hanging, hoping he would furnish her with his name.

'Spiriakis,' he said, bowing again. 'Nick Spiriakis. Very pleased to make your acquaintance, Miss Flood.'

'Please. Do sit down.' Phoebe gestured to the kitchen chair. 'I understand you had a watch you were interested in showing to my father?'

'Yes,' he said, smiling, showing a gold front tooth. 'But

we shall postpone business a while, shall we, Miss Flood? It is not often a poor sailor like me is allowed to enjoy the company of such an exceptionally lovely young lady.'

Dora raised her eyebrows but Phoebe squelched her with a sidelong look and Dora turned her attention back to the Welsh rarebits bubbling within the range.

'You're not from London, Mr Spiriakis?' Phoebe asked.

'I am from everywhere, like all sailors,' he said, with a wave of his hand. 'By birth I am a Corfiote – a Greek – and I cannot tell you how much it pleases me to come here and find a lady who sets such store by hospitality as my own countrymen. It is very important to us Greeks.'

'I'm sure.' Phoebe found herself warming to the little man. Dimly she remembered stories her mother had told her – tales from Ancient Greece and elsewhere – and the glimmer in her mother's eyes as she told stories of wrathful goddesses, archangels who had been slighted by unwitting mortals who didn't recognise them in the disguise of beggars, of Baba Yaga's daughter who was determined to entertain her guest while her fearsome cannibal witch mother was away.

'I remember the stories,' Phoebe said, conscious suddenly that in all her eighteen years her father had never been exactly forthcoming in answering the question as to where her mother was from, only that her family were from Europe.

'You like stories? This is good. Very good, Miss Flood.'

'I love stories,' said Phoebe, settling in her chair. 'My mother used to tell me stories. Wonderful stories. I think some of them were Greek. Perhaps Russian. I'm not sure. I was very small when she died.'

'That's a shame,' Mr Spiriakis said. 'Do you look like your mother, if you'll pardon my asking?'

'Very much, I'm told. I don't know where precisely she was from.'

'There is something of the Byzantines in your eyes, Miss Flood,' he said, abandoning all pretence of politeness. 'In the little gilt flecks. Like the gilding clinging to the looted treasures of Hagia Sophia.'

Phoebe laughed off such gross flattery and flushed. 'I would dearly love to see Constantinople. I'm sure it's wonderful.'

'It is,' Mr Spiriakis said, his dark eyes glinting. 'Constantinople and the carnivals of Venice. The flocks of doves in St Peter's Square in Rome, the navel stone of the world at Delphi – I count myself a lucky man to have seen such things.'

Phoebe inhaled a long breath, fantasies of such places dancing behind her eyes. She could imagine it – Venice during the carnival – faces hidden behind masks, guards dropped and it was every man and woman for his or herself, with no prudery to keep a person in place. If she saw a pretty mouth beneath a domino she thought she might dare to kiss it and nobody would be any the wiser and nobody would care, because that was what they did during the carnival.

'You *are* lucky,' she said. 'It seems to be my fate to sit here while the city floods. There's nothing they can do. One night of heavy rain and a high tide is all it takes. It's been worse. This whole kitchen has been swamped before.'

'It is a curious thing,' he said, nodding as if in agreement. 'They fear the flood and yet they celebrate it in legend. Do you know, Miss Flood, your name is quite the legend? The Hebrews and the Christians have their Noah, the Greeks have Deucalion. Even the Hindus have their legends of the great flood. If we are to believe Plato, the city of Atlantis was destroyed by the very same force that now threatens to engulf London. It is the moon that draws the tides, the feminine force to . . .' He fumbled for the word as if he were suddenly aware that his English had become too fluent. 'To *counter* – yes, to counter the masculine sun. It is the feminine we fear, Miss Flood. It threatens to drown us all like wolves.'

'Like wolves?' Phoebe said, finding his simile unfamiliar. She was suddenly aware that neither she nor Dora had interjected or made a sound during this speech of his, and when Dora set down the plates upon the table she did so quietly and didn't take her eyes off Mr Spiriakis for an instant.

'*Efharisto, kyria*,' Mr Spiriakis said to Dora. 'That is "thank you". This smells wonderful . . . But yes, like wolves, Miss Flood. Perhaps you have never heard of the story of Lycaon?'

'It doesn't sound familiar,' said Phoebe, seeing Dora darting nervous glances at the clock. 'Go on and serve upstairs, Dora. Doesn't do to be late.'

'No, miss,' Dora said, and took the plates upstairs to the men, leaving Phoebe quite alone with a strange man.

Phoebe was pleasantly surprised to find that there was no harm in this whatsoever. The way that most people talked, one would think that a man in a room with an unchaperoned woman would devour her like a monster, but Mr Spiriakis only cut into his Welsh rarebit and seemed determined to do nothing more offensive than entertain her with stories.

'Lycaon was a king who committed an offence against Zeus,' he said. 'The king of the gods came seeking his hospitality, in the disguise of the poorest and most ragged of all mortals – a wretched beggar. The king saw him, and decided that such a pathetic creature was not worthy of his hospitality so he called to the kitchens and said that whatever guts and offal was left of the sheep and goats they had slaughtered for the feast would be good enough.'

'I think I already see Lycaon's mistake,' Phoebe said. She wanted to ask Mr Spiriakis if he was happy with his own supper, just in case.

Dora came back down and brought her own plate to the table and Mr Spiriakis continued. 'But the sons of Lycaon were even wickeder than their father, and thought it would be entertaining to offend the beggar still further. Their youngest brother, Nyctimus, had long been the butt of their jokes and they hated him because he was such a beautiful boy. They killed him, Miss Flood – slaughtered their own brother like a lamb and mixed his guts with the cheap offal stew.'

Dora gasped in delighted horror and Mr Spiriakis smiled a gold-toothed grin at the girl. 'It *is* unpleasant, miss,' he agreed. 'A terrible story, but just a story.'

'Please. Do carry on,' Phoebe urged, fascinated. It was much more gruesome a fairy tale than she had been brought up hearing and although she was supposed to be too resolutely middle class to enjoy such things, it was as sensational as the penny dreadfuls that Dora stacked beside her little bed in the scullery. The fear at hearing of boys gutted like mutton brought the same perverse pleasure, the same little clutch of horror in the pit of the belly.

'Zeus knew what had been done, of course,' continued Mr Spiriakis. 'He pushed away the bowl of offal without even tasting it and revealed himself to Lycaon and his evil sons. To punish them he turned them all into wolves, except for Nyctimus, who he brought back to life, but he was so angry with mankind that he sent his daughter, Artemis, the moon goddess, to raise a great flood to destroy them all. This was Deucalion's Flood, and only the virtuous man Deucalion and his wife Pyrrha were supposed to have been spared.'

'Supposed to have been spared?' asked Phoebe. 'There were other survivors?'

'Indeed, Miss Flood. Lycaon's people heard the wolves baying – the wolves that had once been their king and princes. They were awakened from their beds in the middle of the night by the sound of howling wolves and were alerted to the danger, so they scrambled up the slopes of Mount Parnassus to safety. There they lived for some time – so long that some of them became wolf like. They grew hair on their bodies and ate their prey raw. Some even forgot how to walk on two legs.

'That was many many centuries ago, though – back when the moon was younger, when people worshipped her as a goddess and through their prayers she had the strength to draw up the tides when she was at her fullest. Now, they do not worship her and so she weakens and cannot raise the waters of the Mediterranean much higher than a foot, but it is said the wolves remember. They remember the water rising when the moon was full and remember their fear and so they howl, and sometimes the people who were the descendants of the wolf-people of Parnassus throw back their heads and howl to the moon, remembering the flood.'

Phoebe shivered delightedly. Dora looked uncomfortable, but equally seemed to be enjoying the sailor's story. They ate supper in relative quiet, making small talk now that the story was over, and afterwards Dora went upstairs to clear the men's plates and ask Phoebe's father if he would now like to see Mr Spiriakis.

'You know, I don't think it will be entirely necessary,' said Mr Spiriakis, rummaging in his baggage. 'You have given me enough, Miss Flood. I had this watch and I think it is only fitting that you should have it.'

'Oh, I couldn't,' Phoebe protested. 'I thought you wanted to sell it?'

'I was curious.' He shrugged. 'I wanted to see what price it would fetch, but I suspect it would not be worth much money. Besides, one cannot put a price on the kindness that you have shown to me. Please. Take it as a gift.'

He opened a bundle of worn sailcloth. Inside was a small silver pocket watch with mother-of-pearl or abalone inlays on the face and, when she peered closer, Phoebe saw that the intricate inlays were of dark and light shades, arranged all around the edge of the face to represent the phases of the moon. It was a beautiful and delicate piece of work and she knew her father would have been excited by it.

'I can't,' she said. 'Really. I'm sure you could get a lot for a watch like that.'

She examined the case, back and front, and was astounded by the cleverness of the engraver who had mapped the face of the moon, back and front, onto the silver. The little criss-cross lines and pockmarks so fascinating to astronomers were all marked there, the seas of the moon indicated in writing so miniscule she marvelled that a human hand could etch them.

'Please,' said Mr Spiriakis. 'I insist. I would prefer to give it to you than sell it to someone who did not like it. You like it, do you not?'

'I do,' Phoebe admitted. 'I think it's wonderful.'

'Then it is settled,' he said, pushing the bundle of cloth containing the watch into her hand and folding her fingers over it one by one, exerting only a light pressure but one she felt she could not have resisted even if she had wanted to. 'You shall keep it. Keep it safe. It will bring you luck.'

'Thank you,' Phoebe said. She had wanted the watch,

even though it would have been polite to insist otherwise for longer. She wanted a memento of this evening to remind her of Mr Spiriakis's bloodcurdling stories and she was so pleased that she didn't object when he kissed her hand as he made to leave.

Her hand was not outstretched for kissing but palm up, with the wrapped-up watch inside. He leant forwards and kissed each finger of her hand, quite deliberately, not taking his eyes from her face. For the first time she noticed that in the centre of each of his bright dark eyes was a little rim of gold around the pupil, which rayed outwards like a sunburst, like the gold flecks he had complimented in her own eyes.

He kissed the centre of her upturned wrist and the unexpected shock of pleasure made her gasp.

'Good luck, Miss Flood,' he said, briefly closing his hand tightly over her own. 'And thank you.'

2

Did the watch bring her luck? Maybe, if a change was the same as good luck. Phoebe would find herself puzzling over her reflection in the mirror, murmuring 'you are not the same' to herself, all the while wondering what had wrought the change in her. She didn't look particularly different – at least at first glance. She looked in the mirror and saw the same dark, rather sallow-skinned face that she had seen looking back at her all her life, but there was something different. She knew she was too dark and skinny to ever be considered a beauty, but by the light of the candles she was prepared to believe the little flames lit golden lights in her skin to match the gold in her eyes. Maybe the difference was that she was becoming vain, or it was just because she'd shaken the bars of her cage in committing the tiny defiant act of not coming to dinner on time. She couldn't put her finger on it.

Huddled in her bed in the attic she heard the wind howl and dreamt of people hiding in attics from the water, scrambling to safety like the wolves on Parnassus. At the height of her monthly illness she fancied that the people preserving themselves from drowning might be turning into wolves in attics all over London. When the waters receded they would run through the streets, pink tongues lolling, jowls dripping, their presence sending the rich ladies in Berkeley Square and the gay girls of the Haymarket alike into fits of screaming; skirts hoisted, running and weeping in terror.

Her dreams at that time of the month were always shot with some thread of madness or hysteria, but the wolves had invaded her sleeping mind. She dreamt that she was at St Paul's, where she had only been once, having no real reason to visit, and she didn't know why she was there this time, but scraps of memory had pieced together and placed her, in her dream, high up in the Whispering Gallery. When she looked down at the altar far below she felt dizzy and retreated back against the rounded wall of the dome. She heard a voice in her ear, saying something indistinct, and was frightened by that too, but she knew if she moved away from the wall she would have to look down on the sickening drop once more.

She glimpsed a small ragged man in a red neckerchief making his way back down the stairs just as words were carried back to her by the curving, echoing wall: 'There are wolves loose in the city. They are everywhere. They are everyone.'

She pressed her cheek to the side of the dome and whispered, 'Where?'

'Everywhere. Run home as fast as you can. Stay on the main roads. They're loose in the backstreets.'

'Wait!' she called, but the man was gone. She hurried towards the stairs to follow and more than once her stomach lurched as she glimpsed over the rail. The stairs were narrow, her skirts were wide and she stumbled on her way down and wished she could tear her skirts off with her bare hands, the better to run unhindered.

She rushed down the aisle to the main door, even though the man was nowhere in sight. As she hurried down the steps of the cathedral a flock of pigeons took flight as she rushed into their midst. It was strangely quiet, quiet enough for the beating of their wings to be the loudest noise in the city and when she looked up she saw that night had fallen as fast as a candle being snuffed. The sky was dark and clear, black clouds moving rapidly across the face of a bright full moon. For once there was no fog to obscure its light.

The birds had flown and she knew she must follow their example and go home. She looked for the road but it was gone. She was standing in a round piazza, decorated like the looming floor below the Whispering Gallery. Rayed out around it, like the spokes of a wheel, were entrances to alleys, the hugger-mugger labyrinth of medieval streets that even the Great Fire had failed to straighten and solve.

Phoebe turned on her heel in the centre. This time the cathedral itself was gone and there was nothing but the clouds and the moon and the maze of forbidden backstreets. No place for a lady.

She reminded herself that ladylike behaviour meant only submission and tedium and that she had been a Londoner before she was ever old enough to be deemed a lady. She could find her way home. She turned from where the cathedral had been and walked down the narrow street. There were people there but they wouldn't meet her eye. They hurried away into doorways and off into houses, and the further she walked the emptier the houses appeared. There were boards across windows and no lights and she wondered if she ought to run back and knock on the door of an occupied house and ask for shelter.

When she heard the first howl she knew that she had to run.

The alleyways ran into one another and each intersection led her into darker, emptier streets and she heard panting breaths, the almost noiseless padding of furred paws. She couldn't turn back, because the wolves were behind her. Her heart thundered in her head and chest and throat and she could not remember ever being so terrified in her life. They knew she was alone and defenceless and they would come for her.

As she turned one corner she looked behind her and saw a muzzle, a slobbering tongue and a pair of bright golden eyes peering around the corner after her. She screamed and tried to run faster but her stays were too tight for her to catch her breath properly. She didn't dare turn around again because she knew the wolf was bounding up behind her. She heard it snarl, smelt its breath as it pounced.

It caught her by the skirt and she screamed, prayed and begged as she tried to tear the cloth loose from its huge sharp teeth, but it clung on, shaking its head like a playful dog. The pack rounded the corner, all grey backs, amber eyes, breaths misting the crisp cold air with hot, animal vitality. As petrified as she was some small part of her mind was filled with terrified admiration for how beautifully they were made, how efficiently they were designed to hunt and kill – sleek and solid, their coats thick, their paws velvet, their eyes bright as the moon. She screamed for help and wrenched at her skirt. It came away, torn clean off in the wolf's teeth. She ran once more, but the pack was behind her now, snapping at her petticoats, ripping her stockings. Teeth and claws barely seemed to scratch her skin but her clothes were fast turning into rags. They had her petticoats off, tore away her drawers and rent her stockings into shreds around her ankles. The first one, the great golden-eyed wolf, jumped and ripped at the dangling edge of her chemise, baring her naked from the waist down. She was too scared to feel shame. If anything she wanted to tear off the constricting corset and have done with it all, give them the raw morsel they seemed to crave, so that she could be devoured and wake up from this dream.

'Come on, then,' she muttered, her throat raw from screaming. 'Come on.' She stopped and tugged off the remainder of her dress, so that she stood there in nothing but the rags of her chemise and corset. To her surprise, they stopped too, as if they'd never seen a girl before. She broke the laces on her stays with impossible ease and breathed so deep that the air rushing through her brain made her feel faint, exhilarated. The pack slunk back at the sight of her nakedness, her small dark-tipped breasts, the tangle of black hair between her legs. Only Gold-Eyes didn't seem cowed. He moved closer, but didn't snarl. He seemed merely curious.

Moving slowly, she crouched to his level, aware of how the movement made her thighs open. Maybe that was it. He could smell something between them that he liked. 'I'm not afraid of you,' she told him, becoming more and more aware now that she was waking and the dream was slipping away. She reached out slowly, every fraction of an inch an eternity, and touched the top of his head. So soft, softer than the fur of any dog she'd patted so familiarly. He drew nearer and she shut her eyes, fearful of those teeth, but she felt instead a wet nose on her cheek, the lap of a tongue. She opened her eyes and he was no longer a wolf. He was a man – a young man, crouching and naked as she was, his eyes as golden as ever. His hair was tangled and matted, his skin dirty, but he was beautiful to her; the strong muscles of his arms, the whorls of dark hair around his nipples, the slender thighs that concealed whatever it was between them, because she didn't know and for all she wanted to know the dream was becoming thinner, less substantial. The more she willed herself asleep the more her body woke.

She clutched at him, grasping his upper arms, trying to sink deeper into sleep and wanting to stay. His arms were hard and his skin felt as smooth as silk. He leant forwards and pressed his lips to the hollow between her neck and shoulder. She felt him mouthing at her and struggled to remain sleeping when she felt his tongue dragged over her shoulder, then down to her breasts. His mouth closed over her nipple and suckled, causing an ever-vanishing sensation of pleasure that surged through her body and down between her legs. She knew she was waking up as the feeling ebbed away and he became like ether, like a ghost in her arms.

She woke up. The sweat on her body had dried but she felt the trickle between her thighs and the cramp in her lower belly. Time of the month. Nothing more, nothing less.

When she came down from her bedroom, paler and sallower and thinner than before, she went to work attending to the household accounts, dusting the display cases in the shop and then sewing in her room. She hadn't told her father about the watch. She had just told him that the sailor had tired of waiting and left to take the watch to the pawnbroker, at which her father had grunted and said he was tired of being taken for a pawnbroker anyway.

Phoebe was cleaning the brass edges of the display cabinets one rainy afternoon when a lady came into the shop. She was clearly a lady because for one, she was better dressed than the usual ragged tide of flood victims, and secondly, because Phoebe's father raised his head like a terrier alerted to a rat when she entered.

'Good afternoon, madam. How may I be of assistance?'

Phoebe slunk back behind the display case a little, aware that she was staring. The lady stood side on from her, so that Phoebe could only see her profile, which was partially obscured by a plume of egret feathers on her hat, but even then Phoebe knew that this woman was beautiful.

'Good afternoon ... yes ... filthy weather, isn't it? I was wondering if you could help me ...'

She wore gloves – lovely white kid gloves – and she inched them off, finger by tight finger, as she took the watch from her reticule and handed it to Phoebe's father. Phoebe was only dimly aware of snatches of their conversation ('... broken spring, I think ... family heirloom ... heard you were just the man ...') because she found herself transfixed by the woman's pale hands. Every other scrap of skin below the neck was corseted and buttoned and hooked into a navy-blue costume and her hands looked all the more naked for the contrast. As she passed the watch across the counter Phoebe saw the inside of her wrist, just below the ruffle of her sleeve. She saw the blue veins crossing under the thin skin there and realised with a thrill of shock what Mr Spiriakis must have meant when he kissed her there. The skin looked so fine it was indecent, only just thick enough to cover the workings of veins beneath.

Phoebe watched her father open the back of the watch and screw a glass into his eye so that his eye was magnified and bulbous; the pale eye of a fish. Unable to feign interest in such intricacies, the lady turned her head and, as she did so, Phoebe saw her face for the first time.

It was a rainy afternoon in late January without, but inside the shop Phoebe was sure it was suddenly Midsummer's Day. She found herself looking into a piquantly heart-shaped face perched on a slender neck, rising like a flower stem from the collar of her coat. The woman had blue eyes – a strong, clear cobalt blue – and pink cheeks and a Cupid's bow mouth. Phoebe had never felt so awkward in her own dark snub-nosed skin before, but she had never been so entranced. She realised she was probably staring wildly, because the woman smiled rather uneasily, so Phoebe made the effort to smile back and then ducked behind the display cabinet with the safety of clocks and glass to shield her from further embarrassing herself.

'You know, I might just have the very part in the shop, madam,' said Phoebe's father. 'Let me go and see.'

'Thank you,' said the lady.

Please don't have the part, Phoebe thought to herself. Don't have it, then she will have to come back another day and collect her watch.

Phoebe's father went out to the back and Phoebe was left wondering what on earth to do with herself. Should she attempt to talk to the customer or just pretend not to be here? She cursed Mr Spiriakis's watch for a moment. Bring her luck? It seemed to have done nothing but rob her of the power of intelligent speech.

The lady made up her mind for her. She peeked around the edge of the display case, egret plumes trembling with what Phoebe hoped wasn't suppressed laughter and said, 'Hello.'

Phoebe gulped. She was even more beautiful at close quarters. Her skin was absolutely flawless – creamy pale and tinted delicately with pink. The reflected light from one of the display cases caught the curve of her cheek and the corner of her mouth and illuminated tiny fine gold hairs like the fur on the skin of a ripe peach.

'Do you talk? At all?'

'Talk?' said Phoebe, almost laughing with the relief of getting a word out of her mouth. 'Oh, yes.'

'Thank goodness,' said the lady. 'I was beginning to think I'd committed some terrible faux pas. You looked quite the wild creature for a moment there.'

'No, no. I just dust the cases and things. I'm sorry if I was staring. I was admiring your gloves.'

The lady laughed. 'These old things? I'm sure they're getting a hole.' She turned one inside out and showed Phoebe where the seam was on the verge of splitting.

'Yes, I see,' Phoebe said. 'You really need a strong backstitch to keep the blanket stitch from tearing. It's not easy to do with a sewing machine, unfortunately.'

'Do you do much sewing?'

'Oh yes. I make all my own clothes.'

To Phoebe's intense delight, the lady looked impressed. 'That blouse?' she asked. 'You made that all yourself?'

'Not the lace. But I fitted the panels myself.'

'You're wasted dusting shelves,' said the lady, shaking her head.

Phoebe's father came out from the back, clutching the watch, which made Phoebe hope he hadn't found the part needed to mend it.

'I'm afraid I don't have it, madam,' he said. 'I can certainly acquire it by this time next week and have it fitted for you by next Thursday, if that won't be too much of a delay?'

'That would be fine,' said the lady, turning in a graceful swish of skirts and bustle. 'Shall I pay now or when the job is done?'

'It is policy to request a small sum up front, madam, purely for the cost of requisitioning the necessary parts, you understand.'

'Absolutely, yes.' She moved to the counter and Phoebe listened as she filled in her details. 'Yes ... Mrs LeClerk. L-E. Capital C. And that will be ready next Thursday? Thank you very much, Mr Flood. You've been most helpful.'

She turned back to Phoebe before leaving the shop. 'It was very nice to meet you,' she said, politely, and with some surprising sleight of hand she pressed a small engraved card into Phoebe's palm.

'Likewise,' said Phoebe, standing stunned at the speed and skill with which Mrs LeClerk had handed her the card. She seemed to have produced it from her sleeve with the dexterity of a stage magician. Phoebe slipped back behind the counter to glance at it, feeling she should keep it hidden from her father, but when she read the card it was nothing more than an engraved calling card for Mrs Louisa LeClerk.

Louisa. Her name was Louisa.

'Interesting piece,' Phoebe's father said, peering through his glass once more. 'I've seen a few similar things, but never had one handed to me by a lady before.'

'What's that, Papa?' said Phoebe, giving a cursory glance over at the watch he was examining. She wasn't really interested in Louisa's watch. She was interested in next Thursday, when Louisa would come back to collect it.

'Watch built into a cigarette case,' said Mr Flood. 'Obviously a family heirloom. Probably her father's. A respectable lady like that wouldn't be smoking cigarettes now, would she?'

3

Thursday came and Phoebe talked about nothing the night before but about how dirty the brasses were in the shop, and how the wood was crying out for a good waxing. That way she could stay in the shop and stand less chance of missing Louisa should she come in. It was difficult to keep up the pretence that she was settling in for a long day's cleaning because she wanted to look her best.

'You've been long enough doing your hair,' said her father, when she came down, making her flush self-consciously. 'What did you need to do that for?'

She shrugged and tied a large, worn apron over an old dress. 'It had to be curled,' she said, haughtily. 'It's the fashion.'

'Vanity, thy name is woman,' said Mr Flood with a sigh, flipping the shop sign over to OPEN.

Phoebe rolled up her sleeves and smothered a grin, satisfied that her motives had gone unsuspected. She spent the morning dragging her job out as long as possible, protractedly applying layer after layer of beeswax to wood that probably would have groaned in satiety at so much of the stuff had it been able to do so. Her father was starting to turn his nose up at the smell and Phoebe was beginning to worry how much longer she could keep up the charade when her prayers were answered.

It was Louisa LeClerk, in the flesh. She was dressed in a beautiful costume of dark-green cashmere, and today she had peacock feathers in her hat. Phoebe drank in every aspect of the other woman's looks – her clothes, her piled and curled blonde hair, her gloved hands, her smiling lips, the nipped in waist that emphasised the fullness of her bustle. She was so tightly laced that her breasts were compressed to very little and Phoebe found herself wondering how Louisa would look in a low-necked evening gown, how much of the creamy flesh would be spilling over the top of her stays. She would love to have made something for her; to have Louisa standing in her attic, dressed only in her underthings while Phoebe took the tape measure to her waist, ravelled it around her back and pinched it between her corseted breasts, ran the measure from the nape of her slender neck to the small of her back.

She knew she was staring, and she was positive her smile was perfectly idiotic when Louisa smiled at her.

'Hello again,' said Louisa. 'You look busy.'

'Busy, yes,' Phoebe said, praying she wouldn't lose her nerve and talk in monosyllables all over again. She pushed a straggle of hair out of her face, uncomfortably conscious that she was sweating under her dress and that she probably reeked of beeswax and paraffin wax. 'Cleaning.'

'Yes. So I see.' Louisa looked mildly amused all over again.

Phoebe cursed her own tongue and her own hair – particularly her hair. A stray strand had come loose and predictably it was not keeping the neat, artificial rag-curled ringlet that Phoebe had spent hours torturing it into holding. Her hair had a natural curl, but it was an untidy sort of wiry curl that would have been extremely fashionable fifty years ago but wasn't now. She wanted to push it back into the fastening, but to do so would have meant raising her arms and she knew she would have damp patches under the arms of her dress. She pushed it back from her face again.

'Oh, here,' Louisa said. 'Your hands are probably all covered in polish, aren't they? Let me.'

She moved closer in a haze of perfume – something sweet mingling with the mechanical scents of oiled watch springs and the domestic smell of sweat and wax polish – then she anchored the loose curl back safely under the comb that had failed to hold it in place. The comb scratched at Phoebe's scalp a little as Louisa jiggled it into position. She managed not to wince but she was sure she didn't manage not to blush. Louisa was close enough to hold, to test the span of that tiny waist with her own grubby hands.

'Thank you,' she said, as Louisa pulled away.

'I think that's got it,' Louisa said, inclining her head to admire her handiwork. 'You've just got a little something ...'

She reached out again, and Phoebe thought she was trying to brush away dirt from her face. Self-consciously, Phoebe reached up to wipe it away before it could be noticed any further and her hand collided with Louisa's just above her left ear. She felt something in Louisa's hand, something cold and hard that dropped into her palm, and she must have looked so appalled when she whipped back her hand to look at it, because Louisa laughed.

Phoebe looked down and saw a shining sixpence sitting in her palm.

'Damn! You've sprung me,' Louisa said, with a wink.

Phoebe was torn between the desire to laugh at hearing a lady swear and her absolute terror that her father would have heard the profanity. She realised why she had the sixpence in her hand. Louisa was playing some kind of game with her, the old parlour trick of producing a coin from behind a child's ear, but she remembered how Louisa had slipped her card into her hand the first time they had met.

Louisa raised a black-gloved hand to her mouth, aware of her mistake, but the expression in her eyes was as amused and unrepentant as Phoebe's.

'Sorry. I used to be on the stage,' said Louisa, as if this explained both her language and her quickness of hand.

So she wasn't the respectable lady Phoebe's father couldn't wait to fawn over. Far from it, if she had been an actress. Theatrical folk were notorious for being rather fast and Phoebe was privately delighted to imagine her father's reaction if he knew about Mrs LeClerk's past.

He didn't have a clue. He sailed out from the back-room, his portly belly swelling the front of his coat, and greeted Louisa in his most unctuous manner. 'My dear Mrs LeClerk, what a pleasure and a privilege it is to see you again. Such a fascinating timepiece! I've never seen one quite like it, except perhaps at the Crystal Palace. I shouldn't presume you visited the Great Exhibition. You're far too young, but let me tell you, Mrs LeClerk, such objects of *exquisite* whimsy were quite the thing back in the fifties, you know.'

For all he was such a snob, her father's patter was sometimes redolent of a penny costermonger. Phoebe rolled her eyes and set to polishing an already gleaming display case.

'Are you resident in London, Mrs LeClerk?'

'For now, yes,' Louisa said. She had not flinched under the barrage of nonsense she had just been obliged to endure and Phoebe marvelled at her self-possession. 'The air is better in the country, but I do love London – even if it's rather lonely before the season begins.'

'Your husband prefers the country?'

She shook her head. 'I'm afraid I'm a widow, Mr Flood.'

'Oh. I'm most terribly sorry.'

'Thank you. Yes, it was several years ago now.'

'I find it difficult to believe a lady such as yourself would remain unmarried for long.'

Phoebe glared openly at her father, amazed at his rudeness. If he got any more personal with his questions he'd be asking her how many of her own teeth she had left in her head or the name of her doctor.

'Well,' Louisa said with a shrug, 'I find most of the eligible gentlemen have homes in the country and I imagine I'd be even more starved for company there. I need my diversions, and plenty of company.' She chewed her lower lip for a moment and her gaze lighted conspiratorially on Phoebe. 'Perhaps ... perhaps Miss Flood would care to join me for tea tomorrow afternoon?'

'Yes please!' Phoebe said, so suddenly and boldly that her father had the nerve to give her a reproachful look.

'I don't know that I can spare her,' he said, hesitantly.

'I'll give Dora your orders for tomorrow's meals tonight,' Phoebe begged. 'Please? May I go?'

She could see he had been dead against it, but something changed in his eyes when he looked at Louisa. Her expensive clothes and ladylike manner had clearly touched his social-climbing soul. 'Very well,' he said. 'If only to oblige Mrs LeClerk. Don't be a bother to her, will you now?'

'Oh, I'm sure that's not possible,' Louisa said, indulgently. 'Will four o'clock suit, Miss Flood?'

'It will be fine,' Phoebe's father said. 'Go up and help Dora. If you polish any more you'll wear the wood down to nothing.'

'Yes, Papa.' Much as Phoebe hated the routine cleaning of the house she tripped upstairs cheerfully, thinking of Louisa's calling card still tucked into the corner of the mirror in the attic.

'You look like the circus has come to town, you do,' said Dora, peering up from somewhere beneath Phoebe's father's bed, where she was busy with a dustpan and brush.

'I got invited to tea,' announced Phoebe.

'Good for you, miss. I suppose you got invited to help change the beds an' all?'

Phoebe shrugged. 'That too. Where shall I start?'

Dora stood up. 'Done in here. But you can give me a hand turning your brother's bed over.'

'You didn't try to do it by yourself?' asked Phoebe, going into Philip's room. Philip's bed had a horsehair mattress that weighed about as much as the horse they had presumably shaved to stuff the thing.

'And break my back, miss?' Dora took hold of one edge of the mattress. 'Not a chance. I was waiting for you to be finished with the brasses. One, two, three . . . hup!'

As they lifted the mattress a book fell out from under it and landed on the floor at Phoebe's feet, the pages spread. She stooped to look and stared, unable to believe what she was seeing. The engraving on the page showed a woman in a high white old-fashioned wig and more or less nothing else. She was sat astride the lap of a man, who was naked from the waist down. That organ of his, presumably a full-grown model of the little wen of a thing she had seen between Phillip's legs when he was a baby, was thrust up inside the woman. There was another man standing watching the scene with a shocked expression on his face and the caption read 'Mr H. Surprises Fanny And Will'.

Phoebe let out an involuntary snort of laughter and Dora immediately closed the book with her foot as if to touch the pages would pollute her. 'Oh my Lord,' she said. 'Don't you look at that. It's not decent.'

'Why would he . . .?' Phoebe spluttered, all the more amused for Dora's obvious mortification. 'Why? Under the mattress, of all places?'

'Men,' said Dora, disdainfully, her cheeks flaming scarlet. 'Your brother's getting to be a man, miss, and gentlemen, well – they might look like toffs on the outside but they're beasts, the lot of them.'

'Really?' said Phoebe, attempting to affect an expression of suitable disgust but desperate to steal the book for herself. 'Do they all . . . have those things?'

Dora looked like she might prefer to dive out of the window than answer but nodded. 'You shouldn't know, miss. Not 'til you're married.'

'If we're all to marry ravening beasts I don't think it's fair that we're not given warning,' said Phoebe.

Dora shook her head. 'That's not even marriage, that there,' she said, poking the book with her foot. 'I heard my own brothers talking about that Fanny Hill. She was –' Dora glanced furtively towards the door '– a gay girl,' she added, in a piercing whisper.

'Well, she did look like she was enjoying herself,' said Phoebe, deliberately pretending to misunderstand, flustering poor Dora all the more.

'That's not what I meant, miss.'

'I'm sorry, Dora. I was teasing. I know what you meant.'

'Best not mention this,' she said, tucking the book back under the mattress, out of sight and out of mind.

Louisa lived in a flat in St John's Wood. A prim-faced housekeeper in pince-nez let Phoebe in and directed her across the chequerboard floor and up the stairs, into the flat, where there was a narrow hall with a hatstand and a marquetry-topped chest for carriage rugs.

'Mrs LeClerk will be with you presently,' she said, leading Phoebe into a drawing room with a view of the square.

'Thank you,' Phoebe said, unsure as to whether she should sit, or stand, or stand on her head. She was left alone in the cosy room and so she stood and warmed herself at the fire in the grate, her hands stinging from the cold. The room was full of vases of flowers – hot-house carnations, chrysanthemums and lilies. They weren't the pale funeral lilies, rather the bright spotted trumpet lilies with a perfume that was so overpowering it was almost sickly. Phoebe leant to sniff one to ascertain that it was the lilies that smelt so strong, and the pollen went everywhere. She worried that it had stained her nose yellow and quickly peered in the overmantel mirror to check the damage.

Her nose wasn't yellow. On that score she was safe, but she noticed the frame of the mirror – very thin and fine, gilded and carved, with unmistakable little figures, people, worked into the frame, which couldn't have been more than an inch thick. She strained her near-sighted eyes to see what they were doing and realised that the figures were not those of Greek athletes or wrestlers as she had initially supposed. There were men and women, twined naked together in ways she had never imagined before, kissing, with their hands upon one another's bodies.

She supposed she was meant to faint or scream or flee from this dwelling, clutching her skirts to her as if their touch upon the doorframe might contaminate her, but she found she couldn't look away. She inclined her head to see what the figures up the side of the mirror frame were doing and gasped to see a naked woman squatting with something between her thighs and another tiny panel where there looked to be *three* figures, not two.

She was so absorbed that she let out a scream of surprise when she felt someone grab her by the waist and pull her sharply away from the fireplace.

It was only Louisa, and she didn't look angry, only relieved. 'If you'd been standing any closer you'd have caught yourself alight,' she said, by way of explanation, her hands still on Phoebe's waist.

Phoebe flushed an even deeper red, conscious that this was probably not the drawing-room etiquette she'd been instructed to observe. 'Oh, I'm sorry. How silly of me. I was ... I ...' She couldn't say she was wiping pollen off her nose because she had been too overzealous in sniffing a flower, because she'd look even more of an idiot, if such a thing were possible and it didn't occur to her at the time to say she was adjusting her hair.

Louisa laughed and shook her head. Her teeth were white, her lips very pink. 'Oh, I know,' she said. 'Naughty, aren't they? It's from India.'

'India,' Phoebe parroted, exhaling slowly and furtively examining her skirt for scorch marks.

'You're not horribly shocked, are you?' asked Louisa, sounding genuinely worried.

'No, I don't think so,' Phoebe said. Once the initial shock of realising what she was looking at had worn off she had only felt an intense curiosity, a shortness of breath and a queer loosening sensation in the muscles of her legs. 'You just gave me a bit of a start, that's all. I didn't realise I was standing so close to the fire.'

'Please, sit down.' Louisa gestured to a chaise longue and moved briskly across to a dresser. She wore a dark-brown taffeta shot with red so that she shimmered like an autumn leaf as the silk skirts rippled about her. 'Let me get you a brandy, Miss Flood. Entirely medicinal. You've had a nasty shock.'

'I'm all right,' Phoebe insisted, having never drunk brandy before in her life. 'I'd just never seen anything like your mirror before.'

'No, I bet you hadn't,' Louisa handed her the drink. 'I don't keep it to shock people into self-immolation if that's what you were thinking, but I suppose I do like to shock people. Maiden aunts and respectable married women – you know the type. The ones who think it's just some evil to be endured and never enjoyed.'

Phoebe cautiously sipped her brandy, trying not to flinch at the way it burnt her tongue and throat. She rather needed it, hearing Louisa talk like this, but she was so infatuated with Louisa that she would do anything. She would drink brandy and pretend to understand, if only it meant she could sit here and look at her.

'Were you not married yourself, Mrs LeClerk?' It was the first time Phoebe had spoken the name out loud and since she had always called her Louisa in her head 'Mrs LeClerk' suited the older woman about as well as a moustache.

'Oh God, no,' Louisa said, carelessly, sitting down on a chaise longue. 'And call me Louisa, please. What shall I call you? Phoebe. It's like this, Phoebe – I lied. It's an absolute tissue of lies. I'm not a married woman, or even a widow. Mr LeClerk never existed. It's just easier to explain why you're a woman of means if you say you inherited it from a dear-departed husband, isn't it? That way you can look as blameless as the Queen – mourning, mourning like a bloody lovebird that hasn't had the sense to die. How's your brandy, dear?'

'It's . . . different,' said Phoebe, feeling honesty was the order of the day.

'Drink up. It'll put colour in your cheeks,' Louisa said,

arranging her skirt. She wore the latest fashion – the tie-back skirt – considered indecent by some because it clung to the legs at the front. Women weren't supposed to have legs, and certainly nothing between them. They wore bulky petticoats to keep them neatly covered, like mermaids. The way the taffeta strained over Louisa's thighs when she accidentally sat on the fan-shaped train of her skirt made Phoebe think that maybe tie-backs were rather too much, because the sight of rounded thigh so provocatively displayed made her feel hot and dizzy.

'I'm glad you came,' Louisa told her. 'I get so bored with talking about the weather and clothes and raking over the coals of the latest scandal. People do go on about scandal but the moment you say 'damn' or 'hell' in the drawing room – oh my goodness. The soi-disant *demi-mondaines* go scuttling pretty quick back to *le monde*, I can tell you. You weren't even that shocked.'

'You weren't in the drawing room when you said it,' said Phoebe. 'You were in a watchmaker's shop.' She felt hopelessly stupid, not having that supply of French phrases handy that seemed to come easily to the lips of accomplished, fashionable ladies.

Louisa laughed. 'The unshockable Miss Flood. You didn't even mind that I was on the stage.'

'Were you?' Phoebe asked. 'Really? Or was that a lie too?'

'Oh no. That was true,' Louisa said. 'I'll tell you everything and I'll tell you the whole truth, I promise, but you might be shocked at that.'

Phoebe peered into her brandy glass, annoyed that it wasn't disappearing faster, for all she kept trying to manfully swallow the awful stuff. 'I'm too ignorant to be shocked, I think,' she admitted. 'I don't know French and I don't know how to drink brandy and I don't know a thing about India. All I really know is sewing.'

'But this is perfect,' said Louisa, sounding delighted. 'Would you like to learn French and how to drink brandy?'

'I would love to!'

'Then I think I may have a proposition for you.' Louisa got up from the chaise and unlocked a roll-topped bureau. 'Now, I promise to tell you everything about me before we get started, because that's only fair, and you will be shocked, both by this and me, I expect, but you'll never have made anything like this before. Never. And it will be your masterpiece.'

'My masterpiece?' asked Phoebe, puzzled. Creators of masterpieces had talent and she had never imagined such a thing for herself. She might have taken a measure of pride in a well-made bodice or a tidily finished seam, but there was no art to it. It was just sewing. Most women could do it.

'You think I didn't notice that lace blouse you had on the first time we met?' said Louisa, taking a sheaf of papers from the bureau. 'When I realised you'd made it yourself I knew then I had to get to know you better. There isn't a lady's maid in London who could make something so lovely – well, there might be in Paris, but I've had some perfectly rotten experiences with French maids. One of them drank and the other – well, least said, soonest mended.'

'I don't drink,' said Phoebe, looking self-consciously down at the brandy glass in her hand. 'At least, I didn't.' She was excited by the prospect of what she thought Louisa was proposing. To be her maid. To make her clothes and dress her and trim her hats and listen to her confidences. It sounded like a wonderful dream.

'Oh, she was at the absinthe,' Louisa said, airily. 'Constantly. She could sew, but she was usually too drunk to do it properly. But you're not partial to absinthe, are you? I thought maybe you might like a place here – depending on how you feel about it, of course.' Louisa rushed her words and Phoebe thought she sounded nervous, but nowhere near as nervous as she felt herself.

'Really?' Phoebe asked, heart pounding at the prospect of escape. 'Could I?'

'If you wanted to. Your father wouldn't mind, would he?'

Phoebe put her hand to her mouth, wanting to laugh. Mind? He'd be delighted to get rid of her.

'You should probably know I'm about as famous for my morals as the Prince of Wales,' Louisa said, clutching the papers to her chest. 'That is to say, not at all. So please try not to faint because I don't know where Mrs Dalton keeps the smelling salts, but I have this pattern I picked up in Paris.' She handed over the papers.

'A dress pattern?' Phoebe laughed. 'Oh, I don't think I'd be too...' Her voice trailed off as she opened the pattern book and looked at the sketch of the design on the frontispiece. She felt the blood rush to her cheeks immediately and once again felt the loosening sensation in her knees and thighs that had threatened to overtake her when she looked at the designs on the overmantel. The design was so lewd, so blatantly designed to reveal the body that one may as well have been naked. Her hands trembled and a scrap of fine red velvet, the exact shade of the deepest red rose, fell out from between the pages onto her lap. She picked it up and the material was softer than any velvet she had ever touched before. To wear it would be like wearing a gown made of rose petals.

'That's the cloth I had in mind,' Louisa said. 'What do you think? Can you do it?'

Phoebe nodded. She had already pieced it together in her mind, imagined some of the problems she might encounter and was eager to discover if her means of solving them would work. She wanted to make this dress, even if it meant keeping company that would see her disowned by her family. 'Well, it's a facer,' she said, slowly. 'Looks like it could be quite an adventure to get it right.' She smiled.

Louisa smiled back and looked somewhat relieved. 'Are you up for an adventure, Miss Flood?' she asked.

'I'd say it was long overdue, actually,' said Phoebe.

4

They had been in Paris for four months and there were some nights when Charlie was sure the memory of Naples would never leave him. Nights like this; nights when the full moon hung like a fat chilled pearl in the clear winter sky, casting frigid light over the construction site at the top of the butte. The wind drifted the falling snow into grubby banks rank with straw and horseshit, the snow having little or no time to settle elsewhere. It was trodden rapidly underfoot by the human traffic traversing the Boulevard de Clichy – the drunks scurrying from one café to another, the street-walkers plying their trade, the pimp in search of a missing girl or a rival – all of them cold, tired and relentless. Montmartre attracted the insomniacs, the restless spirits and Charlie wondered if it was fate and a similar instinct that made him want to linger in the cold and wet. He didn't feel cold. He felt as though there was a furnace in his guts, a heat that the weather couldn't touch.

He clutched the heavy parcel in his arms. It was potentially valuable and he knew he should take it home immediately but some part of him shied away from being behind locked doors when the moon was this bright. He was uncertain about what he might do and he could not begin to confide his fears to William. Will was so rational that he scoffed at Louisa's little superstitions, like tossing spilt salt over her shoulder or saluting solitary magpies. If Charlie told him the real reason they had had to leave Italy he was sure Will would worry for his sanity.

As he walked his foot slipped on slush and he stumbled into a girl standing in the street. She was obviously a whore, her shawl pulled tight enough around her shoulders to steal some paltry warmth, but strategically low enough to display the cleft between her breasts.

'Pardon, mademoiselle,' he said, automatically, in an instant catching sight of her face and the stringy brown hair whipped around it by the cold wind. She smiled – a professional's smile, but Charlie glimpsed a hint of gold in her eyes, a burst of winter sunlight around the edge of her pupil that suddenly chilled him to the bone and made her smile assume a different quality. The wind howled.

He tripped backwards away from her, almost falling over into the filthy snow, hurrying towards the nearest lit window, looking for sanctuary behind the stained-glass panes. It wasn't a church. On his first visit to Paris he had found it hilarious that brothels decorated their windows in such an ecclesiastical fashion, but he was in no mood to see the funny side tonight. He realised when he stepped through the door of the whorehouse that he had run from one woman into a den of the creatures.

The girls were keeping warm beside a bright fire. Some wore peignoirs. Others wore nothing but stockings and ruffled garters, but they sat and smoked, talked, played cards and knitted as casually as if they'd been fully dressed. A blonde glanced up and the others followed suit, devouring Charlie with their eyes. Perhaps they'd argue over him – a trick who was young and handsome and wouldn't have to be endured. If there was one thing he hadn't lost in Naples it was his vanity.

A tall, black-clad woman interposed herself between him and the girls – the madam, no doubt. She had dyed black hair scraped so fiercely back from her face that her eyes had the appearance of narrow dark slits, giving an unnerving predatory expression to a face that was already rendered hawkish by a long Egyptian nose. Her skin was dark, her bosom mountainous. She looked like a woman who would take no nonsense from her customers.

She smiled. Her teeth were sharp and white. Charlie backed towards the door.

'Please. Come inside, monsieur,' said the madam. 'Come out of the cold. My girls will keep you warm.'

'I'm sorry, I really can't stay,' Charlie said, opening the front door with his foot. The women were peering at him with quiet consternation, preparing to pounce, he felt sure.

'Of course you can, milord. We will be happy to accommodate you.'

He realised he shouldn't have spoken. She had heard his English accent. All upper-class Englishmen were 'milords' to French whores – rich pickings. 'No, no,' Charlie said, realising he'd have to speak a language she understood. 'You see, I don't have any money. Not a sou.'

A red-haired girl whispered something to the madam and the madam smiled her toothy smile, her sharp jet eyes lighting on the package in Charlie's arms. 'Perhaps you have something of value to trade?' she asked.

Charlie fled, out into the snow where the half-dressed women would be reluctant to follow. They most certainly weren't having the contents of the package. Not that they wouldn't derive a great deal of fun out of the thing, but at present it was the only thing that would raise the money to get the bloody hell out of Paris and off this godforsaken continent once and for all.

He slithered and staggered over wet cobbles, clutching his prize tight in his arms. He had been told to come straight back from fetching it and he hadn't. Will would be angry. He hurried up the Rue Caulaincourt until he reached their lodging and paused for a moment to shut the front door tight, pulling so hard that he heard snow thump from above the other side of the door, then took the stairs two at a time.

Will was shivering beside a meagre fire in the tiny sitting room, and looked more frozen than enraged. 'What happened to you?' he asked.

Charlie shook the snow from his coat and put the package on the writing table. 'Those fucking women.'

'What women?'

'The whores. On the boulevard. Bloody things hunt in packs.'

Will blew on his fingers to warm them. 'I'm not surprised on a night like this. They're probably desperate to go somewhere warm for half an hour. You didn't give them any money, did you?'

'What money?' said Charlie. 'No, I didn't.' He crouched down beside the fire. 'When are we leaving? Did you write to Louisa?'

'I said it depended. If we can't pass the sculpture off as a genuine Hoyland then we're stuck with a porno-graphic curiosity not worth the price of the boat-train to Calais. Let's have a look at it. I hope your marble man had better co-ordination than his absinthe habit would suggest.'

'He was cheap,' said Charlie. 'That's the main thing.'

'Hmm.' Will unwrapped the packaging and opened the box. It was stuffed with torn newspapers and he dislodged them impatiently. Charlie reached for them to put them on the fire but Will stopped him, saying they'd need them to repack the box.

Despite his drink problem the art forger had done an excellent job. Carved from Hoyland's favoured material –

Carrara marble – was a life-size replica of a phallus. It followed the veins and curves of the plaster original Charlie and Will had stolen from Naples and beneath the base was a carefully copied 'FH'. 'All right,' Will said, blinking at it. 'I admit, I'm impressed.'

'You should be,' said Charlie, relaxing. 'It's a very good likeness.'

Will shook his head. 'The things you make me do.'

'I didn't make you do anything.'

'You persuaded me.'

'Persuasion can only accomplish so much,' Charlie said, trying in vain to warm himself at the hearth. The coals were almost ash. 'God, I'm frozen. Isn't there any way we can get paid sooner?'

Will looked censorious. 'Well, we could still be in Naples enjoying the winter sun . . .'

'Don't start . . .'

'. . . if you hadn't been incapable of keeping your prick inside your clothes for more than five minutes at a time.'

'I know. Will, please. I *know* this.'

'Married men do tend to take exception to people seducing their wives, you know.'

'Actually she did the seducing,' Charlie said. 'And you don't know the half of it, so leave me alone.'

'I knew enough,' said Will. 'Which was that he was a certifiable bloody lunatic and when he said he'd kill anyone who touched her he almost certainly meant it. We're fortunate it's only a marble copy of my cock in that box and not *your* actual member.' He blew on his fingers again and sighed. 'It's no good. I'm going to bed. I can't write a thing when my hands are this cold.'

'Give me some money. I'll go and fetch more coal.'

'It's late. We may as well both get some sleep.'

He left Charlie prodding the dying fire. Charlie felt just warm enough to remove his damp coat, but he knew they had to get paid and get out of Paris soon. He was sure he wouldn't make it through this rotten winter. Will was right, as usual. They should have stayed in Naples, although it was questionable how long one could rely on the good humour of a man as unpredictable as Hoyland.

No, Will was right. Charlie had done his fair share of seduction where Mrs Hoyland was concerned, but he had simply never met a woman like her before – or so he thought when he first clapped eyes on her. He hadn't known at the time how right he was.

The fire went out. Charlie went to the small adjoining bedroom, where Will was already curled deep under the covers of the rickety iron-frame bed. He shed only as many layers of clothes as he dared and quickly plunged beneath the covers, wincing at the chill on the sheets.

Will coughed to indicate that he was still awake, but made no complaint when Charlie shuffled closer to him, seeking warmth. Charlie tentatively put an arm around his waist and Will pushed it away.

'Please?'

'No.'

'Why?'

Will rolled over in the dark to look at him. The bright cold moon caught his eye. 'Because I trusted you. Even though I knew what to expect, I still trusted you.'

'Then it doesn't matter, does it?' The furnace-heat was back with a vengeance, licking at Charlie's guts and brain and suffusing his groin with a voluptuous warmth. In the clear light streaming through the thin curtains Charlie could see Will's face, his expression injured but no less handsome for that. He had a narrow face with a strong jaw, a mouth shaped for irony and a long Roman nose. Charlie remembered seeing that same face rendered in charcoals by Hoyland – fine features contorted into expressions that were extraordinary – eyes half lidded, lips pouting around an indrawn breath, or forehead furrowed, teeth clenched around a dirty word.

'It does matter,' said Will.

'It doesn't. Everything's different now, anyway.' Charlie reached for Will and tried to kiss his mouth, but Will turned his face away, resisting.

'No.'

'Why?' Charlie tussled with him, succeeding in grabbing both of Will's hands and pinioning him to the bed. He felt so much stronger than he had before. The blood in his veins felt hot and rich and his muscles sang with their new power, but in the middle of his burning brain was an icy clarity, cold as the moon – an absolute certainty of his physical superiority. He could do whatever he wanted.

'Stop it,' Will said, trying to dislodge his legs to kick.

'No.' Charlie went for another kiss. Will turned away and swore at him, but Charlie was sure he could already smell something salty, a scent he had tasted in Naples when they had 'posed' for that perverted old goat Hoyland. They didn't call Hoyland the new Tiberius purely because he had set up home so near to Capri. The things that man had asked them to do! It had piqued Charlie's curiosity, made him wonder if that might be the reason he caught Will staring at him sometimes, especially the night after they'd visited Pompeii and seen wall paintings of men entangled in the arms of other males.

Will shivered hard and shook his head, muttering 'No, no, no,' under his breath, but when he did surrender to being kissed he did so with such abandonment that Charlie wondered why Will bothered to put up such a fight every time since he enjoyed it so much.

'There. You see? You like it,' Charlie murmured, his lips now warmed with his friend's ragged breaths. Will moaned quietly in response and staunched any further flow of mockery by covering Charlie's mouth firmly with his own, his tongue pushing eagerly between Charlie's lips.

Will could only put up so much resistance. Charlie was certain Will was thinking of the same things as he was himself – the depraved things they had done in Hoyland's studio. It had been warm there, warm enough for them to strip naked and let their hands and tongues roam as freely over one another's bodies as if they hadn't had an audience. It hadn't been like this, half frozen and fumbling in the dark. Charlie promised himself he would make it up to Will once they got paid. They would rent somewhere in London and Charlie would pay for enough champagne to get Will giddy-drunk and more besides – treat him to some warmer, better planned seduction than this chilly coupling.

'Please,' Will whispered, his hips jerking upwards beneath Charlie's body. 'Oh please.'

Charlie had to search his way through several layers of clothes to find Will's cock. When he grasped it in his hand it was as hot as its marble counterpart was cold. The skin was silk soft, veins pulsing in his palm. There was no substitute for the real thing.

Will liked to kiss while they were doing this, which Charlie supposed was the difference between the way he'd done it at school, frigging off the other boys in contests to see who could come first. There had never been kissing and he suspected the mere mention of it would have met with a reaction of pure horror. That was the difference. Kissing marked a genuine desire, rather than a simple schoolboyish urge to blow off some spunk.

Charlie didn't mind kissing. He couldn't mind kissing, not after what they'd done before. There was something so perfect about the way the slip and slide of their tongues and lips became more frantic as they tugged at one another's cocks. The sheer synchronicity of it was delicious. He imagined he could taste Will's muffled moans and he thought that if they had a flavour then they would taste like that first effusion of salty dew at the tip of an erect prick.

Will came first, which according to the rules of school games, made him the winner. His body bucked sharply and he left off kissing, his cheek pressed against Charlie's and his breath exploding in a harsh gasp in Charlie's ear. His fingers tightened with a reflex grip on Charlie's cock and Charlie bit his lip to keep from crying out as he reached his own climax. It was warm in the bed now, not warm enough to sweat, but enough to feel cosy lying there with his drawers round his knees and his shirt hem trailing in his own spendings.

Still panting, Will pulled the covers up over himself. His eyes glittered, although if there was a flush on his cheeks Charlie couldn't see it for the whitening light of the moon that sapped all colour from his face. For a moment Charlie wondered if Will might abandon restraint and curl up beside him like a real lover, but Will hadn't long finished before there were reproaches ready on his lips.

He didn't voice them there and then. He lay on his side and slipped off to sleep, but in the morning Charlie caught him trying to sneak out of bed unnoticed.

'Last night –' Charlie began.

Will cut him off. 'I wish you wouldn't. You know I can't be like this.'

'Who are you hurting?' asked Charlie, unable to see what made 'the Greek vice', as his father called it, so disgusting.

Will shook his head and gave no answer, then he did something surprising and leant over the bed to kiss

Charlie on the forehead. 'I'm going out to get some food and some more coal,' he said. 'Don't get up. It's too cold.'

Charlie wasn't about to argue with him. He curled back under the covers and dozed until he was awoken again by the sound of Will's key in the door. Will had bought bread and cheese, coal and fresh coffee to brew on the little spirit kettle on the sitting-room dresser. So he had had money after all. He just hadn't trusted Charlie with it.

He had also bought a French newspaper and set to reading it almost immediately, ignoring the food and making no move to relight the fire. Will thrived on the written word, to the point where he forgot to eat and Charlie complained that his hips were too bony and hurt him in bed.

Shivering, Charlie bundled himself in an overcoat, his breath freezing where it touched the air. He had no interest in the paper. He just wanted to get warm and get some food inside his stomach. He couldn't precisely recall when he'd last eaten.

'Oh my God,' said Will.

'What?' Charlie asked, not really interested in the answer. He crumpled the newspapers that had packed the box. They had more paper now and they badly needed some kindling.

Will looked shaken as he pointed out the headline. 'It looks as though our sculpture has just appreciated in value,' he said, wryly.

Charlie glanced at the newspaper and felt ill. Hoyland was dead.

Francis Hoyland – famous artist and notorious aesthete. His work had been deemed too racy for exhibition and when he protested the hypocritical condition of morals in England by way of several outraged letters to *The*

Times, a scandal had erupted concerning the daughter of one of his former admirers. Like most scandals, nothing was actually said in print about what Hoyland was accused of, but the rumours were enough to make Hoyland make good on his threat to leave the country.

Hoyland's work became a source of fascination the moment that public galleries refused to take it. When he retreated to Italy it became something of a holy grail for collectors. With hindsight, Charlie now realised why he and Will had been somehow delegated to procure samples. They were young, trusting and at the time they had idolised Hoyland in much the way dissolute boys of the Regency had admired Lord Byron. Hoyland's sense of self-importance was so great that he would not be in the least surprised that two young gentlemen would come all the way from England to worship at his altar of Art and Free Love.

Francis Hoyland himself was as unamiable as his reputation had painted him. He was frequently drunk and while in Naples had developed a habit of eating entire cloves of garlic because he believed they were beneficial to the digestive system. On receiving one of these blasts of garlic and stale wine to the face, Charlie immediately felt sorry for Hoyland's new mistress. Rumour had it he had taken up with some tousled Roman harlot and threatened anyone who didn't show her the deference of addressing her as Mrs Hoyland, even though the real Mrs Hoyland was alive and presumably well in England.

'Let's get out of here,' Will said, when the great artist had lurched off to be sick on the verandah. 'He's all washed up. Stinking drunk.'

Charlie was about to agree with him when he spotted a series of sketches on a table top, sketches which renewed his faith in his pilgrimage. Hoyland was not washed up. In fact, if anything, alcohol seemed to have lent a greater fury to his genius. 'No, wait,' he said, grabbing Will's sleeve and pulling him over to the table. 'Look at these.'

Will looked and it was with satisfaction that Charlie heard him exhale slowly. 'Oh my goodness.'

They were obviously preliminary sketches to a rendering of Leda and the Swan, but neither of them had ever seen anything quite like them before. The basic lines of the drawing – the position of limbs and wings and so forth – were sketched with almost amateurish brevity, but the face of Leda was fully realised. There were tears on her cheeks and her brow was furrowed, but her eyes were closed and her open mouth ambiguous as to whether she was crying out in outrage or unexpected pleasure. Charlie moved an overlying piece of paper and revealed the lower part of the drawing, and they saw that the same attention that had been lavished on her face had been paid to her cunt. The lips were parted and pierced in the centre by the weird serpentine prick of the huge bird. Charlie didn't know how accurate that was since he had never seen a swan's member and had no particular desire to, but he could vouch for the accuracy of Leda's quim. The curls of hair, the layering of the folds – they were all perfect, and so lifelike that one could imagine touching the page between her open thighs and finding the paper wet.

'He'll never part with that,' Will whispered, thinking one step ahead.

'Don't intend him to. I want the finished piece.'

'That's even more unlikely.'

They jumped when Hoyland came up behind them. 'What do you think of my Leda, eh?' he asked. 'Shocking enough for you?'

Charlie turned around, intimidated by the size of the

man. Originally a native of Yorkshire, where he had been born the son of a dairy farmer, Hoyland had a height and solid burliness that made even Charlie feel callow and unfinished by comparison. Hoyland's unkempt red-brown hair grew thickly over his scalp and down the sides of his unshaven cheeks and when he spoke in his brusque, garlic-breathed way the coarse hair seemed to crackle with an untamed animal energy.

'Sir, I've always been in awe of your work,' said Charlie. 'But this ... really. It's quite breathtaking.'

'Breathtaking,' Hoyland said, neutrally. 'Put some colour in your cheeks at any road. Took you for a couple of bum boys. Now I'm not so sure.'

Will bridled. 'I thought you were an advocate of free love, Mr Hoyland.'

'Makes no odds to me if you bugger each other raw, son,' Hoyland told him. 'Just making an observation. I speak as I find.'

'No doubt,' Will said, archly.

'These are preliminaries,' Hoyland said, turning to Charlie, obviously casting Will aside as a lost cause. 'I've had it with painting. There'll be no more paintings from my hand.'

'You can't give up!' Charlie exclaimed, involuntarily. He immediately wished he hadn't. Can't was neither a word for princes or painters, judging by the look in Hoyland's eyes.

'If you listen to me, you'll find otherwise,' Hoyland said. 'I need a drink.' He shouted down the stairs 'Chiara! Bring some more wine!' He hiccupped and shook his huge, auburn head. 'No, I've been wasting my time with paint and canvas. I wanted something I could *touch*.' He held up his big hands, palm out and fingers curved as if squeezing a pair of ripe, invisible breasts.

For the first time Charlie realised why women were

so fascinated by this man. Hoyland was unabashedly sensual, perhaps to the point of grossness, in a world where men treated women like fragile flowers, delicate orchids only to be removed from the hothouse when the purposes of pollination called.

The woman, Chiara, came up with a tray of wine and Charlie struggled not to stare. With that perverse human desire for opposites and being fair himself, he had always found dark women held a special allure for him, particularly the beautiful Italian ladies. This Chiara had the fine dark complexion and jet-black curls that exemplified the loveliest of her breed, and she moved with an impatience verging on anger. There was sweat on her skin and once she had placed the tray on the table she crammed her fingers between her ample breasts and scratched where she was hot. She caught Charlie staring and quirked thick black eyebrows in defiance at her slatternly manners, as if challenging him to wear stays in this suffocating heat and not feel like scratching. He glanced away from her half-exposed bosom and his eyes lit on the face of Leda once more. It was then that he realised that they were the same. Leda had her face, and no doubt her cunt too. It was as indecent as if Hoyland had hitched up her petticoats and spread her out on the table in front of them for them to view. Charlie had difficulty meeting her eyes and when he did she smiled, as if in mockery.

'I've decided to let you see,' Hoyland announced, grandly. 'Come through, gentlemen. You'll like this.'

They followed him down some stairs and through an archway covered by a grubby, paint-stained sheet and there Charlie saw just what Hoyland meant by being finished with painting. He had taken to sculpture. On a table were several miniatures and plaster moulds for

Leda, and there was something huge beneath a piece of sailcloth. Hoyland walked into his domain and began surveying it like a magician in his kitchen, checking this and that, adjusting the sailcloth, blowing plaster dust off moulds. Chiara lingered at the door, leaning on the lintel of the arch with one bare foot pressed up against the wall behind her. She had the knowing look of a street urchin about her and Charlie was certain she knew what she was doing to him every time she turned her black olive eyes and Da Vinci smile his way.

Will beckoned with a slight incline of his head and Charlie went to see what had caught his attention on the table. Cast in plaster, in astounding detail, was a woman's vulva. It looked bizarre denuded of the usual colour and hair – like some kind of tropical seashell – but it was unmistakable what it was.

'Doesn't have the give of the real thing,' Hoyland said, sneaking up on them again and crudely poking a finger into the plaster slit. 'Gives me something to work from, though. The bodies I can do from an anatomy book, but this is the real essence of the piece. You see all these classical studies spattered all over the galleries by these lily-livered bastards and not once do you see realism. *Europa and the Bull* – you ever see that one? They stuck it up where my last exhibition was supposed to go. Bloody rubbish. Pasty little nude capering round a bull with flowers on its horns. The Romans would have chucked a blue fit.'

'But how did you ...?' Will peered down at the quim on the table, looking interested for the first time in a while.

'I was apprenticed to a stonemason as a lad. Should never have bothered buggering about with paintings in the first place.'

'No, I mean, how did you sculpt this from plaster?'

'Had to shave her first,' Hoyland said, leaving Will open mouthed as realisation dawned.

Understanding Hoyland's meaning, Charlie glanced over at Chiara but she was staring up at a fly on the ceiling, twisting a lock of curly hair between her fingers. Her short skirt was almost hitched over her knee, offering a glimpse of the shadows beneath her petticoats. He wondered if she was still shaved bald under there and his blood ran thick and hot all over again.

'Did you see the secret collections at Pompeii?' Hoyland asked, continuing as if he didn't expect a satisfactory answer. 'They wouldn't have let you in anyway. You need written permission. Nobody's supposed to know about those. Classical antiquities that'd make the whole of London society shit its collective drawers if they took so much as a peek. Goats, bulls – even fucking swans. This is where we inherit our culture from, gentlemen, while pretending all the while that we don't. Want to see something you shouldn't?'

His fingers were on the edge of the sailcloth and he laughed at their eager faces. 'Chiara, *dona e mano*,' he said, addressing her in Italian for the first time. Charlie realised she hadn't spoken so much as a word since entering the room. She went to Hoyland and helped him hoist back the sailcloth. '*Europa and the Bull*, gentlemen,' he announced, with an exhalation as he and Chiara loosed the weight of the cloth onto the studio floor.

The sculpture was huge, almost life size, and incredibly obscene. Europa, on her hands and knees on a rock, was being mounted from behind by Jupiter in the form of a bull and no detail or blush had been spared in depicting how wide her sex was stretched by the bull's enormous organ.

'Oh my God,' Will muttered, inclining his head to get a better look. 'It *does* look lifelike.'

'Don't look so worried, Greaves,' said Hoyland. 'I didn't have a bull fuck her to get it right. I just had a bull's pizzle made up in wood, then stuck it up her and plastered around it.'

'How did you work out the ... dimensions?' asked Charlie, hesitantly.

'Worked from memory. I was brought up on a dairy farm.'

'Oh, of course.' Charlie swallowed hard and stared between Europa's legs, uncomfortable with the idea of a woman taking such an enormous object inside her but at the same time madly aroused. 'That's extraordinary. Not painful, I hope?'

'She managed. She's a well-built girl. Can take a whole fist.'

Chiara seemed so unmoved by these conversations that Charlie decided she must speak only very basic English. She seemed quite unconcerned that her flesh was being exhibited by proxy. If anything, she appeared bored. Like most women who appear entirely indifferent to men she was irresistible and when Charlie and Will retreated to their lodgings that evening to discuss tactics, Charlie had only one thing on his mind.

'I *must* have her,' he said, not even realising he'd said it aloud until Will glanced up and frowned.

'Who?'

'Hoyland's maid, housekeeper – model. Her. Chiara.'

Will sighed. 'We're here to procure his artwork, not his staff. Please try and keep your mind on the business at hand, Charlie.'

'My mind *is* on the business at hand. You're never going to persuade him to give up any of his work, not since he made this vow that his art would never be seen in England again. You said it yourself. He doesn't strike me as particularly tractable either, but if *she* were amenable I'm sure she could purloin a couple of pieces.'

Will shook his head. 'Absolutely not. What you seem to forget, my dear Charles, is that this is not a grand romantic adventure. Not this aspect of it, anyway. We are here to do business and furnish collections and we'll get a damned sight less for a stolen Hoyland of dubious pedigree than the genuine article with an official seal of approval from the infamous man himself. This is no time to be playing Casanova.'

'Even if playing Casanova turned out to be expedient?' asked Charlie.

'It never does,' said Will. 'You'd only spend money on the woman and we have a limited amount until we deliver the goods.'

'All right. I'll leave her alone,' Charlie promised, not meaning a word of it. He had a vested interest in drawing this transaction out. Once this was over they would have to return to London and he hated London. It was too crowded, too dirty and too bloody cold. On the other hand he had fallen wholeheartedly in love with Naples, with its warm climate, jewel-bright sea and dark vivacious women.

Will had more conventional methods of persuading Hoyland. He invited him to dinner. Hoyland turned up late and drunk, as if determined to show his disdain for Will's bourgeois sensibilities. He brought Chiara with him and this time introduced her as his wife, which made Charlie realise that he not only didn't have a prayer of seducing the woman but that Will would have even further reason to veto his proposals.

Chiara (he couldn't bring himself to call her Mrs Hoyland; the marriage was obviously bigamous) had dressed for dinner in her own blowsy way. She wore a brilliant-coloured gypsy skirt and a tight scarlet bodice that showed most of her breasts. Her hair was loose around her shoulders and she wore a curious little diadem of what looked like golden daggers and beads on her head. She didn't offer an explanation for her strange costume and neither did Hoyland.

'How's the *Leda and the Swan* coming along, Mr Hoyland?' Will asked, politely.

'Smashed it,' said Hoyland, and took a great swill of wine.

'Oh.' Will looked dumbfounded. 'That's . . . a shame.'

Hoyland shook his head. 'It's not. Leda's a hackneyed old piece. I want something fresh.' He shot an accusatory look at Chiara. Charlie wanted to kill him but Chiara merely looked at her putative husband with something reminiscent of amusement, or perhaps contempt. She caught Charlie looking at her and smothered a smile behind the rim of her wine glass. Her lips were so red they might have been painted. Her lashes were thick and black like her eyebrows and when Charlie looked directly into her eyes he saw that they were not the pure black he had imagined at first glance. Rather they were a dark brown with flecks of an amber green like copper turning to verdigris. Around the pupils were rayed halos of a cleaner copper. She licked the wine from her upper lip.

'The maenads?' Charlie suggested.

Hoyland snorted. So that was a no, then. He drained his glass and rubbed a big scarred hand over his reddish hair. 'Everything's women,' he said. 'Everyone paints naked women. There's more cunt in art galleries than there is in a brothel. I want something new. You two'll do.' He jabbed a fork at Charlie and Will.

'Us?' asked Will, looking surprised. 'What do you mean?'

'Achilles and Patroclus,' said Hoyland.

Knowing the nature of Hoyland's work, Charlie nearly choked on his drink. Will turned crimson to the roots of his hair. Nobody said anything for a moment.

'You will be paid,' Chiara said, in English. It was the first time either of them had ever heard her speak. Her voice was so low it was almost gruff – a strange deep sound coming from the body of a woman who stood barely five foot in height.

'Paid?' said Will, incredulously.

'*Si*. Paid.' She sipped her wine and stared boldly back at them. Her gaze sent a rash of goosebumps over Charlie's flesh and he wondered who really controlled whom in the Hoylands' marriage. Hoyland hadn't even bothered to introduce her when they first met, treated her as a thing to fetch drinks, a face to paint and a quim to penetrate, but the brusque authority with which she spoke made Charlie wonder. She might have been Ariel to Hoyland's Prospero if her lazy, untended beauty were not so earthy and sensual, but as it was Charlie had the sense that she was not in the artist's thrall, rather that he was in hers and that this obscene proposal was her idea.

'Excuse me. I need some air,' said Will, rising from the table. Hoyland poured himself another glass of wine.

'*Scusi*. I did not mean to offend,' said Chiara.

'It's fine, signora,' Charlie said. 'One moment. I'm sure he's just thinking it over.'

He followed Will out to the balcony. Will was leaning on the railing, smoking a cigarette and watching the sun set over the bay of Naples. He looked shocked, which Charlie couldn't help finding funny.

'Are you all right?'

Will exhaled smoke in a sharp, angry puff. 'Paid?' he said, again, shaking his head. 'Paid!'

'I had no idea you were so scrupulous.'

Will turned around, his back to the rail. 'That woman,' he whispered. 'She's a whore. Or was one. It's common knowledge. What kind of creatures does she take us for?'

Charlie laughed.

'I fail to see the humour,' Will said, turning his back again.

Charlie joined him at the railing. 'I would say,' he said, 'that she thinks we're collectors of every kind of filth imaginable. Pornographers. Smut peddlers. And let's be honest with ourselves, Will, that's precisely what we are.'

Will sighed. 'I know that. But really. What they're suggesting . . .'

Charlie nudged Will's elbow with his own. 'I thought we rose above the hypocrisy of conventional morals?'

Will smiled, softened. 'All right. I agree with you on principle.'

'How bad could it be?' Charlie teased, tilting his head to look Will in the eye.

'You're drunk,' Will said, lowering his eyes in a way that seemed both acquiescent and voluptuous at once to Charlie; that dip of the lashes, revealing the smooth skin of the eyelids only normally fully revealed in sleep, in total intimacy and vulnerability. His tone was rueful, amused, as if he'd prefer that Charlie were sober and serious.

It was as if the lid was off Pandora's box now, and there was no closing it. Charlie's whole being thrilled at the idea of seduction – not some cold, mechanical bug-gering – but to seduce Will the way he had seduced girls. Could it even be done with a man? *Should* it be done? He thought not, which made him want to even more. 'I meant it,' he said, quietly, placing his hand on Will's. 'I'm not that drunk.'

Will stared down at the hand covering his and then

looked up again, a weird light in his eyes, one that seemed brim full of corruption, a contemplation of this ultimate profanity. 'We have company,' he finally said, briskly, trying to snap back into his old manner.

'We'll get rid of them,' said Charlie, his voice a lulling siren song to his own ears.

Will disengaged himself and opened the French windows. The Hoylands appeared to be getting ready to leave anyway, Chiara gathering up her shawl and Hoyland draining his glass. 'All right,' Will said, sounding as though he'd surprised himself in saying it. 'We'll consider your offer.'

'Good,' said Hoyland, stomping gracelessly towards the door. 'Don't leave it too long. I have to catch the impulse while it's there.'

'Goodnight,' said Chiara. 'And thank you for dinner.'

The door closed behind her and Will remained staring at it as if transfixed.

'What do you mean, we'll consider their offer?' asked Charlie.

Will exhaled and shook his head. 'I thought that *you* knew? What precisely were you suggesting out there?'

'You know what I was suggesting,' Charlie said, turning to him. He reached out to touch Will's cheek, but Will rebuffed him.

'Don't,' said Will, his tone sharp.

Charlie withdrew, worried that he had made a terrible mistake.

'Unless you mean it,' Will added, reacting to his friend's consternation.

'I do mean it.' Charlie moved closer once again. He was near enough to see where the wine had stained Will's lips, the raw patch on his throat where he had scraped himself shaving that morning.

'It's a sin,' said Will, although he didn't move.

'You're an atheist.'

'You're not.'

Charlie shrugged. 'My soul's hardly stainless anyway. And I think God has better things to do than worry about who I go to bed with. What's He going to do? A repeat performance of Sodom and Gomorrah?'

Will smiled, lightening the moment. 'I really wouldn't advise invoking fire and brimstone *here*, of all the places in the world.'

Charlie breathed in the sulphurous, sultry night air and laughed. 'Yes. Fair point.'

The warmth of the room seemed to close in on him. The smile had slowly receded from Will's lips and his near-sighted hazel eyes had that light in them once again. 'You don't know what you're asking of me,' he said, presently.

'Maybe I don't.' Charlie stepped closer; close enough to feel the heat of Will's body through the thin lawn of his shirt. He wasn't sure exactly what it was they were supposed to do together but his curiosity had reached a point where it would have to be sated. He wanted to know how it would feel to be tangled up in the hard wiry limbs of another naked male. He reached out to touch Will again and this time he wasn't rejected. His hand rested on the slight transverse curve above Will's hip and he could feel the moisture of sweating skin through cloth. He could feel solidity where a woman would be soft in the corresponding spot, but it only stirred him further. He felt Will breathing, slow and deep, controlled; then he wondered how Will might breathe when he lost control, gasping for air as he came, and the thought sent a greedy little shudder of want through his flesh.

Will looked down at the hand on his waist as if he had never seen a hand before. 'You don't,' he said quietly. 'Truly, you don't.'

'Then show me.'

Will glanced up. He looked far too serious but he reached out and touched Charlie's hair, curling his hand around the nape of Charlie's neck and drawing him closer still. 'You don't understand,' he murmured.

Charlie shivered at the touch. It was sensuous yet unmistakably masculine and he was amazed to find his body responded even more rapidly than usual *because* it was a man's touch. This was forbidden, some said unnatural, and Charlie was suddenly sure that it was forbidden because it was so very very pleasurable. It would be wonderful. He was sure of it. It would be delicious and brand new and unbridled. If he was this excited by mere anticipation, then what would the sex itself be like? He was already as hard as oak, his breath catching, his blood rushing and his lips tingling as if they had already been kissed.

'I don't care,' he said, wondering what the hell there could be to understand anyway.

'No, you don't,' said Will, frowning slightly. He moved to hold Charlie's face cupped in both hands, his thumbs stroking the sensitive skin at the corners of Charlie's eyes. 'Close your eyes,' he whispered, his breath warm and winey on Charlie's face.

The tenderness of the expected kiss took Charlie by complete surprise. When Will's lips met his the touch was chaste, until he felt a soft wet lap of tongue, a sharp intake of air as if just that one light touch had robbed Will of the ability to breathe. When it was over Charlie couldn't hold back a small involuntary sound of loss.

'You have no idea,' said Will, his eyes dark and bright

in the lamplight, his fingers still cradling Charlie's skull. 'I want you.'

What threads of Charlie's control remained snapped. He kissed Will hard on the mouth, grasping Will's shirt with both hands, anything to hold him there, although Will showed no inclination to escape; rather he responded with a passion Charlie would never have imagined of him only twelve hours previously. They stumbled against the back of a chair and it fell on its side with a thud as Charlie lost his balance and slid to the floor, dragging Will with him.

Will was on top of him, tugging at his clothes and kissing him forcefully, messily, his strength and shape a constant reminder to Charlie that he was actually *doing* this with another man. He could feel that Will was hard, a rigid bulge crushed up against his own swollen cock, but there was no going back, not now. His body was already straining towards release, so hard that he let out a low moan of relief when his prick was freed from his trousers.

Will stopped to pull his shirt off over his head. His eyes were bright, his lips and cheeks red. With his shirt off and his trousers slipping down over the hard ridges of his narrow hips, his body looked as pure and perfect as a Roman statue, only better, because marble wasn't warm, palpitating, flecked with curls of dark hair and tipped with pale-pink nipples.

Curious, Charlie reached up to squeeze one nipple gently between his fingertips. Judging by the way Will gasped they must have been as tender as the teats of some women. Excited by this discovery, Charlie raised himself up from the floor, enough to kiss and suckle like a child at the breast. Will stumbled backwards onto his haunches, his head thrown back and one hand tangled in Charlie's hair. He was breathing hard and as he fell back his unbuttoned trousers slid the small distance they needed to go to let his prick spring loose. His cock was long and slim, like the rest of him. It poked up from a nest of dark hair, the tip of it rosy red and already leaking drops of clear fluid.

What now? Did he take it in his hand, or his mouth, or kneel and present his bum as if for a school prefect? Charlie didn't know, but his confusion must have showed on his face because Will smiled, laughed breathily.

'You don't know what to do, do you?' he said.

'Do you?' Charlie asked, defensively. He reached for Will's cock but Will shook his head and pulled Charlie down into an embrace. The touch of his body, now naked to the knees, was immediately delicious. The lean flat planes of his hips and belly and chest were thrilling, a promise of strength against which Charlie might brace himself, handle with greater force than even the randiest of women might stand for. They rolled and tumbled on the floor like children wrestling, until Will whispered, 'Look at yourself,' and indicated their translucent reflections in the glass doors of the dresser. Charlie turned his head to one side and saw his own pale naked body, saw Will lying above him. He let out a cry and arched his back, offering his cock for much-needed attention. They really would make a masterpiece for Hoyland – so beautiful the way limbs entwined and candlelight turned flesh to fire.

'You like it,' Will said, softly. 'Don't you?' His roaming hands came to rest on Charlie's hips and Charlie watched his own body twist and buck with need.

'Please,' he moaned. 'Please.'

'Tell me,' said Will, holding him fast. Will's smile was

somewhere between beatific and demonic. 'Tell me you love it. Tell me you want me.'

'I do. I want you. I want this. Please.'

Will bowed his head over Charlie's heart, his dark curls tickling the skin as he pressed and rubbed his cheek against Charlie like a cat. He kissed where his lips rested, breathed deeply, slowly several times over where he had wet the skin with his mouth and Charlie realised with a fresh jolt of pleasure that Will was *smelling* him, breathing in the scent of his skin.

'Oh God,' he whispered, his hips bucking under Will's hands, his balls heavy with the desire for release. 'Please, Will – do something.'

Will dipped his head lower and Charlie felt the tip of his tongue on his breastbone, felt the heat of it travelling down below his ribs. Was he really going to . . .? Oh God, he was. Charlie saw in the glass, saw Will's head move down between his legs and then he had to close his eyes because the sensation of that wet, unholy mouth suckling at his cock was just too exquisite to bear for long.

'Stop,' he managed to say, but Will's tongue was darting over him in such a way on each upstroke that he was losing control before he knew it. He came with a cry that must have sounded so much like frustration to Will that Will laid a consoling hand on him while decorously wiping his mouth on the corner of the tablecloth.

'You needn't think I've finished,' said Will. 'I've barely started.'

Hoyland's studio was a place Charlie associated with erotic expectation, what with the obscene sculptures and the dark vivid presence of Chiara, but when he was dazed with lack of sleep, he felt as pliant as clay. They might do anything with him and he wouldn't care, mould him into whatever filthy pose they thought suitable.

Will had turned out to be a far more accomplished lover than Charlie imagined. Neither of them had slept for the past three nights – barely at all last night, when Charlie had lain half-drowsing, watching with heavy-lidded eyes as the full moon sank into the bay and bathed both their bodies in silver. Will whispered that he looked as though he were carved from ice or marble and Charlie had pressed Will's hand to his sweating skin to show that he wasn't cold, not cold at all, and then they were off again.

That first night, Will had fucked him, lying on the floor in front of their reflections on the dresser door. He had felt drunk, drunker than he should have been on three glasses of thin, Italian red wine and had lain acquiescent to what was being done to him, rocking with the thrusts of Will's body. He thought they might do it again, here in the studio, with Hoyland watching and sketching.

The only furniture was a long, low, Grecian-style couch, perhaps like the one the princely Achilles might have shared with his beloved. There were none of the draperies and bowls of fruit Charlie would normally have associated with an artist's studio. Chiara took their coats, then stood waiting expectantly until they realised they were to hand her the rest of their clothes too. Hoyland, prickling behind his drawing board, was obviously eager to get on with the job in hand.

Charlie undressed first. Chiara didn't react when he handed his clothes to her piece by piece and eventually stood there in nothing but his skin. Perhaps she had seen far too many naked men in her previous profession to be moved by the spectacle but Charlie wanted her to look at him with admiration. She put his clothes down on the floor without saying a word and moved to Will, who took off his shirt without taking his eyes from Charlie's naked body.

Oh, this would be easy, Charlie realised. He knew that look in Will's eyes and when Will was also undressed Charlie could see his eager, slender prick already lifting its rosy head in anticipation.

'Well, touch him, then,' prompted Hoyland, after a long moment. His voice seemed to come from far away. Chiara placed Will's clothes in a neat bundle beside Charlie's and went to the side of her master, or her slave, whichever he was. Charlie couldn't tell.

Will made the first move. He put his hands on Charlie's bare hips, drew him close and kissed him. Charlie was already conscious of how they must look, standing naked, their lips touching, cocks risen like mirror images of one another. Their audience affected him as much as it did Will. In the middle of a long kiss, Charlie peeked through his eyelashes, over the curve of Will's cheekbone, and saw Chiara's impassive face. He wanted to go down on his knees and take Will in his mouth, or lie on the couch and offer himself for a fucking, anything to raise even so much as a blush to her cheeks. As it was, she didn't bat an eyelid, but she would, he decided. He'd show her sights that would made it impossible for her to keep her fingers from her cunt. She'd have no choice but to lift her skirts and frig herself in front of them. Charlie almost laughed at the idea, imagining Hoyland's expression if she did such a thing.

He was determined to stir a reaction from her. He knelt and touched his lips to the warm moist tip of Will's cock, gratified by the way Will inhaled deeply, sharply. Charlie had already learnt to like doing this, because whenever he did Will gasped and babbled and made the most wonderful whimpering noises. As Charlie drew the neat rose-coloured head into his mouth Will cried out softly and reached to steady himself on the arm of the couch. Charlie shifted on his heels, conscious of Chiara's gaze but not daring to look up from what he was doing.

'No,' Hoyland said, suddenly.

'No?' Will's prick slipped out of Charlie's mouth with an undignified wet pop and as Charlie turned to glare at Hoyland it slapped against his cheek.

'The other way around,' said Hoyland, pointing at Charlie. 'You're Achilles. You're broader in the shoulders. I want *you* fucking *him*.'

Charlie looked up, trying to gauge Will's reaction. This was one of the few things they hadn't done over the past few nights. Will said nothing. He wet his upper lip with the tip of his tongue and sat down on the couch. Eventually he said, 'All right. We'll need some ... help though. Some oil, or something.'

Hoyland must have anticipated this because Chiara stepped forwards with a pottery bottle of olive oil. With her usual negligent, indifferent manner she poured a generous slick of the stuff over Charlie's front. It dribbled down between his legs and down his thighs, cooling his overheated skin.

'Up,' she said, directing him to stand, and then she began to massage the spilt mess into his skin. For the first time Charlie was uncomfortably aware of Hoyland because his cock twitched eagerly under Chiara's touch and he couldn't help but stare directly down into the cleft between her breasts. She started with his chest and belly and didn't apologise when the back of her wrist bumped against his erection. Instead she wrapped her fingers around it, making him bite his lip and turn his face away so that Hoyland wouldn't see the pleasure she was giving him. She oiled his cock with smooth, matter-of-fact strokes, her detachment a whore's detachment. He wondered again, what would it take to rouse her?

She poured the oil between Will's buttocks and looked matter-of-factly at Charlie.

'Just . . . like that?' Charlie asked.

Chiara shrugged. 'You did this before?'

Charlie shook his head, still amazed at what he was about to do. He watched the golden-green oil run down the backs of Will's legs and swallowed hard. Will glanced over his shoulder at them both, his expression both expectant and impatient. He arched his back a little, thrusting his bum higher so that Charlie could just glimpse the shadowed entrance. Chiara sighed and took Charlie's hand. 'Use your fingers,' she said. 'Otherwise it will be too tight.'

He wondered if she had ever been buggered. He would have loved to do that to her. Much as he wanted Will he would have loved to have bent Chiara over, thrown up her skirts, pulled down her drawers and taken hold of her large brown buttocks, to listen to her cry of surprise as he stuck it in the wrong hole. Hoyland told her to move away (he had obviously not envisioned having Briseis attend the men in his tableau) and Charlie watched her arse move as she walked away from them. She had a big, round, solid peasant girl's bottom that swayed her skirts provocatively this way and that.

'Come on,' Will muttered.

'Right.' Charlie cautiously pushed a finger into Will's oiled crack and was startled by how easily the flesh gave way. His finger slid inside effortlessly and Will made a soft sound and pressed back into the touch. He was so smooth in there, so hot, and Charlie's cock gave a little jerk and shudder when he wondered if he felt like that to Will.

He remembered Will doing this to him – one finger, then two, stretching and softening the way. He didn't know that he could do this; Will was so tight. He pushed in another finger and fucked Will gently with them. Will moaned very quietly and moved his hips with a sort of wanton sinuous wriggle that made Charlie want this even more. This was definitely something he wanted to do in private sometime, only with Will on his back so that they could kiss while they fucked and he could press his tongue deep into Will's mouth while Will tried to catch his breath and pull away to make those low, lovely sobbing cries he made when he was coming.

'Are you ready?'

'Yes. Yes, I'm ready.'

Charlie lined it up, closing his eyes. He didn't want to think about his audience in that moment. He pushed and his initial thought was no, no, this isn't going to work. Even with all that oil it was just too tight, and then something gave, some knot of resistance, and he was inside. He barely had to push forwards at all to find himself gliding deep into Will's body.

The shock of it was instantaneous – the heat, the tight muscle clenched like a fist around the base of his cock. Charlie bit his lip hard and grasped Will's hips, only daring to open his eyes when he was bent far forwards enough to be unable to see where their bodies were joined. He thought that if he saw that then this would be over before it had even begun.

Will exhaled, a sound of what could have been pleasure or pain escaping with his breath.

'Hold it there,' ordered Hoyland. 'Don't move a muscle.'

Oh, this was unfair. Charlie was aching to thrust, to fuck. He held the pose with difficulty, not least because he could feel every breath Will took, from the inside. He could feel Will's heartbeat deep in the flesh that enveloped him, beating out in tandem with the pulse in his own straining cock.

After what seemed like an age, Hoyland gave them leave to move and Charlie, too keyed up to hold back, began to fuck Will hard. Will moaned louder than Charlie had ever heard him moan before and arched his back eagerly, stuck his arse in the air for further attention and cried out when Charlie dug his fingertips into the sparse flesh of his skinny bum. They had to do this again – had to. Charlie was desperate to see Will's face while he was being fucked like this. Will was always the last to lose control. Whenever he fucked Charlie he watched with a cool detachment while Charlie blasphemed and squirmed and swore. It was only at the crucial moment that Will's control would ever really slip and Charlie thought of his face – eyes shut, mouth open, panting through a ragged, shuddering breath. The thought of his expression was enough to tip Charlie too close to the edge just as Hoyland shouted, 'Stop!'

Charlie would have protested that he could no more stop at that moment than he could fly, but Hoyland was bellowing instructions at them both. 'Head back ... that's it. Hold it, hold it! You, yes, keep your hand on your prick ... no, not like *that*!'

Will jerked beneath Charlie and cried out, his body bucking wildly. Charlie felt the muscle around him clench even tighter, clenching and unclenching in spasms that seemed to suck the spunk towards the end of Charlie's cock. His climax felt thin, a pinprick, a tiny thread of hot semen drawn out of his prick, rather than the luscious gushes he sometimes envisioned himself releasing into Will's clever mouth.

They collapsed in a tangled heap on the couch. Will was soaked in sweat, slippery with oil. Charlie slid out easily and buried his face in Will's back, not wanting to look at him and especially not wanting to look at Hoyland.

'All right,' Hoyland said. 'I've got what I need. You can get up now.'

Charlie sat up on the couch. Will slowly uncurled himself and looked briefly at Charlie with eyes so dilated they looked almost black.

'You can wash downstairs in the kitchen,' Hoyland told Charlie, not even thanking him for a job well done. 'You,' Hoyland added, turning to Will. 'You stay here. I need you.'

It was too hot and the film of oil on Charlie's skin felt as though it was basting him like a roasting goose, so he took his clothes downstairs to wash himself. The kitchen was even shabbier than the studio, plaster peeling from the walls and cracks here and there where the earth itself had shuddered, as if in fear of the great bubbling cauldron of Vesuvius. There was water, soap and a towel, obviously laid out by Chiara because Charlie couldn't imagine Hoyland capable of even such a practical courtesy. She was nowhere to be seen but Charlie heard a splashing, thudding sound from somewhere in the kitchen – perhaps a servant, although he had never seen any servants before. The place was like one of those palaces in fairy tales, neglected and deserted, fallen into a magical torpor until someone kissed the ensorcelled princess and broke the spell. Except that there was no princess, of course, only Chiara, and she seemed the sort to cast spells rather than fall victim to them. Whenever her name was mentioned the Neapolitan women made the sign of the evil eye and muttered some word that sounded like '*strega*', along with another that Charlie knew very well was Italian for 'whore'.

He washed himself briskly and then set out to explore.

There was a broken mangle and a chamber pot in one ante-room, then a small courtyard with weeds pushing through the cracks of the paving slabs. In the centre, a bougainvillea ran riot, untended, giant blowsy blossoms humming with insects in the ashy twilight.

The sound was louder here and Charlie found its source in another ante-chamber off the courtyard. Chiara sat on a low stool, pounding washing in a wooden, brass-ringed tub. She had stripped off her gown in the heat and Charlie could see how wide her legs were spread under her petticoats. She was sweating and she worked at the washing in an angry, exhausted manner, half-heartedly thumping the pole into the water and splashing her bare feet. It was a moment before she saw him and when she did she said nothing, just raised her eyebrows. He thought she was too breathless from her work to speak.

She straightened up and wiped sweat from her face with the back of her forearm.

'Don't you have servants to do that?' Charlie asked, knowing he was being rude but wondering why any gentleman who insisted on his mistress being called his wife would then delegate the woman to tasks more suited to a scullery maid.

She shook her head and got up from the stool. Her petticoats were short, like her switching skirts. As she closed her legs to stand Charlie saw a glimpse of shadowed knee and thigh. 'My husband read Karl Marx,' she said, wryly. 'Good news for the proletariat. Bad news for me.'

'I expect he read Darwin too,' said Charlie, amused by the way she mispronounced 'proletariat'. Her accent lent the word a Latin flourish he found incongruous.

'He doesn't need to,' she said, cryptically.

'What do you mean?'

She shrugged. 'He has never had any difficulty regarding humans as another species of animal.' She moved closer; close enough for Charlie to see the individual beads of sweat on her breasts. He shivered, remembering that not an hour ago she had been holding his cock in her hand.

'It's what he's been saying all along,' she continued. 'It only makes a scandal because people are arrogant – they think they are better than animals.' She looked into Charlie's eyes, her own eyes black in the deepening dusk. 'And what about you?' she asked, her hand on his chest. 'Did God mould you from clay? Did he split me from your rib? Or are you just another monkey?' She grabbed his crotch and leant in and he tried to kiss her, but she screeched loudly in his face in an uncannily convincing mimic of a monkey. When he jumped back, startled, she laughed wildly.

She stood facing him, her back to the wall where there was a little recessed arch – perhaps a window seat long since bricked up and plastered over. He was angry at the way she laughed at him and advanced on her, already thinking of how easy it would be to hoist her onto the ledge and spread her legs apart. 'What are *you*, then?' he asked. 'They call you *strega*, you know.'

'A witch?' She laughed again. She smelt richly of sweat and olive oil, the oil with which she had so recently anointed him. 'They are stupid, ignorant women. Good wives. Good for nothing else.'

He was amazed to think he had ever thought her cold. She hissed the words at him with a sibilance like water on a hot iron. He could feel the heat from her flesh without even touching her, but he wanted to touch her and he would. He pushed closer to her and she shuffled her back against the wall, finding purchase on the ledge and climbing up. She looked knowing and wicked, her eyes bright in the failing light, her lips curled in the sarcastic smile of a whore so accustomed to men's desires that she had grown to find them pitiable and amusing.

'You're not even a wife,' he told her, insinuating his hips between her knees. 'Much less a good one, or else you wouldn't be here.'

She said nothing but she spread her legs wider and hitched up her skirts.

Hoyland, he knew, would probably kill him, but here was an opportunity for revenge. Hoyland had cheated Charlie out of his pleasure upstairs and now Charlie ached to even the score. She couldn't enjoy that garlic-breathed old goat sweating all over her anyway. Charlie could give her things that he couldn't – youth and beauty. And she wanted him. She lifted her chin and stuck out her breasts for his appraisal. Her stays were so tight they made a shelf of her bosom. Her eyes remained fixed on him, her gaze challenging, daring him to touch her. She pulled back her sweaty mass of dark hair and smiled again. Her arms were brown and muscular, with jet-black curls beneath them. He knew something was going to happen. It was just a question of when. She beckoned him with a little incline of her head and without any further ceremony he stuck his hand up beneath her petticoat. Chiara bared her white teeth in a humourless, breathy laugh as he fumbled his way up her smooth, round thighs. She wore no drawers and his prick leapt to even stiffer attention as he found the wet tangle of hair between her legs. So she hadn't remained shaved after all. The hair was thick and luxuriant and he pushed her skirt higher still to look at it. It was as black as the rest of her hair and he could just glimpse the wine-red inner lips of her cunt in the centre.

She breathed hard when he opened her wider with his fingers. The pictures and sculptures hadn't done her justice. He had never seen one so hairy, so red, so wet and so wantonly female. It seemed to pulse already with the promise of an ecstasy that no other woman could offer.

'You want?' she murmured, her accent sounding even thicker and her voice still deeper in her agitation.

Charlie nodded and reached to unfasten his trousers but she shook her head.

'Kiss it,' she ordered. 'Lick it. Taste it.'

He knelt and she held up her skirt for him, nodding imperiously when he hesitated for a moment. Anxious to oblige her, to do anything to be allowed to fuck her, he licked her tentatively, gathering enthusiasm when he heard her gasp and felt her hips rock forwards as she pressed herself against his mouth. He lapped more confidently at her, tasting salt, scenting the musk of her hair. She rocked slowly on the ledge, grasped his hair and pushed his face deeper into her quim.

He felt as though he were drowning in her, his face wet with her juices, spit and salt dribbling down his chin as if he were greedily devouring some exotic fruit. It was glorious to hear her moan for him. She made soft crooning sounds, mingled with broken words in Italian that he didn't understand. When he slipped a finger inside her she became louder and the sound she made was strange, almost bestial, like a low howl, but he took no notice because his cock was pounding behind his trouser buttons in anticipation of following into the soft wet passage now occupied by his finger.

She pushed him away and he staggered back onto the floor, praying that she hadn't changed her mind, but then she stood and began to literally tear off her clothes. She ripped right through the woven tapes of her stays with a strength that was alarming. Her heavy round breasts tumbled forwards as she bent to rip at the fastenings of her petticoat and then she was stark naked before him. She was breathing like someone who had just run a race. Her teeth were clenched and her eyes had a curious, hungry light in them.

'Come,' she said, her voice hard and guttural.

She leant back against the ledge once more, spreading her thighs for him. Charlie scrambled to his feet, finally tugging his cock free of his trousers and thrusting it into her. She was drenched from his tongue and she cried out throatily as he impaled her. For the first time she offered him her lips and she kissed as though she were starved for it. Her black hair spilled forwards, clinging to her neck and to Charlie's sweating, sticky cheeks. Her teeth were sharp and her tongue rough and agile and her kisses seemed to become fiercer as he fucked her.

If only he hadn't come so soon before. She was going to overtake him. She pulled away from his lips and once more she was muttering in Italian, so close that her lips brushed his as they formed the words. Her hips were thrusting, pounding, and he felt her cunt clutch and shudder. He tried to kiss her again to slow her down but then he felt such a sharp pain in his lower lip that he instinctively backed away, stumbling backwards into the dark with his prick out of his trousers and his hand over his mouth.

When he took his hand away he saw, illuminated by the moonlight streaming in from the courtyard, a streak of blood on his fingers.

'You bit me!' he said, turning back to her. 'You fucking bitch, you bit . . .'

He trailed off and backed towards the archway. Chiara was crouched on the floor, her eyes an unnatural shade of gold, her hair an eldritch tangle. She curled her lip at him and snarled, actually snarled, like an animal. He could have sworn that he saw her back arch and *bristle*, with hackles like a dog's, saw her arms and legs change shape and her face stretch and elongate, as if by calling her a bitch he had magically transformed her into one, that he saw her tongue grow longer and her eyes bigger and her teeth sharper. He could have sworn all of these things and more had he stayed to watch, but as it was he crossed himself and ran as fast as his legs could carry him.

5

Phoebe did not wish to become accustomed to her new life too rapidly. She thought that if she did so she might fail to appreciate the luxury and abundance in which she now found herself living. At home there had never been quite enough of anything. The flour for the puddings had to be stretched to the last half-ounce, the rooms were never warm enough and Dora went out to buy provisions with strict instructions as to where she should go and who she should buy it from lest they be fleeced with an adulterated quarter-pound of tea or sugar.

By contrast Louisa didn't seem to care. She treated household accounts as a boring necessity and, to all appearances, she could afford to do so. The fireplaces were always heaped high with coals, the heavy brocade curtains keeping out the worst of draughts on winter nights. The rooms were often fragrant with the festive scents of cloves and oranges. Louisa had a fondness for sticking the orange with cloves and wrapping them in scraps of lace to make Elizabethan-style pomanders of them and the hard, dried oranges would be placed in the drawers where she kept her masses of silk and lace lingerie.

She also had a taste for spicy food, in keeping with the still current fad for anything remotely Indian, and sometimes the smell of roasting spices from the kitchen was enough to catch wheezily in the back of one's throat. Phoebe had been dubious at first about tasting such things but she had taken a liking to a chicken dish made with almonds and coconut. She had never imagined in her entire life that she'd eat such exotic dishes and it recalled Mr Spiriakis to her, with his tales of the spice markets of Constantinople. She was sure that the moon-faced watch he had given to her had brought her the luck he promised.

Then, of course, there was Louisa's dress – the red evening gown that had become such a project for the both of them it had almost taken on a personality of its own. Phoebe thrilled to its purpose. She had guessed quite easily what that purpose was.

'I promised that I'd tell you everything,' Louisa said, when Phoebe guessed the source of Louisa's fortune. It had been perfectly obvious when they had taken a Sunday drive in Hyde Park and met some of Louisa's acquaintances. They were all beautifully dressed and were in carriages driven by expensive, well-groomed horses. They pouted and complained that the city was so dull since those old bores had shut down Cremorne Gardens and didn't a girl need some diversion when the gentlemen were off hunting at their seats? They were all so beautiful that it was clear why wealthy men were keeping them in furs and carriages.

'It really doesn't matter to me,' Phoebe told Louisa. 'Is it any worse than being a wife?'

Louisa laughed. 'Oh, my darling. You're too much. It's better than being a wife, if truth be told. At least a harlot can claim her fortune as her own if she's lucky enough to make one. A wife can do no such thing.'

'I don't see why it's considered so shameful, then,' said Phoebe.

'Neither do I, really. There are girls in far worse positions than me, I know, and it *is* a precarious existence, but then the position of a wife is precarious too. Say your man decided to sink a fortune in some American railway and Indians ambushed the railway and half the tracks sank into a swamp or the contractors froze to death out West – and these things do happen, I'm told. If you were married to the poor idiot with shares in the disastrous enterprise then you'd have stood there before God and said "For richer for poorer, for better or worse," and you'd be quite buggered. Absolutely shackled. Whereas if I found myself in the same position I'd pat the poor fellow on the shoulder, console him for his loss and quietly set about finding myself a more prudent speculator while making excuses to get rid of the old one. In many ways it's a great deal easier, unless of course you're one of those poor little wretches who tumble straight out of the workhouse and land on their back in some gin shop somewhere.'

Louisa's great secret was not such a shock really. Phoebe had been raised to imagine that the sky would somehow fall on her head or the world would cease to turn if her virtue was in any way besmirched by the company of disreputable women or men, and she felt pleasantly vindicated when no such thing happened. When she went to buy patterns in Bond Street nobody stepped aside to avoid her and the haberdasher was perfectly polite and pleasant.

Louisa was constantly entertaining – a never-ending fount of anecdotes and scurrilous gossip, and Phoebe hung eagerly on her every word except for those evenings when they worked on the dress and Phoebe's more worldly mistress deferred to Phoebe's expertise. The construction of the garment was difficult in itself, not least because Louisa had had to have a specially made corset created to go beneath it and the corsetières were taking their time. Phoebe had to pore over sketches and devise patterns and sew silk roses for the time being, excited by the turn her work was taking.

The dress itself was intended to look almost decent on first appearances, although low cut even for an evening gown. A basque bodice with a polonaise would make up the body of the dress with the shoulders left bare except for a garland of red silk roses that sat low off the shoulder. The skirt would be in the fashionable form-fitting style with a train at the back but here, and in the bodice, lay the artifice.

The skirt was intended to be layered carefully so that it could be split apart to show off a leg, and the skimming garland of red roses were designed to hide breasts that would be more or less exposed in the half-cups of the bodice. Even the business of stitching and gathering tiny tunnels of red silk to make roses made Phoebe feel hot and strangely uneasy when she thought of how those selfsame flowers would one day jostle so close to Louisa's nipples and only partially screen them from view.

Louisa helped if she wasn't otherwise engaged for the evening. Although Phoebe never told her so, Phoebe didn't trust her to sew the seams. Louisa was a sloppy needlewoman and often pricked her fingers and dropped cigarette ash on the silk blossoms, but Phoebe didn't care that she would sometimes have to take out the gathers when Louisa had gone to bed and do them again. Those evenings were a joy, just to be near her idol, with Louisa sat on the floor beside the fire in her dressing gown ('God, how wonderful to get that bloody corset off. I think we must all be mad to wear the things'), toasting her toes on the warm tiles before the hearth with her long blonde hair streaming down her back in a fat plait.

Louisa asked questions about dressmaking and shook

her head when Phoebe answered them. 'You must think me a perfect idiot. I only know what the fashion magazines tell me.'

'I think we all have our avenues of expertise somewhere,' Phoebe said. 'I don't know how to palm coins. Where did you learn how to do that?'

'My father was a magician.'

'A magician?' Phoebe put down her roses to rest her eyes and lit a cigarette. She had taken up the habit mainly to spite her own father, who didn't approve of women smoking and plainly didn't approve of Phoebe any longer.

'Well, a conjurer,' Louisa admitted. 'I always say he was a magician because it sounds more exciting. My mother was from quite a good family – gentry, nobody famous or foolishly rich or anything like that, but tediously respectable enough for my grandfather to be monstrously angry when she ran off with a common conjurer from a music hall. Cut her off without a penny and she didn't take well to the life. It's possible she was in the start of a consumption even when they ran away, since it's said she was delicate anyway, but she didn't survive my birth.'

'Oh, how sad.'

Louisa shrugged. 'It sounds awful, but I never knew her. You can't miss what you never had. It was much worse when Daddy died.'

'How old were you?'

'Seven or so. It was typhoid that did for him, poor man. Of course, everyone was quite at their wits' end what to do with me because there I was an orphan, although I really don't believe I would have ever ended up in the workhouse. Music hall people are often dismissed as having lax morals but I still say they're the kindest folk on earth. I daresay someone would have taken me in, and not just because I could sing and dance and perform a few magic tricks, but because they were too good-hearted to see a poor child go to the workhouse. Their kindness was never tested, though, because my mother's cousin had come looking for me. Funny sort of gent – terribly upright and determined to save me from my bad blood.'

'What's wrong with your blood?' asked Phoebe, realising the answer to the question even as she blurted it out.

'No marriage papers,' said Louisa, with a wink.

'Oh.'

'So naturally it was presumed I'd be inclined to vice and *haven't* I proved them right? The taint of being my mother's daughter, as if all women were quite poisonous – which I suppose they can be, but depends entirely on the woman. It's always the so called "good women" who are amoral harpies behind closed doors.'

'You don't like them much, do you?' said Phoebe, stuffing her feet under a pillow to warm them.

'I should say not. It's not that I regret my situation in life at all. In fact, I rather like it, and I doubt a love-child like me would have ever made a respectable match anyway.' Louisa took a cigarette from her case and lit it from the stub of the one Phoebe offered.

'Thanks. No, what I *really* resent,' she said, thoughtfully, blowing out smoke, 'what I absolutely detested was the malice of it, the pure spite.'

'The malice of what?'

'My undoing, dearest. You see my mother's cousin wasn't a bachelor. He was a married man with a little boy four years younger than I, and his wife positively loathed me from the get go, for the usual reasons.'

'Money?' asked Phoebe, congratulating herself on her new-found worldliness.

'The root of all evil. She had no intention of some

orphan bastard eating into the legacy owed her should anything happen to Uncle Charles, so she did her very best to ruin me before I even knew what constituted a young girl's ruin.' Louisa smiled and shook her head incredulously. 'And here was a lady who said her prayers and went to church every Sunday and paid her tithe. Makes you think, doesn't it? Anyway, I'm just about done in, darling. I'll see you in the morning. We may even have a corset to work with by then. Who knows? Miracles *have* been known to happen, after all.'

The miracle in question took another two days to occur. It was morning and Louisa was still in bed when Phoebe looked into the drawing room and found a box from the corsetière on the coffee table. The thing was immediately seductive, made from lavender-coloured cardboard with scallop-shell designs embossed upon it, wrapped in a ribbon under which the invoice was discreetly slipped. Phoebe had opened such boxes before and knew them to be full of rustling tissue paper under which the perfumed constructions of satin, bone and lace would be discovered like a prize fished from a bran tub at a fair. She hesitated to open this one without Louisa looking on because it was special and they had been waiting impatiently for it to be finished for so long. A part of her also dreaded opening the parcel in case the work was shoddy or wrong and had to be sent back again. She thought she should check, but decided against it. Both of them had to be present.

The maid brought up the morning tea and Phoebe told her to leave it on the coffee table, that she'd take it up herself, so the maid did so and Phoebe then found herself wondering how she would carry both the box and the tea tray. She thought about balancing it on her head like an Indian woman with a water jar and giggled at her own silliness, excited as if it were Christmas morning. In the end she ran up the stairs, placed the box outside the bedroom door and then went back for the tea tray.

Louisa was still fast asleep, nothing visible of her except for a bare shoulder and a spill of plaited hair.

'Good morning,' Phoebe called, softly. 'I brought up the tea.'

Louisa stirred and looked up from her bed. 'Oh. Tea. Lovely.' She stretched and slowly sat up. Her linen nightgown was so fine that her firm breasts showed through its weave, her nipples hard and pink from the sudden shock of cold at leaving the warmth of the bedclothes.

'And you'll never guess what,' Phoebe said, placing the tray on the bed.

'A miracle?'

Phoebe grinned 'A miracle.'

'Oh! Where? Show me! Does it look all right?'

'I don't know. I haven't opened it yet.'

'Bring it in!' Louisa said, almost bouncing on the bed and upsetting the tea. 'I can't wait to see it.'

Phoebe fetched the box and put it on the bed.

'You shouldn't be timid about opening things from dressmakers,' Louisa said, tugging at the ribbon. 'You are in charge of my clothes, you know.'

'I know. It's just that I thought we should both open this. As if it were a ceremony. I wonder if this is what launching a ship feels like?'

Louisa beamed. 'If this bloody thing is right at last, we *shall* have champagne. Although I don't know what we'll smash the bottle against. Not my arse, I pray you.'

Phoebe laughed. 'No, let's not. We could just drink it?'

'A marvellous idea,' Louisa said, rummaging amongst the pale-violet tissue paper. 'Now let's see. Oh *yes*.'

She lifted the corset up from its wrappings. It was the same red as the dress, lined and finished in the silk they had been laboriously turning into roses. It looked uncommonly narrow and then Louisa roughly folded it around her torso to show how it would sit. It barely cupped her breasts at all, and didn't quite reach her hips, according to the design they had laid out. This design had meant that no other corset would give accurate measurements and had hampered their progress on the remainder of the dress, but now that it was complete, all that remained was to see if it fitted before continuing.

'It's beautiful,' Phoebe said, admiring the tight stitching over the bone. 'And red. I had no idea it would be so red.'

'We scarlet women have to keep up appearances,' said Louisa, ringing the bell beside the bed. 'I rather fancy champagne for breakfast now, and I don't even care if it's not perfectly cold.'

Champagne was brought up and, true to Louisa's prediction, she claimed it wasn't cold, although Phoebe thought it cold enough. 'This really is better than I hoped it would be,' Louisa said, running her fingers along the padded edge beneath the miniscule bust of the garment. 'Let's try this out.'

She climbed off the bed, a little heavily after the champagne, as neither of them had eaten anything for breakfast. 'No breaking bottles across my arse, now,' she said impishly, and slipped off her nightgown so that she stood in front of the long mirror completely naked. If she had any self-consciousness it was probably on Phoebe's account and not her own because she had undoubtedly been told often how fine she looked stripped to her skin.

'All right,' Phoebe said, taking up the corset and advancing on her mistress's naked figure. 'Let's see.'

Louisa giggled.

'What?'

'Oh, I'm sorry. Now you look like a bullfighter.'

'Because it's so red?'

'That's what I meant, you goose,' Louisa said, positioning herself at the end of the bed. 'The champagne's gone to your head.'

Phoebe passed the scarlet corset in front of Louisa's body, positioning it for lacing. Louisa cupped her own breasts in her hands and dropped them into position beneath it. The corset, carefully lined so as to enable the wearer to do without a chemise, was cut very high on the hips, even higher than Phoebe had imagined, so Louisa's buttocks were completely bare.

'How does it feel?' Phoebe asked, threading the laces and praying that her hands wouldn't tremble. There was nothing between her and Louisa except the space of a footstep and her own thin nightgown.

'Nice and smooth on the inside. So far anyway.'

'Yes. They did a good job sewing in the bone.' Phoebe inhaled in sympathy as she pulled the laces into place. 'Right. Breathe in.'

She pulled hard on the laces, tugging them tight. Louisa shuffled a breast into place and held her breath.

'How does that feel?'

'Go tighter,' Louisa said, her breath-held voice almost a whisper. 'I want to see what this thing can do to my waist.'

Phoebe tugged harder on the laces. The black tapes cut into her fingers. 'Snap you in half, I shouldn't wonder.'

'I'd prefer it on the tight side.'

'All right.' Phoebe pulled until the edges of the corset had almost come together. It formed a scarlet band reaching from just below the bust to just above the hips. Louisa had bent slightly and grasped onto the headboard to give Phoebe some purchase and from the rear her bare bottom stuck out and between her buttocks Phoebe could see a wisp of pale hair and pink flesh. To tie off the laces Phoebe found that she had to lean forwards across Louisa's back and she could feel the warmth of her mistress's skin against her own thinly covered loins. She shivered as she pulled the knots tight and stepped back.

'That's it.'

Louisa straightened uncomfortably. 'Doesn't feel too bad, actually,' she said, and turned to face the mirror. Her white blue-veined breasts were hoisted and bared so that their natural roundness seemed all the more plump and delectable. The corset pinched her in the middle so that the swell of her bosom and hips was accentuated to exaggerated proportions, but in spite of Phoebe's initial misgivings each boned panel of scarlet silk fitted Louisa like a second skin and left her indecently bared where she wished to be.

'Could go a little bit looser, maybe,' Louisa conceded, turning to the side and running her hand over her confined mid-section. 'It looks rather good, though. How do I look?'

'At this very moment?'

'Yes.'

Phoebe stifled a laugh. 'Um ... like the whore of Babylon, actually.'

Louisa preened. 'I do hope so. It's about time the Babylonian fashions came back in.' She caught Phoebe's eyes in the mirror and laughed. 'Oh, look at you – blushing like a schoolgirl. Anyone would think you'd never seen a naked woman before.'

'I haven't, apart from you.'

'What do you do? Wear a blindfold in the bath?'

'No,' Phoebe said. 'I just ... don't look.'

Louisa shook her head and then glanced at Phoebe's nightgown. 'Right,' she said, with a wicked gleam in her eye. 'Off.'

'Off?'

'Off. Take it off,' Louisa said. She looked like an incitement to debauchery by herself. Phoebe had dressed her fresh from the bath enough times but Louisa somehow looked even more naked with that strip of scarlet around her middle, pushing her breasts to jostling fullness and making the light-brown tousle of hair between her thighs stand out all the more sharply against the contrasting white of her rounded hips.

'I couldn't,' said Phoebe, despising her own dark skinny body compared to Louisa's voluptuous figure.

'Why? It's your body. Why shouldn't you look at it?'

'I don't look like *you*.'

Louisa advanced on her and pushed her towards the mirror. 'Good God, I should hope not. If all women looked alike then the world would be horribly boring. Arms up.'

The world turned white for a moment as Louisa lifted the shimmy up over Phoebe's head and then Phoebe found herself face to face with her own naked reflection. Although she didn't have Louisa's beautiful fair skin and luscious curves, there was something aesthetically pleasing about her smooth brownish skin and slender limbs. Her breasts were small, rather pointed, with darker nipples than Louisa's and the hair between her legs and under her arms was thick and black. She had never seen herself like this before and she was surprised to find that she thought herself well made. She had never even seen the way her navel sat neatly in the centre of her belly and she suddenly imagined herself with a jewel stuck in the middle of it like an Arab girl or one of Louisa's naughty Indians from the overmantel mirror. The vision made her giggle.

'There,' said Louisa, triumphantly. 'Aren't you lovely? What a figure. I wish I was so slender. Now, just one more thing.'

She unfastened the ribbon at the bottom of Phoebe's braid and unplaited her hair, pulling it around Phoebe's bare shoulders, exclaiming at its length and thickness. Her spilling, corseted breasts brushed Phoebe's back as she did so and once Phoebe was sure she felt the brush of Louisa's maidenhair against her bare buttocks. Her legs immediately felt unsteady and she felt a prickle of warmth between her thighs.

'I never liked my hair,' she said, rather stiffly. 'It doesn't like me. It just won't behave.'

'It's beautiful,' said Louisa, drawing the strands over Phoebe's shoulders to frame her bare breasts. 'So black! If it were much longer I should think you could sit on it. You look a perfect nymph, darling.' She put her arm around Phoebe and gave her a kiss and Phoebe saw herself blushing from the roots of her hair to her breasts. Her nipples puckered into hard wrinkled nubs like the stones of fruit, startling her even more by the way they tingled with the mere passage of air across their surfaces.

Louisa saw her blush and laughed – a throaty, smoky, seductive sound. 'There is more, you know,' she whispered in Phoebe's ear, her breath stirring the strands of tumbled hair and heating Phoebe's already burning cheek to blazing.

'More?'

'Don't tell me you've never taken a handmirror and peeked at your cunt?'

'My . . . what?' gasped Phoebe, having never heard the word before.

'Your cunt, darling,' said Louisa. 'Your quim. Your Mount of Venus.'

'Oh,' Phoebe said, stupidly, suddenly glad to have a

name for the part of her body that was causing her such agitation. It felt swollen and ached with that curious not-ache that she sometimes felt in dreams. It would never have occurred to her to *look* at it before now. It was just the place from which she pissed and bled.

'I'll show you, if you'd like,' said Louisa. 'Sit up on the bed.'

She rummaged in the dressing-table drawer, bending over so that Phoebe could see that faint glimmer of pink between the tops of her thighs again. Her cunt. Louisa's cunt. Phoebe rolled the words around in her mind, imagining Louisa astride a man like that picture she had seen in *Fanny Hill*.

Clutching a handmirror, Louisa climbed up onto the bed, advancing on Phoebe on her hands and knees. Her breasts dangled like sumptuous fruit and she was smiling wickedly, the tip of her tongue caught between her pearly teeth. She looked like an angel that had lost interest in virtue and taken up a new career as a succubus. 'Legs up,' she said, mischievously. 'Now ... spread your legs.'

Every movement seemed to take forever now. Phoebe opened her thighs slowly, feeling heavy with the weight of her own wickedness, but bathed deliciously in this strange new sin. Louisa gasped. 'What a pretty thing,' she said, softly. 'You're very wet, dear.'

Self-conscious, Phoebe tried to bring her knees together but Louisa laughed and held them apart. 'Don't be silly,' Louisa said, picking up the handmirror. 'You haven't even seen it yet. Look!'

Phoebe leant forwards and looked in the mirror. It was strange, hairy, with a slit of pink in the centre. Tentatively, she opened her legs wider and saw the folds of flesh reveal themselves, shining with moisture as Louisa had observed. It didn't look like much. She thought it rather ugly, really, like some hothouse flower, some hairy curiosity from the tropics that sucked dew from the air and shone like raw meat, but because looking at it like this was new and forbidden she couldn't help being sensible of the sensations it caused her.

'Oh,' she said, stupidly, once again.

'Well? What do you think?'

'I ... don't know.'

Louisa moved on the bed so that she was sat beside Phoebe. 'Give me the mirror,' she said, opening her own legs. Her knee bumped against Phoebe's. 'See? They all look like that,' she said, positioning the mirror between her thighs.

Phoebe stared at the reflection, dumbfounded. Louisa's hair was lighter and sparser than her own and the skin didn't look quite so red, but on a superficial level she could see that the structure was the same. She could feel her heart beating so hard she thought the thuds of it would be visible through the skin of her breastbone. When Louisa reached down with a hand to touch herself, Phoebe caught her breath in a gasp.

'Just here,' Louisa murmured, showing Phoebe the way her index finger lingered on the nub of flesh at the apex of the folds. 'That's the seat of a woman's pleasure. Did you never feel it for yourself?' Louisa rubbed her finger back and forth and closed her eyes. 'You can feel it beating away like a second tiny heart sometimes.'

Phoebe swallowed hard. 'Yes,' she said. 'I think I've sort of felt that before. In dreams.'

Louisa had slumped down on the pillows. She opened her eyes and looked pityingly at Phoebe. 'Dreams,' she said. 'A wretched substitute for reality. Go on. Touch it. I think you'll be pleasantly surprised.'

Phoebe reached down, using the mirror to guide her hand, and slowly pressed her finger to the spot. Somehow she knew she had done this before, at the times of the month when she was so ill she was not herself. She had felt this before, but never understood the how and why when she was back to her rational self. She closed her eyes to begin with, to avoid being embarrassed, but as she touched the tip of flesh she found her eyes closed with a new languor, her head falling to the side on the pillow, like someone falling into an enchanted sleep. 'There,' she heard Louisa say. 'Isn't that better?'

6

A few days passed, days in which Phoebe felt dazed and pleasantly so. She was conscious of the secrets imparted to her and even more conscious of why her face became hot and her flesh trembled whenever Louisa looked at her. She pricked her fingers more while she worked on Louisa's dress, her stomach quivering like a jelly when she thought of how it would reveal Louisa's breasts and tender pink cunt when she wore it. She hated the men that Louisa would wear it for, but she couldn't reveal that to a soul. She knew too little to gauge whether her attachment to Louisa would be frowned upon.

Then one day about a week later, another package arrived.

Phoebe wasn't sure if she should open the box, but Louisa had told her not to be bashful about doing so. Besides, the package came from Paris, and most of Louisa's jewels and furs and feathers came from Paris, either directly or through her milliner or corsetière, so Phoebe undid the package and opened the box. There was a sheet of newspaper crumpled on the top and for a moment Phoebe lost all her interest in the contents of the box because the newspaper was printed in French. She was so pleased with herself for even recognising the language and some of the words that she stopped to read, but thought she must be misunderstanding because it couldn't possibly be what she thought it was about. Things like that didn't happen in the modern age. It was absurd and far from the *plume de ma tante* stuff she was beginning to learn, but she picked up a few words here and there. *L'artiste célèbre* – 'the famous artist', Francis Hoyland – well, she knew of him. He was always in the newspapers. *Mort* – dead. *Les animaux fauves.* Wild animals? A famous artist killed by wild animals in Italy? No, it had to be some outrageous blood and thunder story. Were there even wild animals *in* Italy?

She smoothed the sheet of paper out on the table, disturbed in a way she didn't understand. Some part of her was prickling with anger that a newspaper should be allowed to print such lies. She would ask Louisa to read it to her later, so she could be certain she'd made a mistake.

There was another box inside the box, each shell packed with layers of newspaper. She opened it and pulled away more newspaper and saw something round and white peering back at her. It was cold to the touch, like marble, and when she carefully lifted the object from the box she realised it was marble – part of a statue, but not like any statue she had ever seen before.

She was so shocked she almost dropped it, which would have been a disaster, but she managed to set it on the table and step back from it. She had seen from pictures what men kept between their legs, but this thing looked enormous. Anxious to verify, Phoebe turned to the overmantel mirror and looked at Louisa's Indians capering all over the frame in their various positions. Yes, that was it. The lingam, as they called it over there. And huge. How would a thing like that fit inside a woman's body? It was easily the breadth of four of her bunched fingers and she knew from her own tentative examinations that she could fit two at most.

Was that what they all looked like? All those veins and wrinkles? And there was a curious little helmet affair at the cap of it, with a tiny slit at the very tip. That, she supposed, was what men piddled through. It was all very strange and so interesting that she hadn't even wondered what Louisa would want with such a thing, or whether she should even have opened the parcel. It most definitely hadn't come from the milliner. That much was obvious.

Louisa breezed into the room while Phoebe was still staring fascinated at the thing, making Phoebe start at her arrival.

'You should see your face,' Louisa said, laughing. 'I've been expecting this for a while.'

'I'm sorry,' said Phoebe. 'After what you said about opening parcels ... I saw it was from Paris and naturally I thought –'

'No, no,' Louisa interrupted. 'Don't worry yourself. I expect it gave you a turn though. From Paris, did you say? What the bloody hell are they doing in Paris? Was there a letter?'

'No. Just this newspaper, but it's in French. I can't make much of it, except for a few words.'

'That's to be expected,' said Louisa, taking up the newspaper and frowning. 'French grammar is an absolute beast. Well, this is old news. What happened to my damned painting, I want to know? I don't have any use for a cock in a box. Doesn't pay as well as the real thing.'

She picked up the marble sculpture and turned it upside down to examine its base, then her eyes became very wide and she closed her mouth tightly, abruptly. 'Good Lord,' she said, shakily, replacing it on the table.

'What is it?' asked Phoebe.

'It's expensive is what it is,' said Louisa, sounding breathless. 'Come along. We'll be late for bridge.'

* * *

On Thursdays Louisa played bridge with a mixed assembly of women. There was an actress and an aesthete lady who sometimes dressed in men's clothing and always smoked cigars, as well an ancient dowager countess who loved to recollect the glory days of her youth, painting the Regency with such a sumptuous palette that the modern era seemed cinder-choked and drab by comparison.

The dowager's name was Charlotte and she had once been a famous beauty and hostess, but it seemed that even countesses were liable to fall upon hard times when their men died or deserted them. Phoebe liked listening to her stories and, out of deference to Phoebe's feelings, Louisa stopped fleecing the countess at cards. It was becoming all too clear that the old lady was not long for this world and she looked frailer by the week, shrinking into her bulk as her bones gave out.

The time had gone by so rapidly that Phoebe realised that she had been with Louisa for a whole month. She'd not bled during that time and thought nothing of it besides relief at the respite she had received. It wasn't unusual for her to go three or four months and then become ill, but she had noticed the moon fattening by slivers and wondered what it was that had prevented it wreaking its usual havoc. On the way to the countess's bridge evening she peered at her watch and noticed for the first time a fourth hand upon the face, pointing to the mother-of-pearl disc of the full moon at the outermost edge of the watch. She frowned, sure she'd never seen that before.

The countess lived in Berkley Square, in a townhouse that looked as though it were shut up for the winter. The statues and furniture in the grand hallway were all dust sheeted over and the air was so frigid that Phoebe's breath froze in a cloud. The countess, it seemed, had long ago given up the business of keeping up appearances.

'No wonder her arthritis is bad,' said Louisa, as they mounted the staircase – an overblown design in Carrara marble infested with round-bottomed cherubs and caryatids. The caryatids carried candle holders, but some of them were empty and none of them were lit. Where light had been designed to glimmer on the faces of the stone women there was none. They grasped nothing but the occasional stalactites of cold melted wax that dripped from their frigid, immobile hands. The quantities of marble involved gave the stairwell all the comfort and warmth of an ice house.

'It's very grand though,' Phoebe said, diplomatically, conscious of the butler leading the way with a candle in hand.

The countess rarely left her boudoir except to go to bridge. She lived entirely in a small suite of rooms on the first floor, retreating to the warmest corner of the great house the way Phoebe imagined a very old turtle might shrink within its shell. There was a lively fire flickering in the sitting room and the aesthete lady in her gentleman's finery was already standing in front of it, warming herself like a man.

'Josephine, darling,' Louisa kissed her on both cheeks 'Are we early or late?'

'I should say you're on time,' said Josephine, ostentatiously examining a gold pocket watch tucked into her waistcoat. 'It's Lily who's running late. Sarah can't come. Dreadful headcold, or so she says.'

Sarah was the name of the actress and there was much speculation about the identity of her wealthy patron. It was even whispered that it might be the Prince of Wales himself. Phoebe looked around the room. It was fusty with the smell of dog and the walls were almost entirely covered with pictures of dogs and horses and children. One wall was a floor-to-ceiling mass of sentimental miniatures of lapdogs, Pekes and poodles and miniature spaniels, all hung on little blue or pink strips of ribbon. The overmantel swarmed with pictures of the countess's many children, every surface crammed with mementoes of a long and rich life and in amongst them large bowls of blowsy hothouse roses, the scent of the flowers fighting a losing battle against the smell of dog.

A dog barked and there were scratches, yelps and whimpers from behind the closed doors before the countess hobbled out as if carried on a tide of surging canine bodies. There were two enormous mastiffs, a retriever and six or seven yapping lapdogs, all making for Phoebe as if she was a magnet and they were iron filings.

'Ah, you came,' the countess said. 'I'm so glad. Don't worry about the bitch pack, dear girl. They like you. You'd know immediately if they didn't. Do make yourselves at home, ladies.'

Phoebe wondered what the dogs did to people they *didn't* like. The two big mastiffs were licking her hands and the retriever was capering so excitedly that it knocked over several pictures. The lapdogs scrabbled and chewed at the hem of her skirt. When she sat down the little dogs swarmed up onto her knees, defying her attempts to count them. The mastiffs, defeated, flopped down at Phoebe's feet, but the retriever kept nosing in her lap for attention and agitated the yipping, snarling lapdogs even further so that Phoebe felt herself quite engulfed beneath a mass of flailing, twisting, turning furry bodies.

'They do so love new people,' said the countess, indulgently.

'Yes, they certainly do,' Phoebe said, overwhelmed.

Louisa turned her face away and pretended interest in the miniatures, her lips pressed tight together to keep from laughing.

'Sarah won't be joining us,' announced Josephine, lighting a cigar from a candelabra. 'Bigger fish to fry, I suspect.'

'Yes. Maybe the fish that shalt be king hereafter,' the countess said. 'That's ancient history, Jo-Jo. We really must find some new scandal to chew over. That particular bone is quite bare and my old teeth aren't what they used to be.'

'I'd supply some myself but it's all a question of timing,' Louisa said, having recovered herself enough to turn away from the miniatures and take her seat.

'And what is that cousin of yours up to in Paris, Louisa?' asked the countess.

'Behaving himself.'

'Bloody hell,' said the countess. 'When the men are behaving themselves you can be certain the country has gone to the dogs – pardon the expression, *mes petits enfants*.' She blew a kiss to the hairy swarm piled one on top of another on Phoebe's lap. 'Well, if Sarah shan't be joining us then perhaps you'd care to make up a four, Miss Flood?'

'I can ... try,' Phoebe said, barely able to move her arms, never mind deal cards.

The countess whistled softly and the entire 'bitch pack' as she'd called them moved off Phoebe's lap and arranged themselves around their mistress. 'I should have done it sooner, m'dear,' she said, apologetically. 'But I wanted the girls to get a feel of you. I don't trust people the girls don't like and since they appear to adore you unreservedly I've made up my mind to do the same. What's your first Christian name again, dear?'

'Phoebe, ma'am.'

'Splendid. No wonder they like you. What a marvellous name. It was an epithet for Diana, you know – the virgin huntress. Do you hunt? Although God knows, I shan't ask about the other.'

The women laughed, even Louisa.

'No, ma'am,' Phoebe said, feeling awkward. 'I'm from Blackfriars. I've never really been out of the city.'

'She's a magnificent seamstress,' Louisa said, as if atoning for Phoebe's never having hunted or left London in her life. 'And what she doesn't know about clock mechanisms is barely worth knowing.'

'Clock mechanisms?' asked Josephine, with a snort of laughter. 'What a thing to know about.'

'My father is a watchmaker.' Phoebe felt blood rush to her cheeks. A Pekinese broke loose from the pack and came and snuffled at her skirt.

'It seems a perfectly sensible thing to know about to me,' said the countess. 'Entirely useful, since clocks have a habit of breaking. You should have seen some of the rubbish I was obliged to learn for my first season – all that singing and playing the piano. They may have well have tried to teach a cat since I've always been tone deaf. And as for drawing, well, I really didn't have the patience for it. It always seemed a ridiculous way of netting a husband – learning to swoon prettily and take to your bed when a headache threatened. No, no, no. A good ride, that's what used to blow the cobwebs away for me. A good ride and a clean kill. I had the most wonderful pair of retrievers amongst my wedding gifts from my darling George.' She sighed and shook her head. 'But shan't be long now. Shall we begin, ladies?'

7

She dreamt often of the red dress. The seams, the pattern, the facings, the fastenings – all of those details that go into a gown – they had all sunk so deep in her head that she went on sewing while she slept. Such industrious dreams were welcome compared with what she was used to but she knew when she closed her eyes that night and saw the dome of the cathedral, crouched like a beast under the soiled city moonlight, that she was in for more of the same.

Only this time was different. She felt as though she were observing this oft-played scene of labyrinthine alleys and ravening wolves, whereas before she had always been in the thick of it. But not tonight. Tonight they had fresh prey.

She saw the scarlet heel on the cobbles first – a high red shoe, a flash of delicious white ankle and a leg coyly veiled in vermilion. Louisa was wearing her red dress, under a cloak of the same colour. The cloak had a heavy cowl hood and her eyes were partly screened from view by a black domino mask – perhaps a fragment of Phoebe's Venetian carnival imaginings.

Her lips looked all the more lovely for the mask; the way it screened scraps of her face the same way the dress covered and uncovered her body. She was so perfect. The black of the mask made the red of her mouth look deeper than ever against her white smooth skin, her flax-fair hair covered almost entirely by the hood.

'You can't stay here, miss,' Phoebe told her, with a

dispassion that felt like a stuck scream in her throat. 'There are wolves loose in the city.'

Louisa shook her head. 'I couldn't go now. I'm all dressed up for the Moonlight Ball and I've promised so many men dances.'

'It isn't a ball,' said Phoebe. 'It's a hunt. And they aren't men. They're wolves. They're all wolves, Louisa.'

Louisa laughed and said something in French – something Phoebe couldn't quite translate but she caught the verb form 'vu' and the word for wolf 'loup'. 'Why worry?' Louisa said, in English. 'On a night like this. Did you ever see the moon so bright, darling?'

'Yes. Many times.' Phoebe clutched at Louisa's arm. She could hear the velvet pad of paws already. There was mist rising in the alleyways and Phoebe was sure it was the mingling breath of the pack, slobbering and expectant, each wolf eager to rush along on four sure feet; a pace that they could never hope to outrun.

'It's always bright when they're out,' said Phoebe. 'We have to go home.'

'Do you think a woman like me is afraid of a wolf?'

'You will be,' Phoebe told her, ominously. She could see in the dark of an alleyway a pair of eyes, round, shining like lamps. A pair of phosphorescent eyes, huge with moonlight, a huff of breath in the dark and a thin canine sound, like that of a dog stretching its jaws in a yawn. Phoebe heard it, and pictured the great yawning maw, the killing teeth, snapping back together as it closed its mouth and turned away to rejoin its fellows.

Oh yes. He was out here somewhere – Gold-Eyes. She could feel it in her blood, just as she knew that it was his pack. The other wolves danced to his tune.

'Come on,' she said. 'We have to go, miss. Ball or no ball.'

Louisa looked around her. 'I can't see the road. How are we supposed to get a cab?'

'We can't. This happens every time. They do it to trap you.'

'Trap? Who?'

'The wolves.'

'Oh, Phoebe,' said Louisa, impatient and incredulous still.

'Don't go off on your own, miss. Stay with me, whatever you do.'

'I'll wait here. There's always a cab sooner or later.'

'There won't be.'

Somewhere a wolf howled and Louisa looked up uneasily. She smiled but Phoebe thought that if she could see her mistress's eyes properly she knew she would see fear there. 'A dog,' said Louisa. 'Howling for its supper.'

But even she sounded unconvinced. Nobody can really mistake the plaintive howl of a domesticated dog for the colder, more sonorous sound that issues, so terrifying and strangely musical, from the throat of a wild wolf. Even the baying of hunting hounds is the howl of a creature tamed, to a point. The wolf's howl touches some primitive nerve in the human body, plucks some string of fear deep in the gut. There is nothing else quite like it.

'That was *not* a dog,' said Phoebe, emphatically. The hairs on the nape of her neck prickled and once again she felt the old, familiar terror. She could smell them – the oily canine smell of damp fur, the rank sour stink of carnivore breath. The sound of them – panting, padding, the soft click of claws on stone.

There were eyes peering from every alleyway, wet noses and snarling jaws coming forwards, a slow malevolent growl building in every throat. They slunk, low to the ground, stalking.

'Oh my God,' said Louisa, in a hushed, halting, gulping sort of voice.

Phoebe felt panic prod at the back of her skull like a thin cold needle. There was literally nowhere to run to. They filled every alleyway, circled on the steps of the cathedral.

'Don't move,' she told Louisa, although she didn't know how that would help. Whether they moved or remained stock-still, the wolves would pounce. Of that she felt certain.

And there he was, standing right opposite Phoebe – Gold-Eyes. His tail was up and his tongue hung out, and he tilted his head slowly as he looked at her.

Louisa's face was ashen beneath the mask and Phoebe was no less frightened herself, but she stared right back at Gold-Eyes, determined that he would look away first.

'Up to your old tricks again?' she said, under her breath.

He would – she knew. She knew what she was about. The pack would descend and tear clothes first with their teeth, stripping their prey as bare as raw meat.

'No,' Phoebe said, decidedly. It was *her* gown. She had created that dress and she was damned if she was going to see all of her hard work torn apart by a pack of wolves. All those seams, all those frills, all those bones and hems and silk roses sewn laboriously into place. All those hours of work and devotion. Her masterpiece, Louisa had called it. She realised she had become as protective of the dress as if it were her child.

'You wouldn't dare,' she told Gold-Eyes. 'Not if I strip her first.'

'What are you talking about?' Louisa asked. She sounded desperate.

'You're going to have to trust me, miss,' said Phoebe, not taking her eyes from the wolf. 'Do you trust me?'

'Yes. Yes, of course. Do I have a choice?'

'Not really, no.' Phoebe stared at the wolf, glared at him, almost. She felt angry with him, as if he were the one responsible for dragging Louisa into her dream and scaring the wits out of her. 'Mine,' she told him, taking a jelly-legged step and interposing herself between him and Louisa. 'Mine!' she said again, realising that she sounded much braver than she felt. She bared her teeth at him and his tail dropped a little. Good.

She trembled violently on her legs as she turned but she was for once grateful for her long skirts that concealed the worst of the tremors in her knees. She unfastened the knot of the cloak at Louisa's throat and let it fall to the ground. 'Trust me,' she pleaded, once more. 'I've been here before. I know what they want.'

Louisa nodded, her lips quite white.

Slowly, keeping eye contact with the wolf as much as she could, Phoebe turned around again and stepped to face Louisa's back. She reached down and began to unfasten the hooks and eyes at the back of the dress. Her fingers trembled and she almost laughed, for she had dressed and undressed Louisa so many times by now, perhaps more often than she had changed the clothes of her childhood dolls, but never had she imagined doing it in such circumstances. Moving around Louisa's body to unhook, release arms from sleeves – all the usual steps of undressing – that was enough to almost petrify her with fear because it meant turning her back on the wolf, but she remembered the steps, as if it were a dance.

She peeled off the dress and laid it on the ground on top of the cloak. Louisa stood there in her underwear, and inadequate underwear at that. She was covered only by her stockings and the strip of scarlet around her midsection and Phoebe saw Gold-Eyes lick his chops at the sight of her bare breasts and buttocks.

'Mine,' she repeated, quietly but firmly. Her fear was giving way to rising indignation over his presumption that he could have her mistress just like that. He had a whole pack for company. She had nobody but Louisa.

Louisa had never looked more indecent, or more beautiful. If she felt the cold then the only giveaway was the puckering of her pale-pink nipples. She stood as if transfixed to the spot, her face blank of expression under the mask – a white statue in black velvet and blood-red silk, gilded by the hair on her head and between her legs.

It wouldn't be enough for the wolves, though. Phoebe knew that. The corset would have to come off. The tapes were knotted, the kind of knot that had to be unpicked by fingernails, and Phoebe's fingers were cold. The wolves seemed to be growing restless again and fear made her hands shake. She searched in her pocket and found her smallest sewing scissors, with which she cut the knot and set to the tapes with a vengeance, tugging the laces open and pulling off the corset. She knelt in front of Louisa, offering her shoulder for Louisa to place a hand and steady herself, then she removed the red shoes, one by one, slid off the black ruffled velvet garters, peeled off the silk stockings, until Louisa was naked except for the black mask.

Now what? They had her as they wanted her, but what would Gold-Eyes do now? Lick her all over with his rough, greedy tongue? Transform into a man and take her on the paving stones?

He was at a disadvantage. She would still run from him. She wouldn't run from Phoebe. She trusted Phoebe. Somehow Phoebe felt that all she would have to do was stake her claim and Gold-Eyes would have no power over either of them any more.

Still kneeling on the cold paving stones, Phoebe pressed her cheek to Louisa's thighs. Louisa breathed sharply and quickly for a moment but she didn't flinch away from the touch. Phoebe heard paws pad behind her and felt her own breath quicken, warming Louisa's cold skin. Gold-Eyes prowled into view to the side of them. He wasn't snarling or crouching. He seemed to be simply watching to see what she would do next.

'No,' Phoebe told him again. 'Not yours. Mine.'

She stuck out her tongue and dragged it up the side of Louisa's thigh, in a long, deliberate lick like a cat washing a kitten. She could feel Louisa tremble and felt the tickle of Louisa's maidenhair against her cheek as she reached the top of her thigh. Gold-Eyes slumped, sat, his tail on the ground.

I've got you now, thought Phoebe, exultantly. Her control over him delighted her. The sensation of power tugged at the roots of her belly, teased and insinuated between her legs. She wanted to rub his nose in his defeat and ran her tongue over Louisa's skin once more. She lapped at her mistress's thighs like an animal, only vaguely aware that Louisa quivered and once or twice made low moaning sounds, half plaintive, half eager.

Phoebe could smell her, a strong female scent that overpowered the canine stink of the wolves. She smelt salty, like a fresh, delectable oyster, a morsel of the sea you tugged free from its opalescent shell and slid down your throat in one delicious gulp. She smelt of musk like the warm base notes of her expensive perfume, the scent that pervaded her bedroom and her clothes when Phoebe took them off her at night. The warmth of her took the chill off the night and Phoebe reached around to warm her freezing hands on Louisa's buttocks. Louisa winced only momentarily and then, as she swayed on her bare feet, she stood with her feet a little way apart.

The scents enveloping Phoebe became all the more richer, even more intoxicating and she bent to press her face to the light-furred cleft peeking open before her, but she knew already that she would be frustrated once more, just as she always was. The dream thinned, scents becoming all pervading but the body in her arms becoming insubstantial, the wolves mere shadows.

She woke in the dark of her bedroom, wanting to cry for the loss of it. For a moment, as she surfaced to consciousness, she thought she saw a woman standing near her bed – a woman in a fashionably cut gown, but then as her eyes grew accustomed to the dark she realised it was nothing more than the dress, and that there was nobody inside it but her tailor's dummy – a headless, limbless inanimate woman.

She was quite alone. Louisa was asleep in the next room and Phoebe was alone with her own unnatural lusts.

8

'Sir John Wythenshaw to see you, madam. Shall I show him up?'

'Please do, Mrs Dalton,' said Louisa, leaning over the bouquet she was arranging. She had contrived to tuck the sculpture just behind the vase and was dressed demurely in a high-necked oyster cashmere, the better to demonstrate she was in the business of business rather than pleasure.

'Very good, madam.'

Dear Mrs Dalton – she served as a housekeeper, cook and butler and was as discreet as a nun, for all of her former professions. She had been a prostitute from the age of twelve, but hard living and poverty had taken away her looks too early and her passion for gambling had left her with debts she couldn't pay. She had turned procuress in an attempt to pay them, the career in which Louisa had found her, but the business of luring young girls into a life of vice had left a nasty taste in Mrs Dalton's mouth. Some of them, she avowed, were even younger than herself when she started.

'You'll see none of that in my house,' Louisa had promised her. 'It's not right to take them before they're ready for it.'

And so Louisa had paid off the lady's debts and taken her into her service. Sometimes she still did, securing Mrs Dalton's gratitude and continued discretion. It helped that Mrs Dalton occasionally had an unlucky flutter on the horses – better than if she'd been a drinker.

Drunks were prone to loose lips and thankfully Mrs Dalton imbibed little more than a medicinal brandy now and again. She had seen too many of her former cohorts from the streets die of drink. Perhaps her only fault was this temperance.

Louisa adjusted a carnation in the vase and hoped for good luck with this transaction. If it came off then Mrs Dalton would have the time of her life at the Derby this June.

'Jack,' she said, glancing up as the baronet entered the room. 'How nice to see you.'

'You look as lovely as ever, Louisa,' said Jack, coming forwards to kiss her hand.

'Tea? Sherry?'

'Sherry, certainly. Your cellar is one of many reasons to visit London at this time of year.'

'Sherry and a biscuit, please Mrs Dalton,' said Louisa, noting the housekeeper's sour expression at the request for alcohol. 'I did wonder what you were doing here so soon before the season, Jack. You're hardly ever out of Yorkshire before the spring and always back for the Twelfth.'

'Don't tease, Louisa,' Jack rebuked. 'Are we to play at polite society? I told you I had some pressing business in London.'

'Yes. In Holywell Street,' said Louisa, knowingly, moving away from the vase. 'Do take a seat, won't you?'

Jack took an armchair beside the fire and his eyes fell upon the sculpture. 'Good Lord – what have you got there?'

'Nice, isn't it?' said Louisa, laying her hand upon the shaft and stroking it as she might caress a real man. 'Terribly expensive though. Newly arrived from Naples.'

'Pompeian?' Jack raised an eyebrow. 'You don't expect

me to believe you managed to acquire a genuine Roman piece from Naples, do you? It looks far too new, anyway.'

'It is new,' said Louisa. 'Very recent. Very expensive. Its like will never be seen on these shores again – of that I can absolutely assure you. Whoever buys this particular ... piece ...' She slid her hand up over the shaft and squeezed the tip suggestively. Jack swallowed. It never hurt to titillate a potential buyer a little. 'Well, they'll be the envy of every other collector in England, and possibly even France too.'

Jack made an incredulous noise. 'Come now, you've seen some of those Parisian collections. You're trying to tell me that *that* compares with original de Sade letters?'

He stopped and looked awkward as Mrs Dalton brought in the tray and swept out again.

'Better than De Sade,' said Louisa, confidently. 'De Sade wrote a lot of letters. This is unique. The artist only discovered his gift for sculpture perhaps a year ago until his career was tragically cut short.'

'Why? What happened?' asked Jack, sipping his drink.

'You read the newspapers, didn't you?' said Louisa, with pretended levity, taking a cigarette from her case.

Jack shook his head. 'Not possible,' he said, firmly.

'Entirely possible. My associates were in Naples for much of last year. They managed to strike up an acquaintance with the late Mr Hoyland –'

'And he just *gave* them this piece, did he?' interrupted Jack. 'In the knowledge that they would most likely send it back to England where he vowed his work would never be seen again?'

'I never said he gave it to them.'

'It's *stolen*?'

'Jack,' said Louisa, coquettishly. 'You can only steal a masterpiece provided that someone knows of that masterpiece. You could steal the *Mona Lisa* and the whole world would know. On the other hand, if you purloined a little sketch from a house auction and it later turned out to be a genuine Da Vinci then you'd risk a great deal less infamy. And you'd be sitting on an absolute bloody fortune.'

'And how many people know of this "sketch"?'

'Currently about four people in the whole world, including yourself.'

'Is it genuine, though?'

Louisa lifted the marble phallus from the table and took it over to show him the initials on the base. 'Absolutely genuine,' she said. 'Feel the quality of that marble, Jack. Pure Carrara.'

He touched it squeamishly, as if he were being asked to handle a real cock. 'I'm not disputing the quality,' he said. 'But how am I to compare it with anything else? It's not as if Hoyland was much of a man for sculpture before he left England. He was better known for his paintings. Do you have any preliminary sketches for this?'

'It's possible I may be able to lay hands on some,' Louisa said, guardedly, taking the sculpture back from him. 'I don't know what else my sources managed to acquire. I'm told there was a life-size *Leda and the Swan* but Hoyland took a sledgehammer to it in a temper.'

'Well, that sounds convincing,' said Jack. 'Brilliant man, but arguably mad. Wasn't he a drinker too?'

'So I'm told,' Louisa said, setting the sculpture back down on the coffee table. This was not going to plan and she couldn't imagine that she'd ever get her asking price for the piece. She had put up a fortune to send Charlie to Italy and it wasn't looking likely that she'd get her money back. The only thing she could count on Jack to do was talk, and part of her wanted to give him something to talk about. Ever since she'd clapped eyes on the sculpture she had marvelled at how lifelike it looked and once or twice she'd lain awake in bed fighting the desire to slip into the parlour and sit upon the thing. The only reason she hadn't was a ridiculous notion that it might somehow spoil the marble and the possibility of Phoebe coming in and finding her fucking a spurious work of art. For all Phoebe wasn't as green as she had been, she was still capable of being shocked and Louisa didn't want to scare off such a superb seamstress.

'It's very realistic, though, don't you think?' asked Louisa, conversationally.

'Yes. I suppose it is.'

'I'm told he sculpted the more ... *intimate* details from plaster casts made from his models.'

Jack laughed incredulously. 'You don't mean to say some poor bastard had his cock encased in plaster to make this?'

'Exactly that.'

'Would I know the gentleman in question?'

'No. I don't believe you've met him.'

'Friend of yours?' Jack asked, quirking an eyebrow. He counted himself amongst Louisa's 'friends' and she enjoyed entertaining him. His more than passing acquaintance with the bookshops of Holywell Street had made him a well-read man and he knew of more than one way to please a woman – although thankfully none of his methods had been learnt from de Sade. Louisa had attempted that once and although she was happy to wield the birch, cane or crop on her clients she had not enjoyed being the victim of such a beating, even if it had left her musing on the happy coincidence that bustles had been very much the fashion of the season. She'd been glad of the padding every time she sat down.

'I thought so at first,' said Louisa, 'but his was thicker,

I think. I don't believe I've had the pleasure of the gentleman in question.'

'Perhaps you'd like to?' suggested Jack, sitting back in his chair. He anticipated a show, all right.

'I'm not sure I'm his type, Jack.'

'Nonsense, darling. You're everybody's type.'

Louisa sat down on the ottoman and lazily stroked the underside of the phallus with her fingertip. 'Oh, I don't know. Some men prefer a more saturnine complexion than mine. Others might find me too thin for their liking.'

'Why don't you ask him?'

'I would, dear, but I couldn't afford him,' said Louisa. 'He's worth at least fifteen hundred pounds.'

Jack sucked on his lower lip. 'That's a lot of money.'

'That's the price.' Louisa lifted her skirt a little way, showing the pleats of her petticoat and her ankle – a promise that maybe she might just hitch up her skirts and straddle the table.

'The price of ownership, or the price on his chastity? He *is* chaste, I presume?'

'Chaste, yes,' said Louisa, grasping the thing with her whole hand. 'But as you can see, very easily *caught*.'

Jack poured himself another drink and extracted a cigar from a silver case. 'You haven't caught him yet.'

'Who would want him once he was debauched?' Louisa asked, loosing her grip and standing up. She wanted to do this thing. She had wanted to do it in the first place but a captive audience excited her still further. She wanted to see his face when she dared to do it and she could already feel her blood flowing faster and a little pulse beat thrumming away between her legs. 'His loss of virtue might compromise the price.'

'I doubt it,' said Jack. 'When I buy a stallion I don't

pick him for his virtue. I pick him for his willingness to cover my mares.'

Louisa picked up her skirts and carefully swung a leg over the top of the coffee table, positioning herself above the sculpture. 'Have you ever paid fifteen hundred for a stallion before?' She arranged her skirts to show him her stockings, the lace garters above her shapely knees.

'Once, yes. And I had my money's worth. He sired champions.'

'There you are then. Worth every penny.'

'Well, I had to see his mettle first,' said Jack. 'No use buying a stallion that's a member of the Moral Reform Society, is there now?'

'Perhaps I should convince you of this gentleman's *mettle*?' Louisa asked, lowering herself over the table.

'It might help to make up my mind, yes,' he said, affecting nonchalance, although she could see he was agitated.

She put her hand under her petticoats and positioned the tip of the phallus in the slit of her drawers. It bumped against her flesh, chilly and harder than any real man could ever dream of being. She smiled at Jack as she rocked gently on top of it, letting it find entrance to her body, pushing between already slick lips. When she took it all, the cold of it made her gasp and made her clench reflexively against it, heightening the sensation, and she could see he was excited and fascinated by her reaction.

'Oh, you didn't,' he murmured, on an outdrawn breath.

She steadied herself on the table, gasping at the way her cunt fluttered and convulsed as it tried instinctively to reject the icy thing inside it. 'I did,' she said. 'It's so cold.'

'Warm it up.' He sucked on his cigar, his gaze hot and

hungry. She immediately wanted him, wanted him pumping, animate between her thighs, but not yet. That would be for later, to seal the deal.

She raised and lowered herself as if riding a horse at a trot, panting at the way the sculpture slipped and slid inside her. God, it was cold. It was like fucking a pastry slab. She giggled at the thought and moved faster to cover her laughter. The thing bumped against all those secret, delectable places inside her with a touch like ice, making them tingle and tighten and making her cry out. Sir Jack had his hand on the crotch of his breeches by now and she couldn't wait for the coup de grâce. She wished she hadn't worn this damnable dress. It would have been better to have something low cut so he could see her breasts bounce as she rode the phallus. She thought of her still unfinished red dress – now *that* would be a sight for him, her tits jostling their way out of the rose garland of the bodice and her pierced cunt on show through the slit in the skirt.

'Is there anything you won't do?' he asked.

Louisa moved faster still and shook her head. She could feel the pleasure swelling in her lower belly and she wanted more. 'Come here,' she said, breathing hard. 'Show me your cock.'

'You really are a piece of work,' he said, amused. He stood up and unfastened his breeches. His prick stood to stiff attention, swaying as he moved clumsily, trousers around his knees, to stand in front of her. She leant forwards and lapped at it with her tongue, breathing in the coarse male smell of him. He inhaled sharply at the touch of her mouth and she went on, teasing with little fastidious licks of her tongue. She knew what he wanted. He wanted what was currently being occupied by the chill facsimile between her legs, but she was close now, too close to pull away.

She took hold of his cock and drew the head of it into her mouth. His groan as she did so was nearly enough to send her over the edge. With a smooth movement she impaled herself fully on the marble phallus, greedy for sensation as the shudders inside her rose to a crescendo and she reached her climax, her moans muffled by Jack's cock. She had to draw away and sink down over the table, drained by her exertions.

'Up you get,' Jack said, pulling her unsteadily to her feet and helping her to the chaise. She flopped on it like a rag doll, still tingling and pulsing inside, but he was determined to have his satisfaction and lifted her petticoats and mounted her with one easy thrust.

Louisa laughed at the look on his face when he reacted to the marble chill that still suffused her flesh. 'Told you it was cold,' she said, drowsily.

'Have to . . . warm . . . you . . . up, shan't we?' he panted, as he pumped away with none of his usual finesse, knowing the moment had come and gone. 'Worth a thousand, I'd say.'

'Fifteen hundred,' she said, lazily gyrating her hips. He was hot inside her and she pressed her fingers into his buttocks – hard muscled from riding. Some of these country squires got fat, but not him. He liked an active life, in and out of the saddle.

'Twelve hundred.' He frowned and pressed his lips together, his breathing quick now and a flush on his cheeks.

'Can't be done, Jack.'

'Thirteen hundred?'

She managed to regain control of her muscles enough to gently grip his cock as he thrust into her and he moaned deep in his throat.

'All right . . . damn you. Fifteen hundred. Just let me come.'

She bounced her hips along with his and he shuddered, slumped and fell forwards onto her chest. She could feel the heat of his spendings trickle between her thighs and swallowed down a laugh. That wasn't all he'd be spending. On the coffee table the sculpture gleamed obscenely, glossed with her juices. It had been a pleasure doing business today, and no mistake.

'Fifteen hundred pounds?' Phoebe's eyes were as round as sovereigns. 'For a marble ... thing?'

'It's not any old thing,' said Louisa. 'It's attributable to Francis Hoyland and that makes it fantastically rare.'

'I've never seen a sculpture like that before,' avowed Phoebe. No doubt she hadn't. She'd probably seen nothing of life in Blackfriars. 'I've seen some at museums but they were a lot smaller.'

'That prick, darling,' Louisa said, slipping her arms into her opera dress, 'is a perfect example of that "pornography" you'll hear all the prigs railing against. Gentlemen will pay inordinate amounts of money for dirty books, indecent pictures. They imagine themselves collectors, so I furnish their collections, for a fee.'

'A *fee*?'

'Well, in this case a fortune, but I do have to cover the investment I made sending my associates abroad to get it. Charlie lives up to his namesake – bloody Champagne Charlie. Expensive tastes.'

'My brother had a dirty book,' Phoebe said, meditatively. '*Fanny Hill*, I think it was called.'

Louisa laughed. 'Oh, dear old Fanny. How much we owe her.'

'I looked, or I tried to, but Dora – that's our maid – she pushed it back under his mattress and said I wasn't to look and I'd find out on my wedding night.'

Louisa raised her eyebrows and looked at Phoebe,

reflected in the mirror behind her. What kind of husband would she have found? A grocer? A draper? Some dingy little man who would never give her a moment's joy between the sheets. It wouldn't do. It never did. What was a girl supposed to do – dispatched to her nuptial bed in a state of such extreme ignorance that she didn't even know what her own cunt looked like or even what to call it? It had always been a point that rankled with Louisa and the day she first clapped eyes on Phoebe she decided to do something about it.

The girl was handsome enough in her own way. Phoebe, an epithet of Diana, the old dowager countess had said. The more Louisa thought about it the more she realised that might have been a reason she'd taken such a fancy to the girl. She was as brown and farouche as the Huntress, with her mass of curling dark hair, fierce eyebrows and bright brown eyes. Louisa thought a fancy dress party might be fun if she could persuade Phoebe to dress up as Diana, with a silver bow and quiver and sandals laced criss-cross up to her knees. Aspiring Acteons beware!

'I should think if you'd never looked and never known a thing you'd be scared out of your wits on your wedding night,' said Louisa.

'That's what I said, miss.' Louisa gave her a look. 'Louisa,' Phoebe corrected herself. 'I said if we were all to be married to ravening beasts, as she said all men are, wouldn't it be better to know what we're getting into?'

'You darling,' said Louisa, fondly. 'I'm so glad you're not happy to remain ignorant. Most "good" girls would have fled screaming from this place by now.'

'I don't know that I want to be good,' Phoebe mused, lifting an amber necklace from Louisa's jewellery box. 'I always tried to be good and I just got bored, polishing brasses and reading fairy stories.' She held the necklace against Louisa's throat. 'Girls are always good in fairy stories, ain't they? Do you like this one or shall we try the jet?'

'What do you think?' asked Louisa, deferring to Phoebe's good taste.

'I don't like the amber with that bottle green. I think the jet would be better.'

'I think so too.' Louisa uncorked a scent bottle and dabbed some behind her ears. 'They're not always good in fairy tales,' she said. 'Sometimes they misbehave and get punished. Touch a spindle when you're told not to and fall asleep for a hundred years.'

'As I understood it they took all the spinning wheels out of the kingdom bar that one the wicked fairy managed to sneak in. So she didn't even know it was dangerous for her to get a . . .' Phoebe pursed her lips, as if she realised what she was about to say.

'A prick?' finished Louisa, sending Phoebe into gales of laughter.

'Oh dear,' Phoebe said, wiping her eyes and fastening the jet bead necklace around Louisa's throat.

'Says it all, doesn't it?' said Louisa. 'The state of women today. Sleeping Beauties. Bloody somnambulists, the lot of them. They're not even told what it is they should be afraid of.'

There was a knock at the door and Mrs Dalton poked her head around.

'Is the cab early?' asked Louisa.

'No, madam. Mr Thornton's here, with Mr Greaves.'

'I thought they were in Paris?'

'They're here, madam. And a bit worse for wear.'

'Drunk?'

'No. Not drunk,' said Mrs Dalton. 'But not . . . what they were, if you catch my meaning.'

'No, I don't,' said Louisa. 'But never mind. Looks like

I'm going to have to attend to more business, Phoebe,'
she said, taking out a sheet of notepaper and writing an
apology on it. 'Mrs Dalton, when the cabby arrives give
him a tip and ask him to take this to the front desk at
the opera. I only hope Sarah will forgive me for standing
her up.' She handed the note to Mrs Dalton and took off
the earrings she had only just put on. 'I suppose they'll
want some supper.'

'I've some sewing to do anyway,' said Phoebe,
diplomatically.

'Good idea,' Louisa told her, not wanting her anywhere near Charlie. He had gotten one of her previous
lady's maids pregnant and the poor girl had scuttled off
into a hasty marriage with a pastry cook who was
thankfully mad enough about her not to care that the
child wasn't his. Charlie had always been irritatingly
potent, as she well knew herself.

Louisa steeled herself and prepared to tell him she
would geld him like a horse if he touched any of her
staff this time but she wasn't prepared for the sight that
met her in the parlour. Will looked thin, but then he
always did, but Charlie...

Her cousin looked little more than skin and bone. He
had always been a fair-haired, fleshy, well-built sort of
young man, with rosy cheeks and bright, cheerful blue
eyes, but his eyes looked glassy and haunted and his
skin was pale.

'Oh my God,' Louisa said. 'Charlie? What happened to
you?'

'Nice to see you too,' he said, sarcastically, helping
himself to whisky from the decanter.

Louisa shook her head. 'Oh, bugger the pleasantries.
You look like hell. It's not ... tell me it's not...?' She
couldn't bring herself to say it, even though she was sure
that it probably was.

'It's not consumption,' said Will. He looked tired and his clothes looked worn. 'There's nothing wrong with his lungs. It's his nerves more than anything.'

'There's nothing wrong with my tongue, you know.' Charlie glared. 'I can still speak for myself. You look dressed up, Lou.'

'I *am* dressed up. I was supposed to be going to the opera.'

'Don't let us keep you,' said Charlie. 'Just point us to a bed for the night and we'll have Mrs Dalton bring us some supper.'

Louisa frowned. 'Don't you have anywhere else to go?'

'I'm afraid not,' said Will. 'It was as much as we could do to find the money for passage to Dover. We got to London on a series of farm carts.'

'Fine,' Louisa said with a sigh, 'you can stay. But you –' she glanced at Charlie '– molest my maid at your peril. Besides, I sold your little objet d'art. Fifteen hundred, split three ways. Can't say fairer than that, can you?'

'Five hundred?' Charlie whistled. 'You got fifteen hundred for Will's cock?' He laughed, but his laugh didn't have his usual natural, animated quality. 'You're in the wrong line of work, Mr Greaves, with a prick that pricey.'

'Oh.' Louisa pressed her lips together to keep from laughing. 'It was yours, was it?'

'It was a fake,' said Will. 'I don't suppose he put that in his letter, did he?'

'No,' said Louisa, 'but I guessed. Luckily I have a better eye than my buyers.'

Louisa was worried. Charlie looked like a character from some sensational Gothic novel, as if he'd been in a gloomy haunted schloss somewhere in the depths of the Black Forest, rather than in sunny, saucy Naples. He'd been in Paris, of course, but he'd always loved Paris. It suited him spectacularly. It was full of tarts. Maybe that was the trouble.

'It's not the clap, is it?' she asked, when Will had gone off for a much-needed bath.

Charlie blinked. 'The clap?'

'Don't come the innocent with me, darling. I know what you're like. I was barely sixteen when I found that out for myself. What's the story, Charlie? Got yourself clapped up in Paris, or was it Naples? They say it's the most syphilitic city in Europe, don't they – naughty Napoli?'

Charlie sighed and shook his head. 'I'd be glad of a dose of the bloody clap compared to what I've seen, let me tell you.'

'There was a woman, though? There's always a woman.'

'Oh yes.' Charlie lit a cigarette and slumped down on the sofa. Even his hair had lost its gloss. There were shadows under his eyes. 'Will doesn't believe a word of it, of course. I tried to tell him. He thinks I'm going mad.'

'Tell him about what?' Louisa sat down, stiffly, the bones of her opera gown sticking into her thighs. She would have to get Phoebe to make her some new ones. Phoebe sewed whalebone in so tight and snug that wearing a dress made by her skilful hands was like being sheathed as comfortably as a silk worm in its tailored cocoon. Louisa poured herself a brandy and wondered why she had ever imagined she would last the duration of *Die Zauberflöte* in this bloody get up.

'Didn't you get that newspaper clipping I sent with the prick?'

'The box was full of newspaper anyway. I had to scrub the prick to get the print off it. You might have thought of that, Charlie.'

'There was a newspaper – a French one.'

'Oh, that,' said Louisa. 'Yes. Phoebe got hold of it – wanted me to help her read it. She's dead set on learning French, that girl.'

'Phoebe?' Charlie frowned. 'Never mind, never mind. That's not the point, Lou.'

'It is from where I'm sitting, I assure you. Phoebe's my new maid, the one you are not to touch under any circumstances. Poor Adeline – she was a superb maid and she was getting quite a head for the business. Now she's raising your bastard in a flat above a bakery. I hope you're pleased with yourself.'

Charlie got up from the sofa and stood in front of the fire. 'It was about Hoyland,' he snapped, impatiently. 'How he ... died.'

Louisa felt the blood drain from her face. Her guts seemed to shrink in her belly at the implications of the words and she could feel her corset loose about her. Charlie couldn't have done that. He didn't have the nerve, for one. He might have been a rake and a confidence trickster, but murder? Her mind was working too rapidly, but he looked like a man with something terribly grave on his mind and she had never seen him look like that before, not even the time when he'd made her pregnant.

'It said he'd been killed by wild animals,' she said. 'I just thought it was some blood and thunder nonsense the French newspapers cooked up.'

'It wasn't wild animals. In *Naples*?'

'That's what I thought,' said Louisa, unsteadily lighting another cigarette. 'And if you're going to tell me what I think you're about to tell me, then don't. I won't be a party to it.'

Charlie frowned, then his eyes widened as realisation

dawned. To her surprise, he laughed. 'Me? No! You've been reading far too many novels, Louisa. *I* didn't kill him, although there were times I would have liked to.'

'Well who, then? He obviously didn't kill himself, did he?'

'Not who. What.'

'An animal? You've just said it wasn't an animal.'

'I said it wasn't a wild animal, and I'm not sure it was an animal,' Charlie said, darkly. 'There were moments when she *looked* like an animal, and other moments when she didn't.'

Louisa shook her head. 'You're not making any sense. What are you talking about?'

Charlie waved a hand and sighed. 'Look, it doesn't matter. He's dead and we've got the money. The end of the adventure.'

'It must matter,' Louisa insisted. 'I've never seen you like this before.'

'It doesn't matter. It's just my nerves. Will's right.'

William entered the room at that point, raised an eyebrow and remarked that he would like that in writing, the feeble joke distracting attention from the subject enough to forestall it until supper was served in the dining room. Louisa picked at her cold roast duck without much appetite, the flush of triumph at securing her sale dimmed by Charlie's odd appearance and cryptic conversation. Normally she would have been amused beyond restraint at the thought that just that morning she had copulated with William by proxy, as it were. In all their professional dealings he had never shown any interest in her direction beyond polite flirting and he was such a dry scholarly creature that she had never imagined he would be in any way interesting as a lover. He would translate the filthiest of French pornography without so much as batting an eyelash at the contents, whereas such material would arouse Charlie into a state where he'd plead with her to lend a hand.

She couldn't see the humour in it tonight. She was too busy trying to understand what Charlie meant by this 'she' who looked like an animal sometimes and didn't at other times. Perhaps it was madness. Relatives had always said it ran in the family. Louisa's mother's folly was blamed on madness, which she suspected was a lie. It was easier to accuse a well-bred girl of being mad when she 'went wrong', rather than accept the truth that she might have lusts like any other human being.

'We'll have to put them in Phoebe's room,' she told Mrs Dalton, after supper. 'And Phoebe can come in with me.'

'I'll have the beds made up,' said Mrs Dalton. 'Young Peter asked me to tell you the horses was funny, madam. Thinks you might quiet them, since he's at his wits end with the beasts.'

'Funny?' asked Louisa. 'What do you mean?'

'Skittish, madam. Can't quiet them.'

'Thank you,' said Louisa. 'I'll go and see them.' The night was getting stranger by the moment, she thought. Perhaps Peter, the groom, had fed them something that disagreed with their digestions. They were highly bred horses, after all, a gift from one of Louisa's late benefactors, and she took great pleasure in driving them around the park with their handsome black coats gleaming like jet. They had delicate stomachs, though, and Peter, who loved them, was prone to spoil them.

Nevertheless, she felt an inexplicable shudder of unease as she wrapped a cloak over her opera dress and went down to the little mews at the rear of the building. There were several carriage pairs stabled there, her two in the stalls at the end. Peter, a fat fair-haired urchin of sixteen, was holding a headcollar and standing warily back from Alcestis, the friskier of the two mares.

'My girls playing you up, Pete?' asked Louisa.

'I didn't give them nothing unusual for their dinner, ma'am,' Peter said, immediately. 'I swear, they ain't had no titbits but a bit of apple when I was brushing 'em this afternoon.'

'Have you exercised them?'

'Yes'm. They've had a good trot twice round the park today and I thought Hippy might've had a colic but Alcy's worse, ma'am.'

Alcestis whinnied and shied back in her stall, showing the whites of her large liver-coloured eyes. Not wanting to approach her, Louisa instead reached out to pat Hippolyta, who was less nervous but still not her usual even-tempered self. Hippolyta tossed her head, nearly catching Louisa a glancing blow to the shoulder. In her agitation, Alcestis poked her head over the partition between the stalls and nipped her sister hard on the rump.

'Duncan's horses did turn and eat each other,' Louisa murmured, to herself.

'Pardon, ma'am?' Peter looked alarmed, as if it was likely that the horses *might* eat one another.

'Nothing,' said Louisa, distracted. '*Macbeth*. It's a play.'

'Was that what you was goin' to see, ma'am?'

'No. I was going to the opera – it was Mozart. But that's not important.' She chewed her lip and wondered how they were going to get that collar on Alcestis. 'Are you positive they haven't eaten anything unusual? You didn't let them nibble anything in the park, did you?'

'Some sugar,' Peter admitted, shamefacedly.

'Oh, they've had sugar before. Sugar and apples. They get that everyday.'

'They aren't kicking at their bellies, so I didn't *think* it was nothin' they ate, ma'am.'

'No, you're right. They'd be kicking like furies if it was colic. How very peculiar.' She looked at the snorting, skittish horses and shook her head. 'I don't understand it. Have you tried giving them some brandy in their mash?'

'I haven't, ma'am, but I could do. Might calm them down a bit.'

'Try it,' said Louisa. 'If it gets any worse, summon the vet. I wish I could call on old Charlotte, she'd know what to do.'

'Yes'm.'

Pulling her skirts up to avoid the muck on the floor, Louisa stepped back out into the night. The moon was out and she shivered in the cold air. '"By the pricking of my thumbs, something wicked this way comes",' she whispered, under her breath, wondering why she had a headful of Shakespeare when she'd been so looking forward to Mozart. She knew she was probably being foolish – 'overburdened with imagination' as her uncle had always said – but something about the cold clarity of the night unnerved her.

She slipped back into the building, some primitive part of her eager to hurry back to the security of the fireside and bolt all the doors tight, tight shut. It was all Charlie's fault, with his incomprehensible stories. As if *she* had been reading too many novels! She never read those sort of novels anyway. Why would she go grubbing in penny dreadfuls for sensations when most of the books she read were written by 'Anon.' and contained sensations of quite a different kind? No, if anyone had stayed up too long and too late with Edgar Allen Poe then it was Charlie.

Louisa peered out of a window, seeing her face

reflected in the glass alongside the bright moon. 'Of course, *I'd* be hysterical,' she said to herself. 'Men don't get hysterics, supposedly.'

'What's that?'

She jumped, startled by Phoebe's voice behind her. She hadn't seen the girl approach. Since when was she such a stealthy little beast?

'Christ, Phoebe, don't sneak up on me like that or I *shall* get the screaming abdabs.'

'Sorry,' Phoebe said. She looked swarthier than ever tonight, her big eyes black in the lamplight.

'I was just thinking aloud. I wonder why men are never accused of being hysterical?'

'Because they're men, I suppose, miss.'

Louisa sighed and unfastened the curtain tie from its hook. 'Shouldn't look at the moon through glass. It's bad luck, isn't it?'

'The new moon, I thought,' said Phoebe. 'Bad luck to look at the new moon through glass and if you do, you should turn your money over in your pockets. But that's not a new moon.'

'No.' It was bright and sharp edged, full as full could be. 'Why do people call it a full moon and not an old moon? That looks like an old moon to me.'

'Older than any of us,' said Phoebe. 'It's always old, even when it's new.'

Louisa pulled the curtain across and laughed. 'There's a riddle in there somewhere. What's as old as the earth even when it's new? Come and help me out of this bloody dress, darling. I must get some new opera togs. The bones in this thing are sticking into me like knives.'

They both undressed in Louisa's room, Louisa helping Phoebe with her corset as if she were her maid. Phoebe hurriedly pulled her shimmy over her head and tugged on her nightgown, as if still ashamed to be seen naked.

It was a pity she should still be so timid, because Louisa thought her body quite lovely. There was nothing cuddly about her when she was naked – dusty-brown skin, hard little dark-nippled breasts and long lean legs. She had the look of something feral, quite wild, and Louisa knew that if Phoebe ever took it into her head to turn to the world's oldest profession there were men who would pay highly for such exotic-looking flesh. She thought Phoebe's serious demeanour and flashing dark eyes would lend themselves to specialities, men who enjoyed the whip and the birch and paid money to lick a lady's boots and call her 'mistress'.

'You shouldn't be so shy with me,' Louisa told her. 'You've nothing to be ashamed of.'

'Haven't I?' said Phoebe, with a sidelong look from the dressing table. She sat brushing out her long hair, her lips set in that characteristic purse-lipped, chin-jutting pout she got when she was thinking or worrying about something. The expression made her face wedge shaped and her eyes seem enormous.

'Not a thing,' soothed Louisa, taking the brush from her and running it through the girl's coarse but luxuriant hair. 'What big eyes you have.'

'I take after my mother,' Phoebe said, softly, closing her eyes like a cat being stroked.

Poor thing. She had probably never had a mother to brush her hair. Even when Louisa was a motherless girl herself she had never wanted for mothers – there had been half-a-dozen tender-hearted women amongst the artistes, all who were pleased to brush little Lou's golden curls and sing to her and call her my ducky-doll, my little lamb. Louisa had counted herself lucky. How many other little girls had a wire-walker or a mesmerist brushing their hair?

'You must miss her,' said Louisa, gently parting Phoebe's hair.

'Sometimes. I wish I knew more about her. I think she might have been foreign – an Italian or a Greek.'

'You think?'

'I don't know for sure.'

'It would explain your colouring. What was her name?'

Phoebe pursed her lips and jutted her chin again for a moment and then she said, in a sighing little voice, as if it hurt her to say it aloud, 'Selena'.

'I think that's a perfectly beautiful name,' Louisa said, decidedly, trying not to sound as sentimental as she felt, thinking of her own lost mother.

'It is, isn't it?'

'Yes, it is. You really are the moon's own daughter.'

Phoebe frowned, as if startled out of her reverie. 'What does the moon have to do with it?'

'Selena means "moon". I think it's Greek, like Phoebe.'

'Oh.' Phoebe tipped her head forwards to let Louisa pull the segments of her hair into a plait more easily. 'What was your mother's name?'

'Caroline. Nothing so exotic for me, I'm afraid. Practically all the girls her age were called Caroline. It was a very fashionable name.'

'It's a lovely name.'

'It's the female version of Charles – like my cousin. Well, he's not really my cousin. Something like a fourth cousin, and his father is my third cousin but he made me call him "Uncle" when he adopted me. You'll probably meet him tomorrow, but don't let him try any nonsense. He's a very devil with the ladies, that one. He was always spying on me when I was young. I've a good mind to do some spying on him – get my own back.'

'Spying?'

'Yes. Peeking through the keyhole and so on. He'd always be trying to catch me with my clothes off, or using the chamber pot.'

Phoebe looked alarmed. 'And he's here?'

'Don't you worry about him. I'll cut his balls off if he tries anything. Not that I minded, of course – not that much – but I was never very good at being a good girl. I suppose I should have screamed or fainted when I heard him shuffling about behind the door but I used to tease him, give him something to really look at.'

'Oh, miss . . . Louisa! You didn't!'

'I did,' said Louisa, tying a ribbon at the base of Phoebe's plait and climbing into bed. 'I use to tease him something rotten. I'm sure he thought I couldn't hear him, but I could. I knew he was there all along, staring and playing with himself. So I'd have a little play of my own. I looked at myself in the mirror and stroked my cunt and once I even stuck the handle of a hairbrush up there and all the while I was trying so hard not to laugh because I was thinking of the state he must have been in on the other side of the door.'

Phoebe stared, open mouthed, then covered her mouth and giggled. 'What did he do?' she asked, slipping into bed beside Louisa. She did so stiffly, as if she were uncomfortable about doubling up.

'Probably frigged himself half-blind, I shouldn't wonder. Finally I got to him so much that he threw open the door, came in and said he'd tell his father what a dirty bitch I was. I said he knew that better than anyone since he'd been watching the entire time and what would his father say to that? That shut him up and I said he should show me what he'd got since he'd seen everything of mine, so he showed me his cock and I couldn't resist. I wanted to know what it felt like.'

'What did it feel like?' asked Phoebe, breathlessly. She wore an expression of slack-mouthed wonder and when she relaxed her lips that way Louisa thought the shape of her mouth was beautiful. The corners of her lips were finely finished, the dip in the middle of the upper lip making a bow shape of her mouth. She held her lips a little way apart in her eagerness and her teeth were very white, rather sharp. Louisa recalled the way she bit off a thread, with a brisk, animal efficiency, sometimes marking her underlip with the line of the thread so that she would worry it with the tip of her red tongue for days afterwards.

'It's a bit like riding, only not,' said Louisa.

'I've never been on a horse. Horses don't like me.'

'I'm sure that's not true,' Louisa said, thinking of Alcestis and Hippolyta fretting in their stalls. 'They're very intelligent animals. They know who loves them, and who's afraid of them. If you learn not be afraid of them they won't play you up.'

'I'm not afraid of them. They just don't like me.'

'That's funny. Usually people who are good with dogs are good with horses, and I've never seen dogs take to a person like Charlotte's *petits enfants* took to you.'

'They were hardly *petit*,' said Phoebe. 'I was worried that mastiff was going to try and climb up in my lap.'

Louisa laughed for a moment but stopped abruptly when she heard a noise from the room next door. 'Shh,' she said, straining her ears to hear. 'I wonder what they're talking about in there.'

She got out of bed and emptied the water glass on the bedside table into the chamber pot. Phoebe looked as though she was about to ask what Louisa was doing but Louisa shushed her again and very gently, so as not to make a sound, placed the rim of the glass against the wall. She held her ear to the base and listened intently, unable to make out words. There was just a mumble of male voices, speaking too low to be overheard. In the bed, Phoebe was looking scandalised and smothering her giggles with a hand.

Damn. They were talking even more quietly in there, whispering. Louisa was about to put the glass down when she heard a moan, a sound of pain or pleasure. Her mouth was dry with trying to breathe as silently as possible and she crept to the adjoining door, which she had locked and left the key in the hole. She tried to draw out the key but it was stuck fast and she was sure that the rattle of the lock could be heard for miles.

'Bugger,' she muttered, under her breath, trying to think of something with which to grease the lock. 'Pass me that face cream,' she whispered, pointing to the dressing table.

Phoebe slid out of her side of the bed and handed it over. Louisa smeared it around the base of the key and blew hard on it to force the cream into the lock. She tried it again and the key slid out easily. She hoped that, after all that effort, the men still had the lights on in their room.

'You can't!' said Phoebe, in a piercing whisper, as Louisa knelt down.

'I bloody well can.' She put her eye to the keyhole. Good. There was still light. She could see someone, in a nightshirt, on the bed, their back to the door. She tried to still her breathing so that she could hear what was going on because she was sure she heard panting but couldn't be sure if she was making the sound or whether it was coming from the next room. The man on the bed moved, enough for her to see above his shoulders, see his fair hair and know it was Charlie, and then off came the nightshirt.

She had always liked his body, ever since they were young. It had been the main reason she'd got into trouble, because once they'd started they had never been able to keep their hands off one another. At the time she had never imagined a man could be so soft to the touch. He had the whitest, smoothest skin, almost as soft as a woman's, and, with her uncle's wife pretending friendship and encouraging her trysts with Charlie, Louisa had been at liberty to lie in bed with him and touch every inch of him.

She watched him now, her view confined to his face and upper torso. He lay with his head on the pillow, but he hadn't pulled the covers up over himself. His right arm, the only one in view, was down by his side and when he turned his head towards the door she almost lost her nerve and jumped back, thinking he might remember his own old tricks and quite rightly suspect her of doing the same. His eyes remained closed, however, and he opened his mouth in a short, shuddery hitch of breath, which made her bite her lip hard so that she didn't giggle at the thought of what his left hand might be doing.

'*In flagrante delicto*,' she mouthed, to Phoebe, who probably didn't know what she meant.

'What's going on?' said Phoebe, in a hushed voice.

'He's playing with himself!' whispered Louisa, exultantly.

Phoebe clapped her hand back over her mouth and fell over sideways on the bed, making Louisa struggle hard not to laugh. There was a clearly audible moan from Charlie's room and when Phoebe met Louisa's eyes they very nearly erupted into loud laughter.

'Come here!' Louisa beckoned her over. 'Shh. Oh, I don't *believe* this.'

'What is it?' asked Phoebe, kneeling beside her. 'Put the candle out. He might see our shadows under the door.'

'Yes, blow it out, blow it out, but shh ... quiet as mice!'

Louisa saw Phoebe's face in the candlelight, pretty lips pursed, then a breath and darkness. She blinked in the dark and put her eye to the small light that shone through the keyhole. Charlie's face was flushed, his chest rising and falling rapidly, and he had crammed his clenched fingers in his mouth to keep from crying out. She was just about to invite Phoebe to peep and then she was taken completely by surprise. Charlie arched his back, shifted on the pillows and she saw his thigh folded up against his chest and then someone who must have been William, mounting him as if he were a woman.

'Fuck!' she said, aloud, and then fell back from the keyhole, sure they must have heard her.

'What?' said Phoebe.

Louisa's eyes were becoming accustomed to the darkness and she could make out the shape of Phoebe's face, pale under her hair, and the white of her nightgown. 'They're lovers!' she gasped, half laughing, half breathless. 'They're fucking one another in there!'

'Two *men*?'

'Look, if you don't believe me.'

She could hear Phoebe breathing hard as the girl peeked through the keyhole, but she was so eager to see more that poor Phoebe could probably have only got a glimpse or two. 'Let me see, let me see,' Louisa whispered, pushing her away. By now she could hear the bedsprings quite clearly and Charlie's moans and groans filtered through the wall. They had moved, impelled towards the headboard by their motions, and she could see the slope of Charlie's curled haunches and see William's hips pounding into him repeatedly. Her mouth was as dry as dust but she could feel wetness welling between her thighs at the sight of them. Now she understood why so many clients were eager to procure books about lesbian women, if it was so affecting as watching two men fuck.

'What are they doing?' asked Phoebe.

Louisa didn't answer. She watched Charlie's body arch, shudder and go slack. He was so thin and Will handled him like a doll, turning him over onto his knees with his bum in the air. She saw Will's prick for an instant, before it was buried between Charlie's buttocks, and squeezed her legs tightly together as she watched the motion of his thrusts turn staccato and he finished with hard little jabs of his hips, his hands grasping Charlie's sagging body by the waist.

Someone blew out the candle.

She sank down onto the floor, barely able to believe what she had just witnessed. William, maybe – it wouldn't have surprised her to find that he fancied boys, but Charlie had always been such a lady's man. What a strange turn up. 'Bed,' she said, recovering her senses for a moment. 'Quickly. Before they hear us.'

She plunged back under the sheets, Phoebe bundling in beside her. Her nightgown rode up and she felt the brush of Phoebe's bare leg against her own for a moment and then they both lay very still beneath the covers, as if even breathing too loudly would give them away.

'What were they doing?' Phoebe asked again, under her breath. 'Were they really . . . fucking?'

'Yes,' said Louisa, as if she couldn't believe it herself.

'But they're both men.'

'Oh, for heaven's sake, Phoebe,' Louisa whispered, impatient in her surprise. 'It's in the Bible, you know.'

There was a pause, a gulp from Phoebe. 'I must have been reading the wrong Bible,' she said, her endearingly baffled tone making Louisa's irritation melt away as fast as it had come upon her.

'Sodom and Gomorrah.'

'Ohhhh.'

'"Bring out the men so that we may know them." "Know" is just another word for fuck. Carnal knowledge.'

Phoebe exhaled in the dark. 'Blimey. They never mentioned that in Sunday school.'

Louisa bit down a giggle. 'No, I expect they didn't. I suppose we're going to get turned into pillars of salt now.'

With an audible pop, Phoebe stuck her finger in her mouth and sucked on it for a moment. 'I don't taste like a pillar of salt. Well, not yet, anyway.'

'I can't believe it,' Louisa said, wondering out loud. 'Those two! I wonder when that happened.'

'Wasn't it Sodom where they told them to bring out the men?'

'Yes, I believe it was.'

'So what were they doing that was so terrible in Gomorrah?'

'Do you know, I'm not sure,' Louisa said. 'Maybe it was the women who were misbehaving.'

'The women?' Phoebe raised herself up on an elbow with a rustle of sheets. 'Really? Doing what?'

Louisa laughed. 'Anything they could imagine, I suspect. Maybe they had big graven idols made of stone, shaped like men's pricks, or they just used their fingers to fuck one another.'

'Can women really ... do that?' Phoebe's voice was shaky with what could easily have been more than curiosity and Louisa wondered what she had begun here. She had been overeager to spring the girl from her prison of ignorance and wondered if she hadn't gone too far by showing Phoebe herself in the mirror. Louisa had always loved men primarily, regardless of what attachments she made to other women.

'Darling, you should see some of the books that have passed through my possession over the years. Some men are absolutely fixated by it,' she said, trying to keep her tone light. Her mind was drifting elsewhere, to pictures of naked girls with their quims picked out in red ink, their breasts pressed against one another and their fingers penetrating one another's flesh. She imagined some scene from Gomorrah – a Bedouin fantasy of silk cushions and pierced copper lanterns, the air thick with incense and burning oil. She squeezed her thighs together between the sheets, her cunt already clamouring for attention after what she had seen through the keyhole.

'I wonder why.'

'It's something they can't have for themselves. Men always want what they can't have. And I suppose they imagine that two naked women are twice as good as one – double the softness, double the tenderness.'

Phoebe settled back down in the bed. 'I don't know,' she said, quietly. 'I think sometimes it could be rather fierce.'

For a moment Louisa pictured Phoebe with her hair cut short, dressed in a beautifully cut suit like Josephine, a cigarette between her red lips and her dark eyes heavy and rakish as she looked at some thin-skinned little blonde with the air of a connoisseur, a predator. The thought made her insides give a queer little squirm.

'Not in the books,' Louisa said. 'It's always soft and gentle.'

'Then the books must be written by men,' Phoebe announced, with an air of authority.

'I think maybe you're right,' Louisa said. It was always the same in the books, one girl wordly, like herself, the other innocent, like Phoebe. Then the innocent would ask questions, about men, about kisses and then one thing would lead to another. 'Do you ever feel ... fierce?' she ventured, feeling like the innocent rather than the worldly seducer the books would have her believe she was – the lamb rather than the lion.

Phoebe hesitated. 'Yes,' she said, in a faraway voice. 'Very often. Not tender at all. I wonder if it's right to feel like that.'

'Like what?'

'Like I could just ... I don't know ... *eat*, I suppose. Like I could sink my teeth into what I wanted and tear it all up, only not with pain. Quite the opposite.'

Louisa bit her lip. Her hips felt as though they wanted to stir, to lift off the bed and force her thighs open. The image of Gomorrah in her mind was populated now, by women sprawled naked over cushions, their legs spread while other women feasted on their cunts, the smell of sex pungent in the fragrant smoky air, the room reverberating to cries and moans as they penetrated one another with fingers, tongues, with fetishes carved from Chinese jade or Italian marble.

'It's not wrong, is it?' Phoebe asked, although she sounded as if she didn't care if it was.

'No,' said Louisa, barely trusting herself to speak.

'Is it just for men that women do that?'

'No.'

'Did you ever ...?'

'No,' said Louisa, breathlessly. 'We should go to sleep.'

Phoebe was silent, ominously so. Worried that she had offended the girl, Louisa touched her lightly on the waist beneath the covers and Phoebe made a soft strangled noise in the back of her throat. Looking was one thing, touching another girl like that? That was a whole different matter. Louisa had known girls who had taken so much money from men and grown so disgusted with men and their desires that they had turned to their own sex for real tenderness. She supposed that it was her own fault if Phoebe did turn out to be lesbian – she had taught the girl too much. She felt guilty, remembering the stepmother who had encouraged her to her own ruin, and tightened her grip on Phoebe's waist.

'It's not wrong, is it?' Phoebe asked, again.

'People do it,' said Louisa, faintly, 'whether it's right or wrong.' She could feel the heat of Phoebe's skin through her nightgown and felt her breath against her cheek. For the longest time it felt as though she didn't dare turn her head because she knew what she would meet when she did.

It was still a shock, even though she had anticipated it. She brushed Phoebe's lips with her own. They were warm, soft and when she instinctively raised her hand to cup Phoebe's chin she was reminded starkly of what she was doing. Phoebe's chin was small, smooth and unquestionably a woman's chin. Louisa shivered, thinking strangely of the trinkets in her jewellery box, of the ropes of pearls and the collars of emeralds. How would it be to be given licence to play out her fantasies of the harem – dress up in nothing but jewels and pretend they were diverting themselves with one another's enticing flesh while awaiting the pleasure of a sultan or a maharajah?

She breathed harder and pressed her lips harder to Phoebe's, realising that the girl had probably never kissed anyone like this before. She opened her mouth and then had cause to wonder, because Phoebe's tongue surged between her lips with a hunger she had never imagined from a prim little virgin seamstress. What had that girl been up to on the sly?

No, she couldn't have. That fat terrier of a father

would never have let her out of his sight for a moment. There were some girls you could imagine with their skirts up against walls, eagerly welcoming the attentions of the butcher's boy, but Phoebe was not one of them. She was a nervous bourgeois animal whose world was composed of threads and seams and buttons and bows, not some aspiring tart from Whitechapel.

Nevertheless, she was surprising Louisa with her fervour. Phoebe rummaged at the neck of Louisa's nightgown, unfastening the ribbons with fingers accustomed to dressing and undressing women. Louisa couldn't help a moan escape her throat when she felt Phoebe's wet, hot mouth close over one of her nipples and teeth nip the flesh into a stinging, sensitive point.

This was strange, but not unpleasant. Louisa could feel the moisture welling between her thighs and squirmed, wanting attention. She thought of those men in the next room and imagined their chagrin at not being able to witness this spectacle. Anything they could do, she thought, women could do it better.

She reached down and grasped a handful of Phoebe's nightgown, pulling it upwards and meaning to pull it off entirely. Her hand brushed the small of Phoebe's bare back and she marvelled at the texture of the skin, the narrowness of her waist. She knew that beneath that, where she could not reach, was Phoebe's bare arse, flat little buttocks that curved only slightly to lead the way to her black-haired cunt.

'Roll over,' she whispered, and Phoebe obediently lay on her back.

It was too dark to see anything so Louisa had to rely on touch alone. She had her hand on Phoebe's stomach and she could feel the dip of her navel and when she moved her hand lower and touched the mass of hair she was surprised at its coarseness. It already felt slightly damp to the touch and for a moment she wondered if she'd even know what to do once she moved her hand even lower still, but she told herself that all women were made alike. What worked on her would surely work on Phoebe.

Phoebe was breathing raggedly as she opened her thighs wide enough to grant Louisa access. Tentatively, Louisa felt her way down to the top of the cleft, found the nub that she always thought constituted a woman's cock. It was wet and swollen and Phoebe cried out softly when she touched it. 'Shh,' Louisa said, aware that there was only a partition wall between them and Charlie the arch-voyeur. Not that he'd be able to see anything with the lights off but Louisa felt strangely determined that he would know nothing of this, because all he'd want to do was watch. She wasn't doing this for him, or any man. She was doing this because she wanted to.

Her finger felt the entrance and when she pushed inside she wondered that she had ever doubted Phoebe's chastity. The passage was narrow and ridged, unfamiliar to her own, which felt wider and smoother. Phoebe jerked under her touch and gave a little mew.

'Am I hurting you?' asked Louisa.

'No. Oh no.' Her voice was breathless, trembling, and the sound of it inspired Louisa to greater daring. Louisa rubbed the tip with her thumb, all the while gently introducing a second finger. It was wonderfully slippery inside and she moved her fingers back and forth, thrusting gently as a man might with a cock.

'Is that . . .?'

'Mmm.'

Phoebe's body bucked and she pressed herself against Louisa's hand. Louisa wondered if the girl had ever really brought herself off before and she relished the opportunity of doing it for her. She pushed Phoebe's nightgown up to her armpits and pressed her other hand to the small breasts, wanting to laugh at the absurdity of her own shyness. They had looked at one another, after all. She had shown Phoebe how to tease the parts she was now handling, so why this trepidation?

Phoebe's breasts felt hard compared to her own, the nipples stiff. She took one in her mouth, bringing their bodies into a closer contact. That made a difference somehow. It was no longer a game or an experiment but actual sex. 'Help me,' Louisa whispered, manoeuvring her own nightgown higher by moving against Phoebe. 'Get these nighties off.'

Somehow they wriggled out of their nightclothes. Phoebe just had to raise her shoulders from the bed to remove hers and then she tugged Louisa's over her head and cast it aside. The touch of naked flesh was as exciting to Louisa as it always was with a man, but different, softer, and even more exciting for its strangeness.

'You knew,' Phoebe kept saying, mouthing at the skin of Louisa's shoulders. 'You knew all along ... if only you'd told me!'

'It doesn't matter,' said Louisa, not knowing what she was talking about. What mattered, anyway, was how wet Phoebe was, how soaked she was getting herself and finding some kind of relief. She had Phoebe's thigh between her own and she rubbed against it, praying that it would be enough.

Phoebe moaned into her ear and then she gasped in one breathy rush, 'Oh stop, stop. It's too much ... I shall die, I shall ...'

Louisa smiled, smug that she had accomplished what she set out to do. Phoebe thrashed so hard she almost dislodged Louisa and she sank her teeth into Louisa's shoulder to muffle her cries, but Louisa held tight, determined not to lose the pressure of Phoebe's leg between her own.

'Oh God,' Phoebe murmured. 'What did you *do*?'

'Didn't you like it?'

'Oh yes. I loved it. But is that how? I thought ... well ... I thought it was something different.'

'Different?' asked Louisa, wanting to laugh. 'With a cock or something? I haven't got one, darling.'

'No, I know,' Phoebe said, her breathing still heavy. Her skin was hot and damp all over. 'I thought ... I dreamed, it was different.'

'How?'

Phoebe disengaged herself and sat up in the bed. 'I'll show you,' she said, determinedly and she pushed Louisa onto the bed on her back. Louisa suddenly realised what it was the girl was doing and although she couldn't believe it she was not about to stop her when she felt the tickle of breath ruffling her pubic hair.

Morning came too soon and Phoebe was not as timid as Louisa imagined she might be. There was something deeply unnerving about the way Phoebe was innocent and yet depraved and in the morning she seemed particularly sinful. She said nothing about what had transpired the night before but as she dressed Louisa she lingered over the process, daring to cup a breast before settling it into a corset or brushing her hands over Louisa's naked hips as she helped her on with her drawers. Louisa noticed that the tip of Phoebe's tongue slipped out while she was concentrating on laces and she thought she would never be able to watch Phoebe lick her lips again without thinking of *that*.

It was strange to say goodbye like this, to slip back into the roles of mistress and servant. For a moment

Louisa wanted to invite Phoebe to dine at the head of the breakfast table, to take her everywhere with her, announce that Phoebe was her lover and make cow eyes at her like some silly old dowager infatuated with a young footman.

'I'll see you after breakfast,' she told Phoebe, standing outside the bedroom.

Phoebe nodded, still saying nothing but looking at her with an odd new light in her eyes. When Charlie stepped out of his room and caught her eye Phoebe did not look away but boldly stared him in the face, as if daring him to peek through keyholes or look at her mistress in that way ever again.

'That girl,' Charlie said, hoarsely, watching Phoebe go off down to her breakfast. 'Where did you find her?'

'Blackfriars. You remember that watch I have – the clock fitted into the cigarette case? I took it to be mended at a little shop in Blackfriars and there she was. I thought her clothes looked a bit fine for a shopgirl and asked her about them and it turned out they were all her own work.'

Charlie paced the rug, shaking his head. 'She's not like other girls, that one.'

'No, I know,' said Louisa, biting her lip to hide her smile. Oh yes, she *was* different, and how gloriously different! Louisa shivered at the sense memory of slippery flesh giving way for her fingers and she fancied she could still smell Phoebe.

'You *know*?' cried Charlie. He stopped pacing and stared at her. 'Then why in the name of God do you let her stay here? You heard what happened to Francis Hoyland, didn't you? That was Mrs Hoyland's handiwork, that was.'

'Which one? Wasn't he married bigamously?'

'The other one,' said Charlie, impatiently. 'The Italian

woman. She was just like that girl. You can tell. It's in the eyes.'

'Charlie, you're raving.'

'I'm not raving. If you'd just shut up and listen to me then I'd explain.'

'Sorry.' Louisa sat back and wondered if he had gone mad, but then he had never been prone to melancholy like some members of their family. If Charlie stood any chance of madness it would be from a pox on the brain, but if he'd gone and caught the clap in Naples there was little chance it would have been advanced enough to addle his wits just yet.

'I haven't been able to talk to a soul about it,' said Charlie, settling in an armchair and lighting a cigarette. 'Besides Will. The Great Rationalist. Who thinks I'm mad.' He gave a little snort of contempt and Louisa wondered when she would ever be able to broach the subject of what was going on between him and Will. Now was certainly not the time. 'You know how he is,' Charlie continued. 'Thinks we're all Papists and superstitious peasants. He wouldn't have believed what had happened to me even if I told him. Worse, he'd go and concoct some logical, rational explanation designed to make me feel even more like a lunatic.'

'Go on,' encouraged Louisa. 'You can trust me, darling. I'm probably a more superstitious peasant than you.' She still kept her Tarot cards in the bedside drawer, as an insurance against the day she might no longer be able to rely on her looks to extract gifts and money from men. She saw herself as an old woman, telling young beauties their fortunes – The Lovers, The Queen of Pentacles, The Star – telling the story they wanted to hear, as she'd learnt to do as a little girl.

'It was that woman of his, Chiara. They said she came

from Rome where she'd been a prostitute. That was the rumour anyway. You couldn't mention her name in any of the marketplaces without some woman spitting, making the evil eye and calling her a whore and a witch. I think Naples was proud to be the adopted land of Hoyland, but not her. The Neapolitans seemed to hate her with a passion, even though he'd allegedly married her with the full Catholic rite.

'Anyway, he was drawing her all the time – preliminaries for his sculptures, and no, don't ask. We didn't get any. He'd drawn her in fantastic detail, particularly with regard to her face and her cunt. Oh, Lou, I wish you could have seen this study he'd done for *Leda and the Swan*. It was perfectly filthy. I can't begin to imagine how much we'd have got for it if we'd managed to salvage it from his studio, but the poor bastard frequently went mad and smashed and tore everything up, or so he said. I'm not sure now that it wasn't *her*.

'She had him in some kind of thrall, I believe. At first I thought he had the whip hand of her, because he treated her like a skivvy rather than a wife but then, I don't know. Something changed. I don't know quite what it was that gave away the balance of power between them but I just knew instinctively that she was in charge from that moment on.'

'Really?' Louisa thought of her sudden whim to enthrone Phoebe at the head of the table and wondered if everyone who was in the habit of loving their servants or marrying whores was in danger of sending Charlie into this kind of conniption. For all his pretensions, Charlie was really quite disgustingly conventional.

'I knew,' Charlie asserted, hiding something. 'I knew she was in control.'

'What does this have to do with Phoebe?'

'It's in the eyes,' said Charlie, giving her a weighted,

worried look that made her think he might be irredeemably potty after all. 'Such eyes that woman had! She had bronzy-coloured eyes with a ring of deeper gold around the centre – just like your little maid. I've seen those eyes before. They're a wolf's eyes.'

'Perhaps you need a rest –' Louisa began, cautiously.

'No!' Charlie interrupted, springing up from the chair. 'No, you haven't heard all of this yet, Louisa. That woman? She was *not human*. I saw her with my own eyes. I know what I saw. I watched her turn into some sort of wild animal – literally, Lou. Literally. I swear on my mother's life that what I saw was real. She turned into a wolf, right in front of me!'

Louisa bit her lower lip hard for a moment. 'Charlie, it's not that I don't believe you . . .'

'Yes, of course,' Charlie snapped. 'You don't believe me, do you?'

'I believe that you believe entirely in what you saw.'

'You think I'm insane?'

'I think maybe you're tired,' said Louisa, struggling to hold back the desire to laugh. 'This hasn't been an easy job for either of you, I know.'

'I am telling you the God's honest truth! Bring me a Bible, I'll swear on it. I'll swear any oath you ask me to.'

'But, Charlie,' Louisa pleaded, 'you're not honestly trying to tell me that my lady's maid is some kind of . . . werewolf?'

No sooner was the word 'werewolf' out of her mouth than her sense of humour got the better of her. It was too funny – the idea of shy, inoffensive little Phoebe turning into some hairy beast every full moon and devouring people in Hyde Park. Louisa saw Charlie's face and wanted to apologise immediately but she couldn't stop laughing, and so Charlie stormed out of the drawing room to the sound of her gales of hysterical laughter.

9

From that moment, everything changed. Phoebe was no longer herself – she was a new creature entirely, a thing elevated and sanctified by desire and by being desired. She could never have believed in a thousand years that she could get Louisa to look at her like that, to sway back into her touch every time she undressed her and to make Louisa murmur with pleasure whenever Phoebe placed kisses on every scrap of skin as she clothed it – an insurance that the same place would be kissed later when the clothes came off.

But she had. The red gown took on even more idolatrous significance in Phoebe's mind. Now she finished every trimming with her hands trembling; every detail of the dress, every braid on the bodice and every rose at the neckline – they would all go towards concealing and revealing the flesh she adored. Sometimes she couldn't prevent herself from thinking of the men who would see Louisa in that gown and then she would sometimes grow so clumsy in her anger that she pricked her finger with her needle and a smear of blood would vanish, invisible, into the blood-red silk heart of an artificial rose. By the middle of April the gown was finished.

For the final fitting Louisa insisted on wearing all of the underwear that had been specifically designed for the dress – the red corset, the rose-red ruffled garters that held up black silk stockings. She looked obscene and exquisite, even lovelier than Phoebe had imagined in her dreams, perhaps lovelier for the knowledge that Phoebe had of what was between those round white thighs, the flavour and texture of each pale-pink nipple and the subtly different weight of each breast when cupped in a palm.

The dress was everything they had imagined. It pinched in Louisa's small waist so tight that her breasts swelled like pale fruit in the neckline. Only the garland of roses hid her nipples and when she moved one was sure the eye was deceived by that flash of darker pink against the white of her bosom. The skirt was so artfully constructed that unless Louisa sat down or spread her legs then nobody would have known that it was divided almost to the waist.

Louisa stuck out a leg and posed, putting her foot on the dressing-table stool and looking at herself in the mirror. 'It's still not right,' she said, rather petulantly.

'It's perfect!' protested Phoebe.

'It's not your fault, darling. It's mine. I wish I had your colouring. I look too pale.'

Phoebe took a stick of carmine paint from the dressing table. 'Here,' she said. 'Use paint, then.'

Louisa sat quite still, as if chastised, while Phoebe painted her lips a bright whorish scarlet. Louisa's face looked doughy when she had finished, too pale, so she smeared some of the carmine on her fingers and smudged it over her cheekbones. That looked better.

'If you're going to paint everything red to match,' said Louisa. 'You'd best do my tits as well.'

She pulled down the rose garland to expose her nipples and, laughing, Phoebe smudged the red paint on each pink circle. Louisa's breasts looked strangely artificial when she had finished, like a picture in a dirty book, Louisa said.

'They always pick out the girl's nipples and cunt in the brightest of red,' Louisa explained. 'It's strange. I've never seen anything like it in real life, but then they don't concern themselves with real life overmuch.'

'What about down there?' Phoebe asked. 'Red enough?'

Louisa raised her eyebrows, but she opened her legs all the same. The dress fell easily to either side of her thighs and her legs in their black stockings looked beautifully slender and graceful. Between her legs her quim was bare, a pink sliver beneath light-brown hair.

'Pink,' Phoebe pronounced, decidedly, and asked her to spread her legs wider as casually as she might once have asked her to raise her arms to facilitate the removal of a chemise. Phoebe opened up the folds of flesh with her fingers and rubbed at that spot that she knew now cared most for pressure. Louisa bit her painted lip and groaned softly and the blood flushed between her thighs.

'There. That's better,' said Phoebe.

'You tease me,' Louisa complained.

'I shan't do it again, then.'

'I didn't say that!' Louisa laughed and rose from the dressing table. 'Shall I change, do you think? Or shall I just go and meet Lord X like this?'

Phoebe looked up in alarm. 'A man?'

'A lord, darling. A *lord*. They think themselves better than real men. I'm after a book of his. I should think I'll be quite safe with him.'

'Dressed like that?' Phoebe asked, her own anger surprising her. She knew all along that this was the purpose of the dress but she couldn't help being jealous. It was her creation, hers and Louisa's. It should have existed solely for their pleasure.

'He's as impotent as a child,' said Louisa, airily, spraying her throat with perfume. 'I've tried to ingratiate myself on numerous occasions, being as he's rich and he's got a few texts I'd rather like to get my hands on myself, but I've never managed to excite him. Maybe he likes the boys. I don't know.'

'I don't care what he likes,' said Phoebe.

'Come and chaperone me if it bothers you so much,' Louisa said. 'Although you know this can't continue, don't you? If you want me I'm happy, but I'm afraid a job is a job. I've been doing this for years and I'll do it while my looks still allow me to get away with it. I have to put something aside for my old age, Phoebe. I'm an unmarried woman and nobody provides well for poor old spinsters.'

Phoebe sighed and sat down heavily on the bed. 'I know. I've always known. I never minded much about what you did ... until lately.'

'We'll make the best of it,' said Louisa, giving her a kiss. 'I promise. Come with me into the drawing room and we'll make fun of him after he leaves.'

'I suppose so,' Phoebe conceded, sullenly. It was better than Louisa being alone with him anyway. 'Is his name really Lord Ecks?'

'No. He goes by Lord X to hide his identity, but everyone knows who he is. I think he really quite relishes the sensation when his reputation is whispered about.'

Phoebe thought he sounded like an extremely boring man, but she followed Louisa into the drawing room to meet the lord all the same. She hadn't known what to expect of a lord and only a few months ago she would have been cowed to near speechlessness at the presence of an aristocrat, but being Louisa's lover had lent her a new arrogance that she hardly believed of herself.

She didn't curtsey to the middle-aged man who presented himself in Louisa's drawing room. Instead she looked him in the eye. To her complete surprise, Lord X cut his eyes away first and demurely averted his eyes from Louisa's half-bared bosom when he went to kiss her hand.

'I hope I haven't caught you at an inconvenient time, Mrs LeClerk,' he said.

'Not at all, your lordship. You'll excuse my outfit. I was just trying on Miss Flood's latest creation. It's quite something, don't you think?'

Lord X made a sort of strangled sound in the back of his throat. 'Charming,' he said, eventually. 'Although perhaps a little risqué for the opera?'

Phoebe watched Louisa's lips twitch and realised her mistress's sense of humour was getting the better of her once again. 'Surely you of all people know I have a reputation to keep up, my lord,' Louisa teased. Phoebe didn't know how she could bring herself to speak flirtatiously to him. The man was not at all handsome. He had sandy hair, a large nose and matching sandy whiskers which seemed to drag his lugubrious-looking face even further downwards. He reminded Phoebe of a bloodhound.

Pleasantries were exchanged, seats taken. Louisa pulled a pillow into her lap and carefully curled her legs under her seat to conceal the most shocking revelations offered by her dress. On one occasion she forgot herself and her leg, up to the calf, peeked high heeled through the slit skirt. Lord X stared and Phoebe could not restrain herself from glaring fiercely at him. He caught her eye and flushed like a schoolboy, then he stared down into his lap, as if chastised. That was strange, Phoebe thought, that he should behave so timidly in front of a commoner and a woman.

She still disliked him, because of what he was, because of what he might be to Louisa – more than another poor fool to be conned out of a handful of dirty books. Louisa was talking animatedly about daguerreotypes undercutting the market for everything else these days when Phoebe realised the stupid man wasn't even listening. He was looking at her, hopefully, with sad-dog eyes.

Phoebe gave him a dirty look and to her disgust the man smiled furtively and diverted his attention back to Louisa, who had let fall one side of her dress and sat with her garter showing. Louisa chattered on, leant over for a light for her cigarette and the cushion fell out of her lap.

He couldn't help but stare. Nobody could have helped but stared. Her whole thigh was showing and at the top was a visible wisp of hair. Phoebe couldn't contain herself any longer.

'What the hell do you think you're looking at?' she erupted.

Louisa stared open mouthed at her. 'Phoebe!' she gasped. She had gone so white under her paint that she almost looked green in contrast to her gown.

Lord X gave her that sad-doggy look again and Phoebe was tempted to cross the room and strike him, but he got up from the chaise and *knelt* in front of Phoebe. Shocked, Phoebe sprung up out of her chair and stared down at the kneeling man. His head was bent and she could see the bald patch on the back of his head. Louisa had stood up too and she had her hand over her mouth, but her colour was returning and Phoebe could tell by the familiar tremor of her shoulders that she was trying not to laugh.

'I beg your apologies, Miss Flood,' said Lord X. 'Please, do as you will with me!'

He disgusted Phoebe all the more with his grovelling and she found herself saying, haughtily, 'You're not fit to lick her shoes.'

Lord X nodded. 'Yes, mistress. I'm a worm. It's true. Only I beg you that I might be allowed to kiss the tip of her shoe, if only for a moment.'

Louisa looked at Phoebe and shrugged, as if things like this happened all the time. Phoebe stared down incredulously at the peer crouched at her feet and realised that she was rather enjoying his abasement. She moved away from him, to Louisa's side.

'You want her, don't you?' she asked, tugging at the rose garland to bare Louisa's breasts. Louisa didn't move. She stayed stock-still as she had in the dream where Phoebe was exhibiting her to the wolves.

'Yes, mistress. I am sorry for my depravity.' He began to sob and Louisa sucked her lips tight into her mouth and trembled.

'Specialist tastes,' she whispered to Phoebe. 'Well done. I never thought him the type myself.'

Phoebe didn't entirely understand. She had not yet read widely enough to know that some men liked to be humiliated, shouted at and whipped like dogs, but she disliked him enough to continue. 'You're not sorry,' she said. 'Not sorry enough. Get your nose on the carpet, go on. Right down on the floor.' She was conscious of the cockney sound of her own voice, common, not like him, but he lowered his face all the same, pressed his nose to the rug and stuck his bottom up in the air.

'I don't know why you were staring,' she continued. 'You wouldn't know where to start with a woman like her, would you?'

'No, mistress,' said Lord X.

Louisa pressed her lips even harder together and scrunched her eyes shut. She looked as though she was about to explode into one of her wild fits of laughter. Phoebe pinched her hard on the nipple and for a moment

Louisa looked angry and then grateful as the pain allowed her to restrain herself.

'You're all the same,' Phoebe told him. 'You come in here and think you can buy her off with jewellery and dirty books but you can't give her what she needs, what she likes. I hope you don't believe for a second she could ever love a thing like you.'

'I don't, mistress,' he whimpered, into the carpet. 'Oh please . . . please . . .'

'Please what?' asked Phoebe, bending over him. 'What is it you want? Do you want to lick her shoe, still?'

'Yes please, mistress. I'll do anything you ask of me if only you let me.'

Louisa had calmed down somewhat and now Phoebe was sure that she would herself be the one to burst out laughing. What was wrong with this man? He was a lunatic, surely.

'Look up,' Phoebe commanded. He did so and he was looking directly up at Louisa, up her legs which were only just covered by the skirt of her gown. All Louisa would have to do to give him a view like no other was shift her feet a little way apart. A wicked impulse seized Phoebe and she knew she wouldn't be able to keep from acting on it.

She leant close to Louisa, breathing in the delicious rose smell of her perfume. He was never going to get that close to her. That was Phoebe's privilege, to inhale the smell of her perfume until she was nearly sick on it, to touch every inch of her, listen to her laugh and sigh and moan, taste the sinful salt of her in places and ways that this pitiful creature couldn't even begin to dream about.

She looked down at him and wanted to laugh, wanted to mock him for his impotence. Stupid man, thinking you needed a prick to satisfy a woman. Phoebe managed very well without one. She wanted to show him what she could do.

'Look at this,' she said, opening the folds of Louisa's skirt. Louisa caught her breath in a barely audible gasp but she didn't move. Phoebe had taken a gamble on Louisa enjoying being exhibited in such a fashion but it seemed now that her dreams had steered her true. The velvet clutched in her palm was soft, in contrast to the rougher hair beneath her fingertips. She played her fingertips over the very ends of the hairs, teasing them apart, and thought she saw Lord X shiver.

'You could have this,' she told him, meaning every word, 'but you'd only be renting it. Paying for the privilege. If you wanted it for nothing you'd have to give her pleasure, but you wouldn't know how to do that.'

'No,' he said, in a small pathetic voice.

'No?' Louisa said, harshly.

Phoebe realised she was prompting her. 'No, what?' Phoebe added, taking up her cue.

'No, mistress.'

'That's better,' said Phoebe, still tempted to start laughing uncontrollably. She couldn't believe what she was doing. There was a peer of the realm *kneeling* on the carpet in front of her while she handled her mistress's cunt in front of him and he was begging *her*, a shopgirl from bloody Blackfriars, for the privilege of licking Louisa's shoe! It would have been hysterically funny if the heat of Louisa's body weren't stirring Phoebe's basest instincts and keeping her laughter in check.

'Look up,' she told him.

He kept his head down.

'Look *up*.'

Lord X raised his head with a mock timidity that only

served to annoy her. All very well for him to play at being a poor humiliated creature but where was he during the flood? Probably off in his country house while genuinely poor humiliated people draggled out of the sodden streets of Lambeth clutching whatever they could salvage from their waterlogged houses.

He was probably off shooting things and swilling port like the toff he was, and not caring two hoots about the state of things in the city where he held a seat in the highest court in the bloody land and did absolutely nothing to ease the fate of the poor. He's worse than my father, thought Phoebe. She wondered if she might get away with beating him. She'd like to whack him across the rump with the poker. Trouble was, the sod would probably enjoy it.

She knew how to really make him suffer. He wasn't going to get anywhere near Louisa's feet if she had anything to do with it. But he was going to see plenty of what he was missing out on.

She looked down into his silly sad-dog face, thinking of the wolves. In her dreams old Gold-Eyes had never looked this pathetic but then he was a wolf, or a man, or a something – a dream. Not real like this, however unreal it seemed. She couldn't keep from smirking at him as she cupped Louisa's mound in her hand and then temptingly, like easing apart another layer of her clothes, parted the furred lips with her fingers to show him the pink flesh inside.

'You may as well look,' she said. 'I shan't let you touch. You don't deserve to.'

'No, mistress.'

Louisa shivered and Phoebe knew that she was enjoying this. She could feel the warmth of Louisa's flesh under her fingers, felt the folds moistening. Unable to stop herself, she pressed herself against Louisa's bustle, reaching further forwards, and then slowly, watching the way Lord X's eyes widened, pushed her finger up Louisa's cunt.

Louisa caught her breath in a gasp and moaned, stirring Phoebe's desire almost to madness. She wanted to exhibit Louisa in every imaginable way – bend her over, lift her skirt over her head and show him the way her quim pouted out from beneath her rounded buttocks, cram three fingers inside her, show him how wide she could spread her legs, rip every scrap of clothing off her and lay her out, mother naked and sobbing with need, on the coffee table while Phoebe knelt between her legs and licked her until she came.

Her mind swimming with filthy images and greedy for more, Phoebe pushed two fingers inside, sliding them up and down and by now laughing openly at the expression on Lord X's face. Her desire had reached a stage where it was now unassailable and had to be satisfied. When Louisa trembled against her it was enough to tip her close to madness. Louisa was rocking slightly on her heels, playing up to her part beautifully. She squirmed her hips into Phoebe's touch and pushed them forwards, trying to expose the part of her that was most eager for attention. It wasn't entirely an act; she was soaked and Phoebe's fingers slid in and out easily. When Phoebe pressed her thumb to the tip of Louisa's quim, Louisa arched her back and almost knocked Phoebe onto the carpet, but Phoebe held onto her from behind, crushed against her bustle, and manipulated Louisa like a puppet before the man.

He was breathing hard now and staring wildly. Louisa jerked and cried out.

'Go on then,' Phoebe told him. 'Lick her shoe. If that's what you want.'

'Please, mistress. Oh please.'

'Yes. Go on. Didn't I say you could?'

Louisa tipped her head back. Her breasts spilt fully out of her gown, her painted nipples smudged and sticking up in pretty, messy little points. She was whimpering and twitching her hips this way and that as if Phoebe's touch caused her pain, which it probably did, seeing as Phoebe suspected she'd already come. She was too sensitive to be handled in such a way.

Lord X, sobbing softly with humiliation, joy or a mixture of both, extended his greyish tongue, lapped once at the tip of Louisa's shoe, kissed her ankle fervently and then sprung to his feet with an agility that neither woman would have expected from a man of his years.

'Thank you,' he babbled. 'Oh thank you, mistress.' Then he fled from the room, obviously with every intention of seeing himself out.

Louisa swatted Phoebe's hand away and flopped gratefully into a chair. Her legs were sprawled, exposing her to the waist, and her breasts were bared, her hair disordered. She looked flushed, sated and completely debauched.

She covered her hand with her mouth and giggled. 'Oh, Phoebe, what *have* you done?'

Phoebe sat down on the chaise and squirmed. Her face must have betrayed her desire for relief because Louisa murmured, 'Oh, you poor thing,' and knelt down before her. It wasn't easy – there seemed to be acres of skirt in the way – but when Louisa's mouth touched her it took almost no time at all. She had found the whole business too exciting.

'Bath,' said Louisa, abruptly, afterwards. 'Come on. Let's jump in the tub. I hope you haven't lost me one of my favourite suppliers, although I doubt it. I think he rather enjoyed himself. Clever old you. I didn't think he was the type.'

Only that evening, the book that Louisa had been trying to acquire arrived at the flat. It was wrapped in brown paper and tucked inside the flyleaf was a note. Lord X, it announced, would be happy to assist in furnishing her collection in future.

10

The old countess was dying. Louisa heard it from the actress, who had heard it from the aesthete, who had heard it from her lover, who had heard it at a tea party given for some charitable ladies' foundation. Phoebe heard it first hand, as it was she who received the summons from the old lady.

'You'd better rush before you're sent a letter edged in black,' said Louisa. 'She's on her last legs and she's been waiting to die ever since her husband went, poor old girl.'

'Aren't you coming?' asked Phoebe.

'Ask her if she wants me when you see her.' Louisa shrugged and popped a cigarette in her mouth. 'I'll go if she wants to see me, but she's asking specifically for you. You must have made a great impression on her.'

'I can't think why. Even if she was strong enough to play bridge I doubt she'd want me to play with her. I'm bloody awful.'

'You have other gifts, darling,' Louisa said, mischievously. 'Oh, and you sew quite well too, I suppose.'

Phoebe glowed, unable to believe she had this beautiful, worldly and witty woman in her bed each night. 'I'll tell her you asked after her,' she said.

'Do. Poor thing. I hope she's not too terrified.'

Phoebe didn't imagine the countess would be terrified of dying. She had always spoken of death like a lover she had been awaiting for too long – Juliet lingering long past the dawn and into the next night and the next for a voice beneath her window. It was hard to imagine her as a girl, because she was so ancient, a relic of the Regency who yearned for days past. It had been hard enough to imagine her without a kind of fear. She was a countess, after all, born the daughter of a ducal house and Phoebe was just the motherless child of a watch-mender from Blackfriars. Phoebe even felt presumptuous climbing into the carriage to be driven to call on the old lady's deathbed. She was scared. She had never seen anyone close to death before and wondered if she would stand up to the experience, but she reminded herself that she was doing this for the countess and not herself.

The big cold house was alive with lights. There seemed to be a light in every window, the curtains opened to the world as if the countess wanted the world to know she was dying, or perhaps because she wanted to defy the usual convention of dying behind drawn shades. The marble caryatids on the stairs clutched lit candles in their hands and the scent of the wax was overpowering. Servants bustled here and there, sweeping the halls, throwing wide the curtains, refreshing the rose bowls, as if the house had come awake now that its owner was preparing herself for her last and never-ending sleep.

The countess herself lay in her bed, surrounded by her dogs and so many flowers it looked as though her funeral had already begun before she had died. 'People are so kind,' she wheezed, gesturing to a bouquet of lilies. 'So very kind. Thank you for coming, my dear.'

'It's the least I can do, my lady,' said Phoebe, feeling as if she should curtsey.

The countess laughed a weak laugh with a ghastly death rattle in it. 'Call me Charlotte. I shan't have any such rank tomorrow, child. I'll be a dead woman, a corpse who was once the daughter of a duke and the bride of an earl, but a corpse much the same as any poor wretch who died of gin in the gutter in Whitechapel. I should think that tomorrow you'll outrank me, my lady.'

'You'll still be a countess,' said Phoebe. 'And I'll still be a maid.'

'Sit down, child. No more of that. I'll be a dead woman and you'll be a living woman. Now which outranks the other, tell me that?' Thankfully she didn't give Phoebe time to reply but looked approvingly at the Pomeranian that had already attempted to leap up into Phoebe's lap. 'Ah, they love you, don't they? That's what I wanted to talk to you about, you know. I find myself terribly talkative now that I know I shan't be chattering away for much longer.'

Phoebe uneasily petted the little dog and prayed that the countess was not going to entrust her with her dogs. She could imagine Louisa's reaction if she came home with those two enormous mastiff bitches and worse still she could imagine the great hounds shredding holes in Louisa's elegant rugs, knocking over vases, desecrating dresses and slobbering all over visitors, leaving a pungent whiff of dog in their wakes.

The countess paused for breath and Phoebe could hear the rasp of her failing lungs. 'Is there anything I can do for you?' Phoebe asked.

'No, no. I have everything I need right here. I wanted to tell you a story. I know it sounds strange, but you'll indulge the whim of a dying woman, won't you, my dear?'

'Of course,' Phoebe said, taking the countess's proffered hand and leaning closer to the bed. Her hand, for all its thinness and the papery skin that barely hid the workings of blue veins beneath, was cold and clammy and felt heavy, leaden. The Pomeranian in Phoebe's lap whined at the disturbance but clung onto Phoebe's skirt.

'There was only one other person I ever saw with your way with dogs, you know,' said the countess. 'And it's a curious thing, but I witnessed it with my own eyes, a very long time ago when I was a girl of your age, before I was married. I was very handsome then – I suppose I may be allowed to say that now that I'm old.

'I was born in the North and it's a hard life if you're not lucky enough to be born into wealth like I was. The cold takes it out of a body, especially the women. The wind and the rain and snow took their looks away and made them old before their time – the shepherds' wives. Hard hands, work worn. They used to make me feel so very lazy. These hands had never known anything harder than a bridle and if I stayed too late riding on the fell my brothers would come and fetch me in from the cold. Feared my complexion would spoil, perhaps. Wouldn't have made a difference, of course. I could have been hunchbacked, pockmarked and one legged and still been a catch on the marital market – one of the oldest ducal families in England, my dear. They were all after me, so perhaps I wasn't so handsome. Just rich and well bred.

'Besides, they didn't like me out late after the trouble started.'

She sat up and coughed, leaving Phoebe terrified that she was going to die there and then, but she didn't. She spluttered into a lace-edged handkerchief and asked if Phoebe would be so kind as to pass her a glass of water, sipped and resumed her tale.

'There was talk in the village, you see, child. A woman. An unmarried woman with a string of admirers and she was picky, she was. That wouldn't do, set people against her from the off. Girls married young, before the bloom went off 'em, so who did she think she was, presuming she could pick and choose? And the other girls in the village were angry. Half their sweethearts were mooning after miss up in her cottage under the fell. Didn't like it, but what woman would?

'I only spoke to her the once. I was out riding, exercising the hounds and they'd caught a whiff of something and run off. So I went after them and there she was, feeding them titbits. The dogs loved her, but I could see why the village girls didn't like her right away. She was a handsome bitch. Rather favoured you in looks, only taller, bigger across the shoulders.

'"You want to get those dogs home," she said to me. "The moon'll be coming up." 'Course, I was about your age, maybe younger, and I said who did she think she was talking to me like I was a farm girl, I was the duke's daughter. She didn't say a word. Just looked at me, and I remembered her eyes. Brown eyes are common enough, but I'd never seen the like of hers before, until I saw you, Miss Phoebe Flood.'

Phoebe swallowed. 'What had the moon got to do with it?' she asked, thinking of her dreams.

'That's what everyone wanted to know, dear,' said the countess, rather ominously. 'Every full moon they were finding sheep ripped to pieces and the shepherds were up in arms. They were demanding to see my father and find out which of our hounds had gone bad so they could shoot the brute.'

Phoebe knew somehow how this story would end. It was as if the countess could see into her dreams. It was said that people's whole lives flashed in front of them before they died but the countess seemed to be able to see inside of Phoebe and understand things she had only dimly made sense of herself. 'Why are you telling me this, my lady?' asked Phoebe.

The Countess coughed again and frowned in pain as she settled back on her pillows. 'Chalk it up to a whim, dear girl. I have a feeling you'll find out for yourself sooner or later.' She gave Phoebe a long calculating look, her blue eyes clouded with age. 'I know your sort. You're not named for the Huntress for nothing. I don't think London will suit you for long.'

Phoebe felt an irrational desire to look behind her. The hairs on the nape of her neck prickled, but the question burnt inside her. She had to ask. 'The dog,' she said, 'that was menacing the sheep. It wasn't a dog, was it? It was a wolf.'

'A wolf, yes.' The countess went into a protracted fit of coughing and Phoebe held the water glass for her to sip. The old woman waved it away and shook her head.

'You'd best leave the city,' said the countess, in a breathless voice. 'Get away. Go away somewhere where there's nobody for miles. They'll come after you, just like they did with her.'

'Where?'

'Anywhere. Time for you to go, child. Time for me to go. Thank you for coming to see me.'

She coughed again so noisily and with such a horrible rattling sound that her nurses rushed into the room and Phoebe was shunted out into the corridor before she had a chance to say goodbye properly.

Phoebe knew that that was the end, even before she glanced through a crack in the door and saw one of the women pass her hand over the dead woman's eyes to close them. What had the countess meant? That the woman was the wolf? That was impossible, absurd. Such things only happened in stories, not in London in the nineteenth century.

Raving on her deathbed, thought Phoebe. The poor old thing. She listened to the sounds of weeping coming from the room and wondered what was the correct way to leave a house whose owner had just died. She paced up and down the corridor for a moment until her eye happened on a painting she hadn't noticed before.

It was a full-length portrait of a young Charlotte, dressed in a hunting outfit. She held a brace of pheasants at her hip and looked out from the canvas with an expression that might have been imperious if it hadn't been for the roguish curl in the corners of her small red mouth. Her hair was thick, wavy and dark brown and her figure slender and graceful.

'That's you,' Phoebe said, under her breath. 'That's what you look like now, wherever you've gone.'

A maid came out of the room, her eyes wet. 'She's gone, miss,' she said. 'Couldn't do nothing more.'

Phoebe touched the girl on the shoulder. 'I know.'

'Should you like a drink, miss? Terrible thing to see – might need a nip of something?' The girl looked furtive for a moment. 'Just to brace your nerves up, like,' she added, as if she was in the habit of bracing up her nerves.

'I'm all right,' Phoebe assured her, exaggerating her accent somewhat. She felt strange to be addressed as miss by a maid and realised why Louisa had used to constantly correct her. 'I'll see myself out. You must have a lot to do.'

'Yes, miss.'

'I'm very sorry.'

'Thank you. Me too, miss. She was a great lady. A *proper* lady.'

'That she was,' said Phoebe, and took one last look at the portrait of Charlotte before making her way down the stairs.

The sky was clear and cloudless when she stepped outside. The moon was a bright crescent and the stars were as brilliant as the candles lining the countess's staircase. Phoebe could make out the Plough and a bright reddish star whose name she didn't know. She tried to connect the dots and make shapes, to identify the constellations but she couldn't be sure if she was looking up at Perseus or the Charioteer. Louisa would know. Louisa kept star charts in her desk and made complex astrological wheels which allegedly could tell you everything about a person's fate providing you knew their time, date and place of birth.

Strange how these clear nights kept following Phoebe about. Usually the air was much fouler, but once in a while the sky would be as clear as it was in her dreams. Had it something to do with the countess's mysterious story? she wondered. Something to do with the moon and people who changed into wolves like the sons of Lycaon who had escaped the flood?

That was, Phoebe told herself again, completely impossible. People were people and wolves were wolves and there were no wolves in London anyway, aside from the miserable-looking creatures in the zoo. The countess couldn't have known what she was saying. She had been dying at the time. Who knew what went through people's minds when faced with the Eternal? The ones who'd been there couldn't come back to tell. It didn't matter, she told herself. What mattered was that the countess was dead and that she should be sorry. She didn't feel as sorry as she thought she ought to be. Death seemed too much like a victory for the old woman, a reunion with a lost love she had missed for many years.

The carriage rounded the corner and Phoebe turned back to look at the house for one last time. There were still no shades drawn in the traditional manner. The countess must have given orders. 'Sleep tight,' Phoebe murmured and lifted her skirts to climb into the cab. As she stepped inside she heard a howling start up from inside the house and she started, wondering if she was mad or dreaming. The howls were so much like the ones she always heard when she was caught in the maze of the city, with or without Louisa but always with the wolves.

The howls grew louder, chilling, as more voices joined in. She realised what it was at last – the dogs. The countess's bitch pack, as she'd called them. They were howling their loss.

Even so, Phoebe shuddered and knew that sleeping tight would be the last thing she'd be doing tonight.

11

Although the bridge club had disbanded after Charlotte's death, there were still no end of diversions to be had living with Louisa. Louisa sometimes took Phoebe to the theatre, or shopping on Oxford Street.

The opera had been something Phoebe was unlikely to forget in a hurry, not because of the music, although that was glorious, but on account of a toy Louisa kept hidden in her safe.

'Jade eggs,' Louisa had said, opening a Chinese box and displaying two little green jade balls resting on red velvet. 'They were a present from an old admirer, since gathered to God, sadly. He was a nice old bugger. It's always the way. The good ones go first.'

'What are they?' asked Phoebe.

'They're a bit of a rarity. All the way from the Orient. He told me that they were what Chinese courtesans used to keep their muscles in trim – you know, *those* muscles.' She dipped her eyes to her lap and Phoebe realised what she was talking about and where the jade eggs were supposed to go. She imagined Louisa must have used them quite often because Louisa could gently contract her muscles and clip Phoebe's finger snugly within her cunt. Sometimes when she came her muscles rippled and pulsed in there and on one or two occasions they'd done so so powerfully that they had pushed Phoebe's fingers clean out and splashed warm salt-smelling juices out onto the sheets.

The old gentleman who had given Louisa the gift, she

said, had never been particularly interested in fucking. He was far too ancient for that, but he had liked Louisa to read to him from her books. The words, spoken immodestly aloud, had had an effect on Louisa and the game progressed. If she squirmed in her seat he would politely ask if she was uncomfortable – perhaps she would be happier without her stockings, or her drawers.

'I was surprised by how it made me feel,' Louisa confessed. 'You'd have thought I'd read so many porno-graphic books I'd be immune. Jaded, I think must have been the word I used. I'm sure it was. I think that was why he bought me these. "You're not nearly jaded yet, my dear," he said to me. "Try these and you literally will be."'

Louisa had been persuaded to slip the things inside her on one of their customary drives around the city. At this point in her story she had held them up out of their box and Phoebe could see that they were drilled through and held together on a leather thong with a little jade bead at the bottom. They slid back and forth on the thong and when Phoebe handled them she couldn't help but think of the cold round stones warmed inside Louisa's body.

'They move around,' Louisa explained. 'And when they do it's sort of queer, but you feel like you have to hold them inside you. Wouldn't want them sliding out and falling down your leg, would you? Anyway, he had me put them in and we went round the park a couple of times and, oh, you wouldn't believe how it felt, especially with the carriage bouncing all over the place. "I haven't had my story today," he said, and I said, I hadn't brought a book with me. So he said, "I'm sure you have a few stories of your own, Lou," and so I said yes, naturally. Given my profession, you know. He said no, he didn't want to hear any of my professional exploits. No. I was to tell him about the first time I ever saw a cock and what I thought of it. Well, you know that story, don't you, Phoebe darling?

'So I told him about peeping Charlie and the hairbrush handle and all that business and I don't know if it was those things stuffed up my quim or the tale I was unfolding; it's naughtier if it's your own story, and he knew that damn well, cunning old bugger. Oh, Phoebe, you would have laughed yourself sick if you'd seen my face when I stepped out of that carriage. I was as red as a beetroot and grinning from ear to ear. I thought I'd scream and scare the horses while we were driving. Good job it was a bloody brougham with curtains. God, can you imagine if we'd been in an open carriage?'

Louisa had looked at Phoebe and smiled rather evilly. 'Lucky for you we'll be in a secluded box at the opera.'

Phoebe had wanted to protest, but like another woman who had once peered into a box, curiosity got the better of her. For all she pleaded with Louisa not to, she felt a thrill of anticipation when Louisa slipped the little box and its contents into her reticule. It was more exciting than if Louisa had insisted she insert the things right away. The delicious anticipation carried on throughout the drive to the opera while Phoebe wondered when she might be called upon to tuck up her skirts and push the jade eggs up inside her. The longer Louisa left it the more eager Phoebe became to see what all the fuss was about and by the interval she was so wet she wanted to just ask Louisa to give her the damn things to try.

With the curtains pulled across the box, Phoebe was able to lift up her skirt, put a foot on the chair and let Louisa put the jade eggs in her. The effect was immediate. She felt the heavy balls slide downwards and clenched her muscles against them. As she did so they moved inside her, making her already tormented cunt quiver and twitch. 'I must sit down,' she said, resuming her seat and accepting a glass of champagne. Although when she sat the motion wasn't so fierce, the knowledge of what she was doing and where she was doing it was making her blush as red as the curtains and making the titillating little nub of her quim ache and pulse in time with her racing heart.

The champagne made her giddier still and she discovered that with a twitch of her muscles she could make the jade eggs move. That, she thought, must have been how they worked. The courtesans probably couldn't help but move their muscles because whenever they did it gave them so much pleasure. By the time they were ready for the emperor's bed they must have been able to clutch the imperial prick as tightly as a fist. The thought made Phoebe giggle – the imperial prick. He probably was a silly prick, keeping all those women at his beck and call. She wondered how many of the courtesans had cuckolded the emperor with one another. She knew she would have put some horns on the sod if she'd ever found herself in such a seraglio.

Louisa kept darting her sly little sidelong glances, which only thrilled her further. She wondered what Louisa's reaction must have been the first time she had tried them and pictured Louisa gasping and shivering in the carriage, blurting out words of her dirty story in-between pants and moans of pleasure. How strange it seemed to imagine that there had been such a thing as a life, or the semblance of one, before knowing what her body was capable of feeling. Phoebe thought she must have been dead before then, because she never felt so alive as she did when she was in bed with Louisa or sitting here nursing her obscene secret at a box in the opera house.

When the Queen of the Night came on stage Phoebe imagined that her impossibly high shrieks were not of vengeance but of pleasure. Mozart was lying when he wrote that aria – certainly a woman could scream at such a pitch in rage but surely he'd first imagined taking a female voice that high when he was down between some woman's legs, lapping at her cunt and making her come so hard she shrieked as loud as a peacock.

Phoebe barely managed to restrain her own shriek when it became too much and slumped, sweating, in her chair. For the rest of her life she would never be able to hear 'Der Hölle Rache' without smiling at the memories the tune engendered.

She wasn't likely to forget the opera in a hurry, but there were other things to do, other places to go. The men, Charlie and William, had recently taken up a bachelor flat near Marble Arch and Phoebe and Louisa always exchanged giggly glances at the thought of them. They came sometimes to join Louisa on rides in the park or to take tea or supper and Phoebe supposed they weren't so bad, even though Charlie's reputation preceded him. He showed no inclination to plaster his eyes to keyholes in Phoebe's presence, which was fine by her. If anything he seemed to go out of his way to avoid speaking to her. He probably thought she was no better than a servant, Phoebe concluded, and left it at that. He'd been brought up in grand style and she was just a watchmaker's daughter. She preferred William to Charlie. Charlie always looked nervous and avoided speaking to her. He didn't tally with the picture of the genial joker that Louisa had painted so Phoebe assumed he loathed her and was suspicious of her. He had reason to be suspicious, she thought, although it was nothing short of pure hypocrisy on his part. Phoebe had, after all, seen him with his heels high in the air, even though he had no way of knowing that she had.

Will was just generally easier, a calm, wry, serious young man with hazel eyes and curling dark hair. Louisa said he was like a brother to her and Phoebe thought she wouldn't have minded him as a brother herself. Anything was better than that fat stupid Philip.

'We'd stick out like a sore thumb in the music hall,' Will protested, as the four of them strolled through the cool of a late spring evening. 'We'd be better off at the opera.'

'I've seen the damn opera,' said Louisa, impatiently. 'Have you never been to the music hall? It's much better, songs to sing to and all kinds of turns – mentalists, acrobats, comedians. Used to be good enough for the toffs when they offered it up as entertainment at Cremorne Gardens. I don't see why it should be any different in the halls.'

'That's as may be,' said Will. 'But that was more of a mixed crowd.'

Louisa rolled her eyes and tucked her arms into Phoebe's. 'Sorry I dragged you into this,' she said. 'That's the trouble with money. The moment you have it you're expected to live up to it and act flash.'

'This is more than flash enough for me,' said Phoebe. It was like a different city to the one she had grown up in. During the winter she had thought the streets would never dry and the filthy waters would just keep on rising but away from the banks of the river the city had escaped the flood unscathed and in a better position to hold onto the veneer of prosperity.

The weather was beautiful, the trees in blossom and hanging over a garden wall here and there were strategically planted lilacs whose sickly strong fragrance didn't entirely mask the smell of horseshit on the street. There were carriages out everywhere, ladies in bright summer dresses, flower girls in tattered boots and aprons, lamplighters going from post to post as the sun dipped and the darkness deepened. People seemed to be determined to enjoy themselves, to drink sherbets and stroll under the trees, as if they were trying to chase away the memory of the gloomy winter of the flood.

'It's not what Charlie would call smart,' Louisa said, in an undertone, glancing at her cousin who was walking ahead with Will. 'He'd say we were slumming it.'

'He ought to try Lambeth one of these nights.'

Louisa's laugh was drowned by a woman's scream further up the street. Phoebe heard a horse whinny and a man shout, 'Whoa!' and the commotion spread as people hurried to see what was going on. A horse had bolted and overturned a carriage and a lady was being helped ungracefully out of the carriage window. The horse lay in the road, a wide circle of people around it as it flailed its legs in pain. Someone, everyone agreed, needed to shoot the poor beast, but nobody dared get near those flying hooves. The cabman himself was bleeding from his head, clutching a wadded-up coat to the wound and screaming furiously at a man in a purple velvet frock coat who waved his hands and shouted back in French that he didn't understand.

'Bloody hell,' Louisa muttered, looking at the horse. Its eyes were white around the edges and there was blood-flecked spittle around its mouth. 'Isn't there anyone with a pistol? That poor horse.'

Phoebe shuddered. The man in the purple velvet coat tried to advance on the horse but the cabman pulled him back by his sleeve and bellowed in his face.

'Why are you stopping him, you cruel bastard?' A woman's voice rose above the crowd like a seagull shriek and Phoebe realised it was Louisa, who had left her side and rushed forwards. Phoebe elbowed her way through the crowd and found her arguing with the cabman.

'It's his fault!' the cabman shouted, pointing to the man. 'It was his bleedin' fire jugglers spooked 'im in the first place!' The cabman jerked his head towards a building bearing carnival-type signs outside the door. A painted cardboard giant straddled the door and within the doorway were a couple of boys in outlandish outfits clutching recently extinguished torches. The largest sign read THE SENSATION OF PARIS – MONSIEUR GUILLAUME'S WORLD OF WONDERS!

'It doesn't *matter*!' Louisa screamed, red in the face with a fury Phoebe had never seen before. 'Just shoot him, *now* – can't you see he's suffering?'

The Frenchman, presumably Monsieur Guillaume himself, spoke too rapidly for Phoebe to understand but Louisa answered him in French. Phoebe caught enough words of Louisa's invective to understand that Louisa was demanding a pistol from him but the cabman was determined to start a fight with the Frenchman and kept getting in the way. Will and Charlie had pushed their way through the crowd to see what the fuss was about. The horse brayed – a high, horrible sound – and still the cabman kept up his tirade.

'I don't bloody care!' Louisa shouted at him, drawing a gasp from the ladies present who fluttered and murmured in horror as if they weren't drawn by the spectacle of a dying horse. 'I don't *care* who's at fault. Just get out of my way so I can shoot that poor bloody horse!' There were tears of anger and upset starting in her eyes and Will and Charlie restrained the cabman.

The Frenchman stepped up and Phoebe covered her ears and shut her eyes. She heard the gun fire even with her hands over her ears and when she looked back she saw the horse was lying dead and still in the road, a puddle of blood spreading from behind its head. Louisa was crying.

'All very well for you to cry, miss,' snapped the cabman, 'it's my livelihood, not yours.' He glared at the Frenchman. 'Shouldn't be allowed,' he said, grimly. 'Killing decent horses like that. Suppose you're going to want it for your supper now, you bloody frog.'

'There's need for that,' Will said. 'Anyone could see that horse had to be put down.'

Phoebe felt like saying the horse could have done with a steadier temperament in the first place if it was unnerved by fire, but she didn't, to spare Louisa's feelings. Louisa loved horses almost as much as Phoebe detested the nervous, overbearing creatures.

The Frenchman introduced himself as Monsieur Guillaume and consoled and fussed over Louisa. Phoebe caught a few words of his speech – 'pretty', 'kind', 'free to you' – and watched the man gesturing towards the door of his establishment. Louisa shook her head and insisted she would rather not but Monsieur Guillaume took Phoebe's arm and invited her to view the signs. Phoebe managed to stutter out that her French was not very good but Monsieur Guillaume took her often practised phrase to mean she was a lot more proficient than she pretended to be.

'*Non! Très bien!*' he insisted, steering them towards the door. '*Gratuit, mesdemoiselles, gratuit!*'

'We shan't be a minute,' Louisa said with a sigh, glancing over her shoulder at Charlie and Will. 'He's determined to show us his sideshow. Wait here.'

Monsieur Guillaume ushered them into the building, still chattering away in French. It had probably been used as a shop at some point but the windows were plastered with signs and brightly coloured posters so it was quite dark inside. In a chair by one of the darkened windows a white-skinned girl with pink eyes sat combing her long white hair. A misspelt sign proclaimed her BLANCHE, THE PRINCES OF SNOW.

Phoebe had seen such things before – freak shows had been popular forms of entertainment when she had been a little girl, although they had declined since the death of Mr Merrick, the famous Elephant Man. The Sensation of Paris seemed a rather limp little affair in contrast to the spectacles that had come before.

Behind a screen was 'The Venus of Montparnasse' – a very beautiful armless woman posing in fleshings to resemble the *Venus di Milo* and then there was a tattooed man covered from head to toe. Louisa sighed and seemed impatient to get away.

'Wait,' said Monsieur Guillaume, speaking English for the first time. His accent was so strong it was almost impossible to understand him. 'For ladies, we have special attraction. He very . . . risqué, but he special.'

'What do you mean?' Louisa asked, in French.

Monsieur Guillaume reverted back to French and spoke to her in an undertone. She nodded and listened then, as he made a great show of rummaging through a bundle of keys, she turned back to Phoebe and translated. 'He says he's got a boy who was raised by wolves,' said Louisa. 'An *enfant sauvage*.'

'What's so risqué about that?'

'Maybe he doesn't like to wear clothes,' Louisa said, raising her eyebrows, with a flash of her usual good humour.

Monsieur Guillaume unlocked the door and opened it for them. Inside an empty room was a large cage, which appeared at first glance to be empty but for a bundle of rags in one corner.

'Garou,' said Monsieur Guillaume, gesturing proudly.

The bundle uncurled and Phoebe saw that there was a boy beneath a ragged blanket. He looked to be maybe eighteen years old and at first it was hard to make out what part of his body was which because he was so flexible he seemed almost boneless. He blinked up at them with dark eyes and stretched like a dog, his arms out, hands palm down on the floor, bum upthrust in the air.

Louisa was horrified and immediately began remonstrating with Monsieur Guillaume about the cruelty of keeping him in that cage with not so much as a pot to piss in.

Phoebe didn't hear her. She couldn't stop staring. The boy was brown, his black hair matted and his limbs bare. He wore nothing but a scrap of cloth around his loins and his eyes were like nothing she had ever seen before. She moved closer to the cage and he padded forwards on all fours to inspect her, lifting up his nose, which was long and rather pointed at the tip. She realised that he was *sniffing*.

Maybe he really had been brought up by wolves. When he raised himself to look at her it was as if he sat on his haunches, reluctant to take his hands from the floor. One hand came up off the floor and he held it like a forepaw, the wrist bent and the fingers dangling, useless. She thought he had the most beautiful hands she had ever seen – long brown fingers and knotty knuckles – but his hands were nothing compared to his eyes. They were large, with long, thick, black curling lashes like a girl's and they were shadowed almost to black under the dirty matted forelock of his hair.

She didn't know what he'd do and there was only a faint voice in the back of her head that warned her that he might bite, but she couldn't help herself. She pulled the glove from her right hand and pushed her bare hand through the bars for him to sniff. He drew back for a moment, wary, looking so much like an animal that she wondered if he was able to talk at all, but then he moved closer again, tilting his head to get the measure of her.

He sniffed audibly, then he opened his mouth and she saw his teeth for the first time. They were surprisingly white and sharp looking. His tongue seemed long and red at the tip and she had to bite her lip to keep from making a sound when that tongue snaked out and licked – first at the pad of flesh at the base of her thumb and then, slowly and (she was sure of it) voluptuously, over the inside of her wrist.

She knew immediately that she would have to see him again.

12

Somewhere in the depths of his memory he understood that the sounds they made had some meaning, but when they captured him he did not even have a word for what he was or the means of articulating it. He understood his siblings by way of growls, the high loud yelps, which told a playmate to be gentler, the greedy, overlapping whimpers of cubs as they nestled and jostled for milk. He understood the nosings, the playful arch of the back, the warning bare of teeth. He understood that when the fat hens in the coop clucked and flapped in panic he should be still, silent, crouched on his belly while he waited for them to be calm once more.

Had he understood what the black stick in the farmer's hands signified he might have been less bold, but he was hungry. His mother had a new litter to nurse and if he tried to suckle she snarled and snapped at him as if he were a stranger to her. He had been taught that the hen coop yielded rich pickings and he thought that if he growled then the man would flee in fear like the others.

Although his hearing was sharp he didn't understand the significance of the bang and didn't associate it with the sudden, numbing pain in his haunches.

He had looked forward to the toothsome bloody mess of fresh fowl in his mouth and he howled in anger when he found the pain would not allow him to move.

There were lights – lights like the moon but golden like the sun, trapped in little cages that hung from their forepaws. The cage was familiar to him and he didn't know why, or why he detested the sight of it and he growled at the lights, at their shadowed faces beyond and at the incomprehensible noises they made as they gathered around him.

He tried to bite them so they tied him up and carried him into the house. There, they tried to make him drink milk, eat something whitish and dry that had none of the relish of chicken and they tried to prise back his fur to see his face. He wanted to writhe and bite at this outrage but it hurt him and he saw that his hindquarters were marked with many little round black holes, all of which were bleeding.

For years he had claimed that that was all he could remember, but he remembered that one of them spoke softly to him and the shape of her waist and wide-swelling skirts stirred some understanding in him that this was the female.

He had seen the likes of women before and he was not afraid of them the way he was afraid of the large rough-voiced males. He snapped at their hands when they tried to touch him, whimpered and scurried into a corner to crouch and shiver and shit.

He had no sense of days without the moon and sun to guide him. Later he recalled a perpetual day, lit with the caged lights that seemed like scraps of the sun trapped the same way as pieces of the moon became trapped in rivers and rippling pools. During such times the woman sat nearby, her head nodding as she fought against sleep. On one occasion he reached for the caged sun, wondering if he could cause it to sing, and she struck him on the paw. He whined and ran back to his corner, hating her in that instant. She hung the caged sun higher on a beam and shook her head at him. When he tried once more to slink towards it she made sounds.

'No. Fire. Lantern. Bad. Bad boy. No touch.' He tried to mimic her but she didn't understand him any more than he understood her.

He remembered when a man came, a man who was all black but for his face and a patch of white fur at his throat. The other men held him down, forced some burning liquid into his mouth and made him bite on a stick while the black man did something to his hurt hindquarters. It hurt excruciatingly and he spat out the stick and bit several of the men in the process. When they finally released him even the woman could not coax him from his corner. She brought him milk and yellow things that looked like the sun surrounded by white clouds and she ate part of one to show him he should do the same. He ate, suspiciously, eyeing the men with hatred, but they didn't bother him any further. They talked amongst themselves, most particularly to the black man.

When they had gone and he felt bold enough once more, he slunk over to the table on his belly and propped his hindpaws on the wooden surface to try and gauge some idea of what they had been doing to him while they held him there on the table. There was a piece of cloth, stained red with blood. It held little black things, hard black objects round as rabbit droppings. He stuck his tongue out to taste one but the woman stopped him with a flick of the wet cloth she held.

He watched the woman, trying to tease out threads of recollection in his mind. He had liked to think he had always been a wolf, for his own comfort, to buoy up his kinship with the pack, but some treacherous scraps of memory remained, memories he knew his brothers and sisters didn't share. The woman, with her narrow-middled shape, bare forearms and soft voice, stirred something in his mind, so that when he slept he dreamt of a different woman, a woman who was browner and somehow brighter than the one who fed him now. A woman with white teeth and a pink tongue, pink and white as the mouth of his mother, the she-wolf. He remembered being held above her face, looking down into her laughing mouth and squealing, giggling as he was held aloft – half laughing, half hysterical with the most childish of all fears, the fear of being devoured.

I could just eat you all up.

The black man came back, this time with a cage. He knew he would be put in the cage but the woman hid her face when he tried to plead with her in his most affecting tones. Well, they hadn't worked on his mother, he supposed. Why would they work on her? Later he learnt that the priest had seen fit to take him away because he was indecent to the young woman, his nakedness was an affront to her modesty. In those days he had not known how to wear clothes and tore at the cloth the first time the Fathers tried to wrestle a shirt over his head.

He had not known that he wasn't a wolf.

After the fact he maintained that they had been kind to him – the Jesuits who took him in, their interest in him as scientific as it was charitable – but at the time he knew that he had protested. He had fled when they tried to scrub him, dress him, teach him to say his prayers. On four feet he outran them on two and he would run away and hide in the woodshed in the priory's kitchen garden. He growled and howled when they tried to dress his wounds or untangle his hair, and finally they were forced to restrain him while one of the priests wielded a razor on the lice-ridden matted hair. They washed him, dressed him and made him look at himself in a mirror, as if it might remind him that he was not a wolf but like them, human.

He snarled and bristled as best he could with his hackles shorn. The hollow-eyed thing he faced frightened him and when it snarled back he knew it for an enemy and backed away, surprised to see that the creature also backed away at the same time he did, as if mocking him. It didn't look like a wolf.

At the beginning they locked him up at night, in a bare white little room with a sloping ceiling and a narrow bed. Once they became more sure of him, sure that he could be trusted not to tear into the chicken coop and devour the fowls, they began to teach him to fetch and carry around the kitchen, and he took to it so well that he made the kitchen his permanent berth. The scents of bread, meats and herbs were a feast for his exceptionally sensitive nose and he stayed so late in the kitchen that he took to curling up beside the hearth and sleeping there. He had no appreciation of the human comfort of a bed, having been raised in a heap of whimpering pups and he liked to drift off while looking at the lamp that hung beside the door.

When he slept he saw the woman again, the bright brown woman. He saw her washing herself, standing naked in a tin tub, her long black hair down the middle of her back. She laughed to see him staring and bent down to pick up the cloth, a motion that made her breasts swing like bells. Her house was small, but it smelt pleasantly of the garlic hung in braids beside the stove, of the bundles of rosemary and wild thyme dangling and drying near the hearth, the rich rank smell of hanging game – pheasants and rabbit and sometimes even a haunch of a deer. She would strip the rabbits of their skins, leaving them pink and small and bare and then he would watch her cut them up, put them in the pot. The skins she kept, stitched them together and made him a bed of such softness in the little closeted alcove where he slept that he would strip as naked as a rabbit before he crawled in to sleep, the better to feel the soft fur against his skin.

... mother's gone a hunting, to fetch a little rabbit skin to wrap my baby bunting in.

The dream was so vivid, but so strange to him that it may as well have belonged to someone else. Clothes and cooked meats – these had been alien things to him for so long that it was all the priests could do to keep him from stealing the raw hearts of oxen from the chopping block.

But he learnt, slowly. He learnt that the black man's blackness was not black fur but black cloth, and similarly the white at his throat was not a marking like that of his younger brother, but the sign of a priest. This was the one who tried to teach him to say 'Father' but he stumbled over the word so the priest tried for 'Papa' with a greater degree of success. Soon he could say 'Papa Roux', which was the priest's name – Father Roux – and Papa Roux patiently tried to impress upon him that he was not a wolf, but a boy – *le garçon*.

He fudged the word and could never get past the first syllable, but he determined that he was a boy in the charge of Papa Roux, Papa Roux's boy, so when he one day announced himself as 'ga-roux', one of the younger priests thought it a good joke and he became known as Garou. It was the only name he could ever remember having.

Papa Roux impressed upon him the need to do the things that boys do, such as eating with a knife and fork, the wearing of clothes and shoes (Garou hated shoes with a passion) and walking on two legs. Sometimes, however, if he was startled or simply forgot himself,

Garou would drop on all fours and scamper along at his old pace, and if caught would slump in shame as if he'd been discovered touching his forbidden genitals.

He had begun to understand that the thing in the mirror was himself and not some cadaverous apparition presented to frighten him. He thought that the priests liked to frighten people. He had never forgotten the first time he saw the crucifix in the chapel, the man nailed there, stretched and bleeding. He had run yelping from the chapel on all fours, causing the eldest and most superstitious priest, Papa Villepin, to cross himself in fear of such an unsanctified creature as Garou. At first Garou thought the thing in the mirror was there to scare him into good behaviour, like the pictures of St Sebastian shot full of arrows, St Agnes with her breasts cut off, St Peter hanging on an upside-down cross. Horrible pictures, full of inhuman cruelty.

He came to realise, as the reflection cast back at him became less hollow eyed, less rangy and filthy and more upright, that it was himself. He knew he wasn't like the priests, who walked with their legs straight. Garou walked with a stooping, knees-bent lope, his head held forwards as he sniffed the air, his arms bent as if they could only be straightened on all fours. His clothes were not the same as theirs either – moleskin breeches and a loose white shirt. They were all black and buttoned from head to toe and he wondered if they were the same as him beneath all that black.

When he was alone in the kitchen at night he would remove his clothes, an act prohibited except for the necessity of bathing. He liked the heat of the fire on his skin, liked to inspect himself as he might once have inspected himself for fleas and ticks. He sniffed and tugged at the new hair that had grown beneath his arms and between his legs, curious as to what had effected this transformation. His cock became a source of fascination to him and he lay naked on the floor for hours at a time, his legs open and his prick standing up stiff. He discovered that a twitch of the muscles in his groin made it jump slightly and bob under its own weight, the tug of gravity giving him an all too fleeting little shudder of pleasure.

He didn't dare touch it. Papa Duclosse – the young priest who thought it such a joke to name him Garou – had caught Garou clutching himself down there and flown into a rage about it. Garou lacked the words to plead that he had only been doing so because his bladder was full to the point of pain and so Papa Duclosse had tied the boy's hands behind his back and then beat him when he pissed on the floor. There had been angry words exchanged between Papa Duclosse and Papa Roux at dinner that night.

Garou hated Papa Duclosse. He had red hair and a pointed nose and moved as stealthily as a young fox, particularly whenever the laundress came to the priory. She was the only woman Garou ever saw there and he thought she was probably not young, like the woman his nakedness had affronted, or the brown woman in his dreams. Still, he thought her beautiful, with her waist so small over her wide skirt and her little hands red from the boiling water in which she scrubbed the priests' shirts. Her hair was black and parted in a straight line down the middle, wound into a knot at the back of her neck, and like the other woman her voice was soft and her smell infinitely tempting. She smiled at Papa Duclosse more often than Papa Roux, who was quite grey, or Papa Villepin, who was so old he reminded Garou of a dead leaf hanging on a branch just before the smallest breeze took it and bore it to the floor of the forest to rot. For all his nose was pointed and his hair was red, Garou supposed Papa Duclosse must be accounted handsome by the laundress.

But for all he was sneaky, Papa Duclosse could never outsneak Garou, who had learnt stealth before he was even weaned. Garou could slip off his hated shoes and move in absolute silence, and if he committed the further transgression of taking off his clothes, his skin was sensitive enough for him to register the movement of the air that might signal another's approaching presence. He was able to hide in corners and watch Papa Duclosse lift the woman's skirts and his own long black skirt. He hadn't understood what they were doing until one day they did it in a posture he recognised – she leaning over and he mounting her hindquarters.

If he didn't understand the pose, then he understood the smell, or at least, his cock did. Just the recall of that rich salt scent made his cock so hard he thought the poor thing would burst. He pitied it. It seemed hungry for something when he lay there contemplating it. The more he recalled his punishment for touching it, the more excited he grew thinking he might be risking more of the same – but of course, he had no intention of getting caught. He knew it was bad to be staring at his cock but he liked to do it in defiance of the priests. He liked to be naked because it disturbed them – even worse if he took off his clothes and tore out of doors for the pleasure of the cool air and the rain on his skin. The rain was the best, when it drummed down hard on his prick as he lay on his back.

He liked to creep out after dark, stark naked, his penis as hard as a stone and quivering with his every move-ment. It became his friend, his co-conspirator. When he shambled along on two legs the tug of its weight on his belly made him wriggle with pleasure and when he ran on all fours it bounced beneath him, slapped against his stomach until it almost hurt him and he had to lie down and roll in the dewy grass to rub against it and go some small way to ease the exquisite and unbearable sensation. One moonlit night he dug a hole in one of the empty vegetable beds and shat in it, an act strictly forbidden since he had been taught to use the privy. He was harder than ever at the feeling of his body stretching to let his waste out and he wanted to howl with joy at this flouting of the rules. He dreamt more frequently now, not the wolf-dreams of childhood that had been crammed with rabbits to be chased and young deer drinking obliviously at forest streams. He dreamt of the brown woman and a man, a man he hated for the interloper he was. The man smiled at the woman a great deal, showing big white teeth, and he brought her haunches of venison and a bird in a metal cage. The bird was as yellow as a buttercup, yellow as a piece of the sun and the man would purse his lips and whistle to it to make it sing.

The woman smiled at the singing but Garou was unconvinced by her smile. He knew her true smile, the one she directed his way. When the man had gone she sighed and said it was sad that the bird should be shut in a cage, but what could she do? The bird was a gift and the man would be angry with her if she opened up the cage and set it free.

The dreams were so distant that they might as well have belonged to someone else, but some deep part of Garou's mind, a part that he wasn't fully in touch with, knew that these were not quite dreams, but memories. Although he was still unable to pronounce her title he knew that the woman was his mother, as the Virgin in the chapel was the mother of the infant Christ in her arms. He knew the man was not his father. How could he be? Garou had never known a father and so he had so little understanding of the concept that for many years he believed that all children were fathered by God.

Papa Roux was patient with him. In time he gained an understanding of speech but for the rest of his life he would always struggle with what he was trying to say. He knew how others would say the words he was attempting to arrange but when they left his lips they never worked quite right, so he kept hold of his own secret language. He supposed that the priests could not understand the language of smells as he did, otherwise they'd prick up their ears and pay attention whenever the laundress came into the room, like Papa Duclosse. Garou attributed this sensitivity to Papa Duclosse's long nose and his resemblance to a fox. Had he liked him better then there might have been an attempt at conversation, at questions aimed at discovering whether Papa Duclosse had been the child of woodland foxes.

As it was, Garou kept his keen nose and his hairy body a secret from them, because he thought they would be disappointed and angry the way they always were if he urinated on the floor or pawed, doglike, at the bottom of a closed door, but he revelled in his secret defiance all the same. He became more and more daring. One night he gave in to his urges and invaded the hen coop and was discovered by the priests, who had been awoken by the panicked cluckings of those indiscreet birds. Seeing him naked, bloody and surrounded by the strewn feathers of his kill, Papa Villepin had said his rosary, Papa Duclosse had insisted on turning him out of doors for good and Papa Roux had redoubled his efforts to civilise Garou.

'Civilising' consisted of being shown cards with words and pictures on them, being encouraged to write his name, count pebbles and understand that God was good, God was love and that he should love God too. He found it boring at the best of times and painfully confining at the worst. He was sorry that he made Papa Roux unhappy when he tugged at his shirt collar or howled along with the hymns played on the piano but he couldn't help it. It was just so boring shut up with Papa Roux and his cards in that white-plastered room with the crucifix on the wall and so little to amuse his nose or his tongue. He wanted to go back to the kitchen where there were smells to investigate, textures to lick at, from the grained wood of the chairs to the smooth cool ceramic of the fireplace tiles. The scents of ash and bread bewitched his nose, but no smell was as seductive as that of the laundress.

He knew everyone by scent. Papa Villepin smelt like something dry, something close to death, Papa Roux of books and ink and the wine he sometimes sipped late at night to soothe nerves shattered by the superhuman effort of remaining patient with his unwilling pupil. Neither of them smelt like the laundress and Garou concluded that her entrancing scent was something female, something that rubbed off on Papa Duclosse when he visited her in the kitchen.

Garou took to watching her, curious as to what set her apart from men and made her a woman. He slunk around after her, sometimes unnoticed and other times attracting her ire, like the time he followed her to the privy and peeked through a hole in the outhouse door, interested to discover what it was between her legs that Papa Duclosse found so addictive. He didn't see anything but a flash of her round white buttocks as she lifted her skirt. She caught him sneaking away and for a horrible moment he thought she was going to scream and it would be like being caught in the hen coop all over again, but she was a self-possessed woman, the sister of many brothers and a mother of sons who knew what boys could be, even strange feral boys who sniffed and pawed and walked as if they would rather be on four legs than two.

'You're a bad boy – a bad, wicked boy,' she rebuked, but she must have seen the fear in his eyes and pitied him. She took his hand and pressed it to the softness of her breast, as if that might satisfy his curiosity, and after that she smiled a little whenever his eyes followed her around the kitchen.

He knew well enough to keep out of her way when Papa Duclosse came down to the kitchen. He hid himself beneath the table when the young priest came to pay his attentions to her. She seemed to barely tolerate him and smiled less often in his presence than she did in Garou's, which pleased him strangely. He once saw Papa Duclosse handle her breasts, loosening her stays enough to make them spill out into his hands. She had protested and frowned while he did it and Garou thought of how she had taken his own hand and pressed it there on purpose. On another occasion he saw her hand go between Papa Duclosse's legs and he saw the priest's cock – red like the rest of him and standing up straight from a lot of red-brown hair. He was interested to see it but more interested to see how she moved her hand up and down it and for the rest of the day he was in a fever of anticipation as he waited for night to fall so that he could take off his clothes and attempt the experiment on his own prick.

The first time he did it he was frightened because he imagined he had done himself some terrible injury. Whitish stuff came out of it like blood and the pleasure was so great that it was akin to pain. He didn't do it again but he seemed to have set something in motion because he woke more often than not with the stuff dried and sticky on his cock, clumping the hairs between his legs and staining his clothes. He worried that the stains would give him away because he was sure this couldn't be something the priests would look kindly on, least of all Papa Duclosse, so he took to rising earlier than usual in order to scrub his nightshirt under the pump and lie in the morning sun until the incriminating damp patch dried. He daren't sleep naked any longer in case the mess transferred itself to the sheets of his little bed.

One night was especially messy and he had slept late, evading morning prayers and knowing he would already be in disgrace for doing so. He tore off the nightshirt and rushed naked to the pump, but he heard Papa Roux's voice and ran back into the kitchen. He collided with the laundress and once again he was sure she would scream, seeing him naked and clutching his soiled nightshirt all balled up in his hands, but she retained her presence of mind and saw his frantic glance in the direction of the priest's approaching footsteps.

She took up her usual stance at the washtub and lifted her voluminous skirts. 'Quick. Hide under here,' she said, with a rather resigned look on her face, as if already tired of keeping him out of trouble.

He hurried under her huge skirt, curling himself up as small as only he could make himself between her feet. The first thing he noticed was the smell. It was that enticing female scent, distilled and concentrated. His prick, rebellious now that he had given it free reign, rose and strained towards he didn't know what, but the richest smell was emanating from between her legs.

'Morning, Father,' she said, casually, unseen above him.

'Ah, good morning, Hortense. I don't suppose you've seen Garou have you?'

'No, Father. Is there something wrong?'

'Oh no, nothing that isn't usually wrong. He didn't attend mass again this morning. I despair for that boy's soul.'

'I expect he just overslept, Father.' She said this last rather stiffly, because Garou was breathing rather hard against her bare leg, just below where her drawers ended. The flesh was white and plump and he had a strange urge to sink his teeth into it. Above him he could see the slit in her drawers – an opening Papa Duclosse so often invaded – and he thought that when she moved her leg away from his mouth he saw fur, black fur, like he had between his own legs.

'Yes. Poor child. Nobody ever told him that sloth is a sin.'

'Thank the Lord he's in good hands now.'

'Indeed, Hortense. Well, I shan't keep you.'

'Yes. Good morning, Father Roux.'

She seemed to be breathing hard like she did when Papa Duclosse mounted her and Garou thought the scent was becoming more and more intoxicating. He couldn't help himself and reached up to put his fingers in the slit in her underclothes, drawn by unbearable curiosity. She kicked him on one of his knees and drew up her skirts to let him out.

'You don't touch me there,' she snapped. 'You understand? Oh, you are such a bad boy – you just made me lie to a priest. I risk my soul for you and that's how you repay me!'

She kicked him again and he sprawled back on the tiled floor, uncharacteristically losing his balance in the face of her anger and the glorious smell that was still lingering in his nostrils. He fell onto his back and not only was his nakedness an affront to her but he was hard, achingly hard. He knew he wasn't supposed to be naked in front of women and he supposed that he shouldn't be hard either. At the sight of him she put her hand over her mouth but her eyes were enormous. When he tried to close his legs to cover himself she put her other hand on his knee and shook her head.

'No,' she said, taking her hand from her mouth. 'Look at you!'

'Bad boy,' he said, solemnly, ashamed.

She pressed her lips tightly together, her eyes glinting. 'Yes, you are. But a big boy. Who would have thought it?'

He didn't understand so he just stared mutely at her. She bit her lower lip and leant closer, reaching out and touching his prick with the tip of a finger. 'Well,' she murmured, 'here's a surprise.'

She ran her finger down the length, making him close his eyes and shiver. Nobody had ever touched him there before and it felt even better than when he touched himself. Suddenly he remembered what had happened the last time, all that white stuff coming out like blood from a wound, and he closed his legs and ran off on all fours, afraid of doing himself further injury.

For the next few days he was afraid he might be dying. It kept happening night after night and for all it was either white and sticky or clear like the white of raw egg, it was hot like blood and smelt salty like blood. He was beginning to remember the meaning of blood – like the blood that had dribbled over his haunches when he had been shot and the blood that poured, painted, from the wounds of Christ. Christ had died and Christ had bled. His mother had bled and she had died – not his wolf-mother, the other one, the brown woman in his dreams. He remembered how sometimes there were bloody rags amongst the washing but it wasn't until the Man came to stay and she grew round with promises that he might have a brother or sister. It was after that that she had died, probably of the bleeding she could never staunch. He didn't understand it. The bleeding holes in his rump had healed into little pockmarks but he couldn't stop this other pale blood from springing from his cock in his sleep.

He didn't die. He didn't understand it either, but he didn't die. The next time Hortense came to scrub the priests' collars and nightshirts Papa Duclosse sidled up to her once more and Garou secreted himself behind the kitchen door to watch. Papa Duclosse bent her over and lifted her skirts clean above her head, pulling down her drawers and sticking his cock between her legs. Eager to see more, Garou peered around the door. Papa Duclosse had his eyes closed but Hortense looked directly at him and her eyes widened in shock and fear when she saw him there. Frightened of her reaction, he hurried away and hid behind the hen coop, equally worried he might be caught lurking there and accused of trying to kill the chickens again.

He kept himself hidden and then a few moments later he heard the swish of her skirt and her voice calling softly to him over the kitchen garden. She found him and he stared up at her, scared that she might be angry. 'Come in,' she said, beckoning him back to the kitchen. She didn't seem angry. She just looked very pale. Her voice was very quiet.

Garou slunk back to the kitchen after her and watched her carefully. Her hands were all knotted, her fingers twisting and twining, and she frowned. 'You must never tell,' she said, looking as though she might cry. 'Promise me? I know you're a good boy really. You must never tell of what you have just seen. Do you promise?'

He nodded and she leant close to him. 'Do you understand me?'

He nodded again, although he didn't know why she was so agitated.

'It's a sin,' she said. 'I won't be forgiven for it if the other Fathers know. You know what it is, don't you? To not be forgiven?'

Garou blinked and waved vaguely in the direction of the hen house, finally managing to articulate the word 'chicken'. He didn't think they had forgiven him for that if not being forgiven meant that you had to be civilised all the more whenever you did it.

'Yes,' she said, frowning for a moment before understanding dawned. 'Like that. A secret. It's not allowed so you must keep it a secret. Not tell.'

He wanted to know what secrets she kept under her skirt – that secret that smelt so delicious and which Papa Duclosse was party to. He crouched closer on the floor and pawed at the hem of her skirt. She stiffened but she swallowed and nodded, lifting her skirts for him.

'All right,' she said, her voice barely more than a whisper, and she put her hand under her skirt to tug at the drawers that Papa Duclosse had pulled around her ankles. Garou stuck his head under her skirt and whimpered with pleasure as her underwear fell down and the elusive scent he had been chasing grew all the more powerful. It was between her legs, where there was hair but no cock. He nosed at the juncture of her thighs, crowded by the shadowy folds of her voluminous skirt, and she lifted up her garment to let him out.

'Wait,' she said, slipping one foot out of her drawers and sitting down on a chair with her skirt lifted for him. She beckoned him closer and opened her legs so that he could see. It was strange, he thought, that she had no cock. Instead she had a pink slit amongst all the black hair and it seemed to be wet and salt smelling like a wound. His cock ached and thrummed at the smell of her and the sight of this curious thing seemed to make it harder still.

He was still more the child of a wolf than the son of his mother, so he did what came naturally to him and sniffed at her, then pushed closer to sniff more deeply. Hortense leant back on the chair and gasped but he was too engrossed in the smell to pay much attention to her reaction. He lapped at her and she stiffened and cried out, making him back away this time.

'It's all right,' she said, breathlessly. Her cheeks were red. She beckoned him back to her. 'It's all right,' she said, again. 'You're not hurting me. Don't be afraid.'

Timidly, he approached her once more, standing with his awkward knees-bent stance. She reached for the button of his trousers and he understood, suddenly. He took off all his clothes and showed her his cock, the way he had done so unintentionally when she had called him a bad boy and touched him. She darted a nervous look at the door and took hold of his prick, stroking back and forth and guiding it to the slit between her thighs. He knew now what was going on – this was what she did with Papa Duclosse.

The heat of her flesh on the tip of his prick was exquisite. He felt the prickle of hair and she shifted her hips and opened her legs still wider. It felt as though his cock was being swallowed up and he couldn't keep his hips from moving forwards. It was like his prick had a will of its own and he could no longer resist it. He knew why Papa Duclosse did this. It was warm inside, warm and slickly wet like blood, like entrails. His cock jolted inside her and he was suddenly scared because he could feel that sensation that meant he would bleed too. She made a little sound in the back of her throat and smiled at him.

'There,' she said. 'Do you like that?'

He couldn't speak. He buried his face in her shoulder as the stuff came out of him and for a moment he was reeling with pleasure-pain, before he heard her scream. She pushed him away and he tumbled, naked and oozing white stuff, onto the hard kitchen floor. He looked up and saw why she had screamed. There was old Papa Villepin, crossing himself and staring in horror at the pair of them.

The priests stayed up late that night, talking and shouting and quarrelling. Garou listened and garnered what he could from the conversation. Papa Duclosse seemed to be of the opinion that Garou should be thrown out on the streets to starve. Papa Villepin claimed he would leave the priory if Garou wasn't gone by the end of the week. Papa Duclosse then said the same and it was left to poor Papa Roux to try to defend his charge.

Shortly before sunrise, Papa Roux came out of the room, looking tired and unhappy. He looked at Garou and shook his head. 'You've landed me in a pretty fix, my boy,' he said. 'There'll be a scandal if you stay here and I won't see you out on the street alone. Pack up your bags, Garou. We're going to Paris.'

Any other boy of Garou's years would have been ecstatic at the prospect of Paris, but he was more sheltered than any other boy of his age and so it meant more or less nothing to him. He was afraid of the horses – they showed the whites of their eyes and frothed at the corners of their mouth when they saw him – but thankfully they didn't travel far by coach. There would be a train, said Papa Roux, whatever a train was.

Garou soon found out. A train was a noisy, malodorous thing that rattled fit to make his sensitive ears burst and reeked of tobacco and some kind of oil that stank foully, unlike the sweet-smelling olive pressings he knew from the priory kitchen. The whistle made his ears hurt abominably and he circled the compartment madly, pawing at his ears and convinced that they were bleeding.

Papa Roux was disturbed to see him revert to this feral state and tried to convince him to sit up, drink milk and look at the scenery out of the windows. He cajoled Garou with stories of the delights of Paris and said that there they would find like-minded people, scientists like himself, who could make Garou into a Real Boy – and wouldn't he like that? To be a Real Boy who rode on trains and went to the circus and said his prayers? If it was what Papa Roux wanted for him, Garou supposed that it must be good. Although at first he had hated Papa Roux for hurting him, he had observed that the holes in his backside that had bled so much had healed after Papa Roux's painful ministrations and he hadn't died, so Papa Roux must have been telling the truth when he said he only wanted the best for him. Papa Roux had never beat him or tied his hands either, or shouted at him when he pissed on the floor. No, it was always Civilising with Papa Roux, which was boring but never cruel.

'Try to sleep,' Papa Roux told him, putting a blanket over him. 'We'll be there before you know it.'

Garou closed his eyes and fell silent, remembering the yellow bird in the cage. The bird had always fallen silent when his mother hung a blanket over its cage, so he supposed that blankets must make you quiet.

He dreamt about her, and the Man, the interloper. The man did to her what Papa Duclosse did to Hortense, and what Garou had done, albeit very briefly. They thought Garou didn't know but he peeked out from the alcove where he slept and saw them in his mother's big bed. The man was as hairy as she was as smooth as silk and the first time he had leapt out screaming, certain that the man was killing his mother.

The man shouted and scowled at him but she got up off the bed, her brown breasts swaying and her hair tangled, and she lovingly, laughingly, put him back to bed. He mustn't worry, she said. It was what all men and women did together and he would understand and want to do it too when he grew up. It didn't hurt a bit. The reason she cried out was because it was so nice. He mustn't be afraid but go to sleep like a good boy, go to sleep like the bird under the dark of the blanket.

Paris was like nothing he had ever seen before. There were people everywhere – people in rags, women in satin dresses, horses and carriages, buildings so huge he didn't understand how they didn't fall over. Papa Roux took him to a giant place – a cathedral, he called it – and Garou stared up at ceilings taller than the tallest trees in the forest, at glitter and gleam brighter than the sun on a rippling river, all the while struggling against the temptation to howl into the great open space above his head.

For the most part, in this city built by giants, Garou stayed in a little room in a seminary. It was like his old room at the priory, small, white and with a cross upon the wall. The priests there looked at him curiously and talked so rapidly to Papa Roux that he couldn't understand what they were saying. Sometimes they came to see him and brought a man who looked in his eyes and in his mouth and pressed an ear to his chest. Papa Roux told him he mustn't mind this because the man was a doctor and that was what doctors did. They looked at you to determine if you were well or not.

Garou felt quite well, if bored. He longed to stretch his legs and explore and he missed the kitchen, the hen coop and the vegetable garden – all his old haunts. He couldn't get out of the little white room because it was high above the ground, not like his old room at the priory where he could open the window, slide down the hen-house roof (luxuriously scratching his bum on the rough lean-to roof) and caper about in the rain and watch the mouth-watering spectacle of the fat hens brooding in their roosts.

He still wondered why he wasn't dead after what had happened with Hortense but by experimental degrees he began to tug at his prick again and learnt to be devious. If he did it while he was naked then it splashed all over his belly and it could easily be wiped away at the washstand. Then he would rinse the cloth and hang it over the edge of the ewer and nobody would pay any attention if the cloth was damp. He realised that it was something else that men did, like the thing they did to women, and it did feel nice. If the priests were angry with him for doing it, well, that was their loss. They should learn to do it themselves and maybe they'd understand that it was good.

One day Papa Roux made him dress in his best clothes and took him in a carriage to a great big circular room with wooden seats that curved all round. It was full of people and Garou seemed to be required to sit quietly in the middle of the room beside Papa Roux, who stood and talked. Then Papa Roux put Garou through his paces. Tell me your name. What shape is this? A square – good. This one? A triangle. Well done. How many fingers am I holding up? Who is our Lord and Saviour?

He answered all the questions, puzzled but indifferent, and the people all clapped when he was finished. 'They will understand you,' said Papa Roux, afterwards. 'And others like you. Then we can help you and others better. Do you understand, Garou?'

He didn't, but he said he did just to make Papa Roux happy. The priest seemed happier since they had come to Paris, not fraught and constantly navigating his way around the other priests' objections, the way he had been at the priory. Besides, when Papa Roux was happy there were rewards for Garou – trips to see giant places, treats like chocolate. The first time Garou had tasted chocolate he had laughed with joy and wanted to eat it at every meal.

After he had answered the questions for the people, Papa Roux promised to introduce him to a thing called ice cream and took him to a café. The ice cream was as cold as snow and as sweet as chocolate and Garou thought he loved it more than chocolate. That wasn't the only thing on that afternoon of delights – Papa Roux took him to the ballet. The doctor, Papa Roux explained, was famous, and he had a box at the ballet. He had been so interested in Garou that he was prepared to loan them the box for the matinee. At first Garou was confused because he didn't see what would be so wonderful about sitting in a box. A box was something you kept things in. He was surprised to learn that a box was also a place with velvet curtains and red velvet sets and gilt all over the edge, from where he could watch the stage.

The stage looked rather like the room in which he had stood answering questions all morning and he wondered what was going to happen on it. Was there someone else like him who would come on stage and answer questions?

He was surprised and delighted when the stage was filled with women – slender-legged women in dresses as white as snow who moved as gracefully as flower petals in a breeze. He was hypnotised by them and more than a little excited. They were women, so they must have that mysterious slit between their legs, just like Hortense, only they were more beautiful than her. Some of them were even more beautiful than the Madonna in the priory chapel or the rich ladies on the streets. He immediately knew that he wanted to be famous like the doctor, so that he could have a box all of his own, and watch the women dance night after night.

He was never the same after that – not content to lie in his little room and play with his prick while thinking of the ballet dancers. He peered out of the window and wondered if there was anything like the hen-house roof to climb down, but thought better of it. It still seemed too high.

The solution came to him in a dream. He dreamt of the man. His mother was dead, presumably because of the bundle of bloody rags the midwife had carried out of the house, shaking her head and muttering Aves.

'What shall I do?' the man asked the old woman, all the while looking at Garou with ill-disguised loathing in his dark eyes. 'The boy isn't mine. I can't be expected to care for him. He doesn't even like me.'

The midwife bowed her head and said something under her breath about God taking care of his own and then she left them there, the man and the boy and the bird in the cage, and the woman who lay dead and bleeding in the bed. That night the man took Garou by the hand and led him into the forest, telling him that someone would come to take care of him presently, to be a good boy and wait.

And then he left. He left Garou alone in the forest.

Garou woke up with tears on his face, as if he'd been a child capable of crying all over again, the son of a human mother. He remembered the wrong done to him now – remembered his stepfather abandoning him. He remembered hearing the wolves howl in the forest and climbing into a tall tree while the wolves circled below and looked up at him with their amber eyes and grizzled, slavering chops shining in the moonlight. He had forgotten that he could climb at all and he assumed that if he could climb up he could climb down. While he was a wolf he had forgotten that he could climb, but Papa Roux had demonstrated to Garou the agility of his unwolflike fingers – fingers that could be trained to hold a pen even if they could only make a cross on a piece of paper.

He got up and looked out of his window for some kind of substitute for a tree, something that could be climbed to give him access to the ground. Twisting his head he could see a length of pipe down the side of the building and thought that if he could only climb out onto the ledge then he could climb down that and get out.

He was delighted by his own agility. He had no real fear of heights beyond an instinctive self-preservation and he managed to shin halfway down the drainpipe before working out a route onto the lintel of the back door and thence to the ground in a jump.

Paris by night was his at last.

Garou gravitated naturally to the ballet. He remembered to walk as straight backed as he knew how to and not to draw too much attention to himself. If he croaked out *Ou est le ballet?'* in a broken, ill-accented voice then the Parisians paid him no more attention than they would any other peasant, absinthe fancier, opium eater or Argentine who came to Paris to mangle the language and act like a fish out of water. They politely but contemptuously dished out directions and Garou proceeded on his way, almost bounding in his eagerness to see the dancing girls once more. When he arrived at the ballet he found that the doors were closed and he heard the music behind them. The clerk at the desk said that he couldn't go in but he said the name of one of the girls – Cecile. Papa Roux had read her name from the programme.

The clerk eyed Garou suspiciously. 'You're a change

from her usual admirers,' he said, in disgust. 'But it shouldn't surprise me that the little slut has become jaded with rich men. Backstage.' He gestured to a door. 'And I didn't just tell you that.'

Garou thanked him and went in. He was disappointed. He could hear the music loud and clear but this backstage place had none of the velvet and glamour of the box where he had sat only a few days before. It was dark and dusty and although when he looked up he could see it was as big as a cathedral it didn't seem big at all because it was crammed with rails full of the dancers' dresses and all kinds of strange things – coaches, pieces of cardboard houses, even a whole balcony, which had been removed from the side of a house and dumped there in the dark and the dust.

Sniffing at the dust and a smell he would later know to be greasepaint, he walked forwards and found himself standing in the centre of a hive of activity. There were men carrying things – clothes and spears and hats and even trees. The dancers scurried about checking their hair in mirrors before rushing away again. He glimpsed one of them pulling off a costume soaked right through with sweat and he saw all of her for a second, through the forest of artificial trees and gas lamps. He shivered and stiffened at the sight of her small pink-tipped breasts and the little brush of hair between her thighs and he knew he'd been right. They were all like Hortense, only there were so many of them.

He lurked behind one of the trees and watched the girls. Their thin legs were like spider legs, poking out of the gossamer web of their huge gauzy skirts. They had red red lips and their eyes were like nothing he had ever seen before. There was some kind of black and blue stuff on their lids that made them stand out bright like stars.

They dressed and undressed rapidly, casually, all the while chattering to one another and sometimes quarrelling. One fair-haired girl sat down at a dressing table and powdered her breasts and armpits, giving him time to look at her breasts. They were as pale as her dress and her nipples seemed redder than those of the other girls. When she thought she had an instant's privacy in the melee she furtively looked around and then dabbed her finger into a pot of something red and deliberately stained her nipples before pulling her bodice back up and lacing up her shoes. Her nipples showed like stains through the thin cloth of her costume. He wanted to leap out from behind the tree and ravish her.

'Cecile!' someone called. 'Will you hurry?'

'Fuck you! I'm going as fast as I can!' she shouted back, but she paused to smooth her bodice down and inspect her nipples in the mirror before she straightened up, fluffed out her skirt and hurried away on tiny satin-slippered feet.

Garou huddled behind the cardboard tree, tempted to follow her but wary after his encounter with Hortense. So this was the famous Cecile who liked rich men. He wished he were rich and famous and he knew he was neither. He knew he was strange and that normal people ate with a knife and fork and didn't prefer their chicken raw. But did normal people go backstage to look at the dancers? He supposed they must do or they wouldn't have let him in.

He sat and waited there for a while, his cock aching in his trousers, wondering what he should do. Should he stay and introduce himself to the dancers, or would they laugh at his halting speech, his stooped gait and his peasant clumsiness? He didn't have to wait for long as the music came to a crashing conclusion, he heard the applause from the other side of the stage and shortly after backstage was awash with women, sweating, complaining, congratulating, crying.

The blonde, Cecile, was back at the dressing table, smirking at her reflection as she wiped black paint from around her eyes. The other girls shot her looks and whispered behind her back but she kept on smiling, her little red mouth a perfect bow.

She turned to glare at her detractors for an instant and as she turned her head back to the mirror she must have caught sight of Garou behind the tree. She stood up and laughed loudly. 'Come out!' she said, boldly sticking out her chest, even though she had breasts like a boy. 'Come on. Don't be shy.'

He stepped nervously out from behind the tree and greeted her as best he could – with a little bow, which he had been told to give in front of the people when he answered the questions for Papa Roux. Cecile laughed even harder and pushed him back behind the tree. She followed him into the shadows and giggled madly.

'Oh, what do we have here?' she asked. 'Where are you from? The Languedoc? I've seen some peasants but you . . .' She covered her mouth with a hand. Several of the other dancers had come to peek between the gap in the trees and were protesting loudly that he'd watched them undress and should be thrown out.

'Now now, ladies,' Cecile said, waving a hand at them. 'He's obviously come from some place in the arse-end of nowhere and thinks ballet girls will do *anything*.' She rolled her eyes, which, he noticed for the first time, were large and brown, then she pulled down the top of her costume and showed him her breasts. The other girls gasped and giggled. Her nipples looked smudgy from the red she had coloured them with and he couldn't do anything but stare.

'Is this what you came for?' she asked, coquettishly.

He went to cover the bulge in his trousers with his hand and she gaily swatted his hand away. 'No, no,' she chided. 'You've seen what I've got. It's only fair.' And then she had unfastened his trousers and his cock stuck out. He was mortified at the size and stiffness of it. Several of the girls shrieked behind their hands and Cecile opened her mouth wide.

'Look at it!' she cried. 'Did you ever see one that size? Oh, now this *is* a challenge.'

She pulled off her shoes and began to pull down the silk that covered her legs. 'Cecile, no!' whispered one of the other girls. 'You'll lose your job.'

'For a good reason,' she replied, shedding the frill of her skirt and standing before Garou quite naked. The hair between her legs was lighter and not as thick as the stuff that grew between Hortense's thighs and both of her slender little dancer's legs would not have made up the width of one of the laundress's. She lay down on the floor in the dust and spread her legs wide, opening her slit with her fingers. 'Come on, peasant boy. I want to see if I can take it.'

The girls had fallen silent and one or two of them were keeping lookout. Garou didn't know what he should do but his cock knew exactly what it wanted to do. This was, after all, what he had dreamt about, wasn't it?

'What are you waiting for, you imbecile?' she said. 'Fuck me.'

He didn't like her tone and backed away, so she softened her voice and beckoned to him. 'Come here, little peasant boy,' she crooned. 'Come to me. Come and fuck the most notorious cunt in Paris.'

He had never heard the words 'fuck' or 'cunt' before and he didn't know their meaning, but he assumed he knew what it was she wanted. He lay down on the floor and she encouraged him, yes, that was the way. She pulled him on top of her and guided his prick between her legs. She winced and complained when he tried to put it in. She said it was too big and indeed she did feel smaller in there than Hortense, but with her smallness was a silky tightness that was delicious and made him forget that he had an audience until she reminded him of their presence.

The girls murmured incredulously and laughed behind their hands. 'What does it feel like, Cecile?' one asked, in a piercing whisper.

She panted and gasped beneath Garou and said, 'Like I won't be able to sit down for a week!'

The girls seemed to think this a great joke and plastered their hands more tightly over their mouths. Garou couldn't have stopped what he was doing if all the priests in the world had walked into the room at that moment. She was so soft, so small in his arms, and she bounced her hips against his every time he thrust into her. It didn't take long before he felt that overwhelming pleasure that accompanied the end and he knew he would have to pull out before the pleasure became so acute it shaded towards pain.

He slid out of her and quickly pulled away, vaguely disturbed by the experience but flushed with his climax. She lay back on the floor, her legs open and her eyes still fixed on him. 'Well,' she said, breathlessly, 'he's got the size of a racehorse but none of the stamina!'

The girls laughed loudly and Cecile quickly called for a dressing gown, which she pulled over her body. 'Oh God,' she said, looking Garou up and down. 'Put it away, you idiot. Don't they teach you any manners out in the country? What are you doing in Paris anyway?'

Garou fastened his trousers, fumbling for the words. 'I

want,' he said, slowly, 'to . . .' He thought he was getting it right. The girls laughed but it seemed they laughed at anything. He knew words but it was stringing them together in what Papa Roux called 'sentences' that he found difficult.

'Famous,' he finished.

The girls collapsed at that. They fairly screamed with laughter. Cecile laughed so hard that tears smudged her eyes and black stuff streamed down her cheeks. Her mouth was one big red hole and he wondered why he had ever thought her pretty.

'Famous!' she shrieked, dabbing her eyes with the sleeve of her dressing gown. 'Oh God . . . famous! Darling, the only place you'd ever be famous is at Monsieur Guillaume's down the street!'

The girls reeled around in hysterics.

'Can you imagine?' continued Cecile. 'Roll up, roll up! Come and see him – Hung Like A Donkey And Twice As Stupid!'

Garou slouched, curled in on himself and scurried out on all fours to the sounds of feminine laughter. He had changed his mind about the ballet girls. They were horrible and Cecile was the most horrible of the lot of them. He found the stage door where he had come in and kept walking, ignoring the looks he got from passers-by. He was so angry and humiliated he wanted to howl and he would have thought nothing would have arrested his attention at that moment if that girl hadn't spilt out of a doorway in front of him, cursing and shouting.

'Give me my fucking money, Guillaume!' she screeched. 'It's none of your damned business what I do with it!'

She smelt strongly of wine, but what caught Garou's attention was her hair. It was absolutely white – not white and grey like Papa Roux's but white like Papa Villepin's, only not thin and straggly. It was thick and fell right the way down to her waist. When she stumbled backwards against Garou she turned sharply and he saw that her face was white too. Even her eyebrows were white. Her mouth was stained pink from the wine she had been drinking and he realised that her *eyes* were pink too.

'What the hell are you?' she demanded, not stopping to listen. She reeled off into the gutter and vomited.

Garou crouched on his haunches and watched her, since he had never seen anything like her in his life. He looked back at the doorway from which she'd came. A huge statue of a giant straddled the doorway and beside it was a figure of a tiny man about three feet high. On the windows were plastered pictures – a woman in man's clothing, a pair of identical men with fish tails.

'What?' he asked, pointing to the window.

The white girl gulped and gasped and raised her head. 'That,' she said, bitterly. 'Is M. Guillaume's World of Wonders.' She waved her arm in an unsteady oratorical gesture. ' "All The Wonders of The Unnatural World".' She burped. ''Cept *money*. That's a fucking given.'

Guillaume – that was what the girls at the ballet had said. Maybe it would make him famous, Garou thought. That would show them. He got up on two legs and went inside.

13

Ever since she first laid eyes on him Phoebe had a sense that things were never to be the same again. Something had changed within her, something profound and something she could not yet put her finger on. She had recognised some strange kinship with the boy in the cage and it permeated her consciousness in a way that her dreams had never quite managed. It was one thing to dream of wolves, one thing to act out her dreams in front of lords who grovelled on carpets and begged to be allowed to lick Louisa's shoes, but quite another to be assailed by daydreams that seemed alien to her nature.

She had thought she had no time for men, especially men with predatory reputations like Charles Thornton, but she couldn't stop thinking about the boy, Garou. She had never seen another human being like him. She didn't even know if he could speak, dress himself, walk upright – do any of the things that distinguished men from the animals – and she wasn't sure that she cared if he couldn't. She couldn't sleep for thinking about his tongue flickering over the inside of her wrist and imagining his tongue elsewhere, probing parts of her body she had scarcely been aware of six months ago.

She could only partially voice her concerns to Louisa, hoping Louisa would believe that her interest in him was the same as hers – that he was being cruelly treated.

'No, you're quite right, darling,' Louisa said. She had been brought up in the grand tradition that even spurious ladies should apply themselves to the business of

Charity. 'I never liked that Guillaume fellow. We'll have to spring him somehow.'

An expedition was arranged back to Monsieur Guillaume's, in the hope that he hadn't packed up and moved on. Thankfully he hadn't. When Phoebe looked out of the cab window she could see the sign was still there and she was determined to go inside. 'I'll just be a moment,' she said, opening the door.

'I'll come with you,' said Louisa. 'I'll give that sod a piece of my mind, keeping him locked up like that.'

'No.' Phoebe was surprised at her own firmness. It seemed Louisa was too. She had been making to rise from her seat and sat back with a bustle-muffled thump on the banquette, knocking her toque hat askew.

'I'll go,' said Phoebe, more quietly. 'You were rude to him. He'll not be so short with me.'

'How will you manage? Your French . . .'

'Is bloody awful, yes. I know. But I think I have enough to make myself understood.'

She stepped down out of the cab, crossed the street and handed a couple of pennies to the man at the door of Monsieur Guillaume's. The albino girl continued to brush her white hair. A couple of girls were sitting, giggling, while their friend sat for Venus, the armless woman, who was astonishingly painting her portrait with a pencil held between her teeth.

Monsieur Guillaume greeted Phoebe with a rush of French in which she could make out a few words – that she had come back and it was a pleasure. Surprising considering how much trouble Louisa had made for him before. She had been right to leave Louisa in the cab, although she knew she had other motives for seeing the boy alone.

Phoebe fumbled for the words. *Je voudrais* – I would like ... now, was it an infinitive? To see? Bugger and damnation – what was the bloody infinitive for 'see'? She was sure she'd never get the hang of it. Nevertheless she managed to make Monsieur Guillaume realise what she was saying, enough for him to give her a look that was both regretful and reproachful at once.

'He is ... *méchant*, mademoiselle. Not today,' he said, in broken English.

'I don't particularly care,' Phoebe snapped back, annoyed by the revelation that he spoke some English when he had been forcing her to limp along in bad French the whole time. 'I want to see him.'

'*Non*, mademoiselle,' said Guillaume. 'Not for ladies. He is bad.'

'I want to see him,' Phoebe repeated, and opened her purse. 'How much?'

'*Il est méchant. Vous ne comprendez pas, mademoiselle.*'

'How. Much?'

She produced a sovereign, irresistible with the dull oily sheen of real gold. Monsieur Guillaume looked furtively up and down the hallway for a moment and then took it with a sigh. 'He is bad,' he said, again, shaking his head.

'He's caged,' Phoebe said, tartly. 'How bad can he get?'

He muttered something that she presumed probably meant something like 'don't say I didn't warn you' and unlocked the door.

'Garou,' he called, softly.

Garou stirred from a bundle of rags in the corner and looked up with dark keen eyes. Phoebe immediately realised why Guillaume deemed him unfit company for ladies that day. He was naked, the curve of his hip completely bared. His skin was nut brown and smooth, his crotch obscured by a long lean thigh. He tilted his head like a dog when he looked at her and the tip of his red tongue hung out, reminding her with a shiver of where she had imagined that tongue touching her body.

'Go,' she told Guillaume. 'Get out.'

'Mademoiselle . . .'

'*Get out.*'

She was only dimly surprised by her own quiet ferocity. At that moment she thought she would be prepared to maim anything or anyone who came between her and Garou. That bared hip drew her hand so compellingly that she wished she had demanded the keys to the cage so that she could step inside and damn the consequences. If he was fierce then he couldn't be as fierce as she felt in her desire to touch him.

Guillaume backed out of the door like a subservient butler and Phoebe approached the bars of the cage.

'Garou,' she whispered, just to see his response to his name. He tilted his head to the other side and his tongue swiped over his full upper lip, making it shine. Damn these clothes, she thought. She was laced in so tightly she may as well have been wearing a suit of armour and she badly wanted to see what he would do if she showed him her breasts, lifted her skirt and opened her legs to him.

He uncurled his body and she realised that his nudity wasn't the only reason he was being kept out of sight. He was huge, hard. Louisa had assured Phoebe that the sculpture that had arrived (being modelled from real proportions – Will's, as Phoebe had later learnt, with some hilarity) had been a fairly good representation of the average size of the male organ.

Garou's was half as large again. It curved up from a tangle of jet-black hair and when he stretched she thought that maybe she saw a hint of pride and defiance in his eyes.

'You have every right to be proud of *that*,' said Phoebe,

under her breath. The size of it! No wonder Guillaume thought it would scare off lady customers, but Phoebe wasn't any lady customer. She was no longer some bored, cloistered, miserable thing who had to sneak peeks at such things from her brother's pornographic books. She knew now the extent of her own lascivious imagination and wasn't afraid.

She clutched the bars of his cage. Her knees trembled with the desire to be lying down with her legs apart. She could feel the heat welling between her thighs. He lifted his chin and she saw his nostrils flare subtly and wondered if he could smell her, if he could sniff out her ardour as if she were a bitch in heat.

He crept closer, still on all fours. His movements were uncannily canine and she wondered if he could speak at all. She didn't think she cared if he could or not. Slowly, his back bent as if from disuse, he got up onto his feet, his gait unsteady as he padded towards her on bare dirty feet. She wasn't afraid of him. She had no reason to be. There were bars between them, certainly, but she recognised something of herself in him. She recognised something of anyone. Anyone could become like him if they'd been abandoned at a young enough age. He was the queerest conundrum – a raw, unfinished human who was therefore more human than a civilised man but didn't seem to know how to be human.

He lurched a little as he walked, his huge swollen prick bobbing obscenely as he moved. He walked like an infant finding its feet, only not quite, because although a baby was unsteady, a baby didn't convey the impression that at any moment it could drop swiftly to its hands and feet and scamper off with astonishing speed.

It seemed like an age until he was standing facing her through the bars. She hadn't realised she had moved closer herself until she felt her thighs press against the cage through her skirt. She had plastered herself against the bars and was not aware of it and now she was face to face with him, staring into his dark-gold eyes. She could smell his sweat and feel the heat coming off his naked body. It seemed to flame upwards and warm her face. That or she was blushing, but she didn't feel ashamed. It seemed like the most natural thing in the world to be so close to him.

She wanted to ask him if he could speak at all, but it didn't feel as though this was the time to talk. She wanted to stretch this moment out as long as she could, just to be near him. He moved a hand, slowly, as though he was afraid of startling her, and reached through the bars of the cage. She was afraid for the first time, because for all he was so thin he was muscular; his hands looked as though they'd be efficient at breaking the necks of birds and so she struggled not to flinch when his hand moved towards her neck. Maybe there had been something in Guillaume's warning – this was what Garou did. He lured young women to the bars of his cage by exhibiting his beautiful body and then reached through the bars and snapped their necks.

But instead of strong fingers clamping around her throat she felt his fingers gently touch a curl of her hair that had fallen out of place. She froze to the spot as he touched her hair with the very ends of his fingers, tentative and shy. Perhaps he was more afraid of her than she was of him. His fingertips moved to her cheek, over the arch of one eyebrow, and she closed her eyes to let him feel the ends of her lashes and the lids of her eyes. He touched the slope of her nose and down to her mouth, like a blind man she had once met who 'saw' the faces of people by exploring the shape of their faces with his fingers.

She exhaled as he touched her lips. She opened her mouth and let the tip of her tongue brush the tip of his finger, opening her eyes to see his reaction. His eyes grew large and he swayed even closer to her so that she was conscious that his protruding cock must be pressed against the folds of her skirt. A new smell joined that of sweat – a salt scent rather like that of arousal but with an unfamiliar musk that she supposed must be male. She reached up and grasped his hand, her thumb fondling the veins in the wrist where he had lapped at the corresponding spot on her at their first meeting.

Garou squirmed slightly and she realised that he was rubbing himself against her. Did she dare? Guillaume could walk in at any moment and catch her with nothing but the bars of the cage keeping this naked man out of her arms. May as well be hung for a sheep as a lamb, she thought, and with her free hand she fumbled through the folds of bunched up skirt in search of his prick. She could feel the warmth of it even before she touched it. Her fingers wrapped slowly around it and Garou uttered a low sound deep in the back of his throat, as though even a human-sounding moan was beyond him.

It was warm and solid in her hand, the skin like fine velvet. It was the first she had ever touched in her life. She stroked experimentally up and down the shaft and breathed harder and faster when she imagined how it would feel sliding up inside her. She knew she had to do it but there was no time now, no way of getting him out of her cage or her out of her clothes. He was panting, his eyes shut, and he winced when her fingers found the head and were dampened by something oozing from the tip. She could smell it the moment it seeped onto her fingers – it was the same smell as before, only concentrated and with a richness that made her stomach tighten and her cunt twitch and water.

There was no time. Louisa would be wondering where she was. Worse, Louisa might come and find her. Phoebe released him and stepped back. 'I'll come back,' she said. 'I promise. I'll find a way.'

He looked uncomprehendingly at her. He pressed himself against the bars of his cage, his own hand on his cock now, looking pleadingly at her as if he thought she should finish what she'd started.

'I'm sorry,' she said. 'There's no time now. I'll come back.'

He frowned and shook his head. She didn't think he understood her.

'*Je reviens*,' she said, wondering if that would make a difference. Doubtless he'd been spoken to in French more than English in his life. Maybe he understood something of that language.

He tilted his head but gave no other sign of comprehension. She assumed he must have understood because he made no protest when she walked away. She didn't dare glance over her shoulder. She thought if she did she would find herself plastered up against the bars of his cage all over again, while Louisa grew impatient in the cab.

Monsieur Guillaume looked knowingly at her as she left the room. He had been waiting in the hall, probably listening at the door. She was glad that little or no conversation had passed between herself and Garou. She didn't want this man intruding.

'He is five pounds,' said Guillaume, in heavily accented English. 'For the night.'

'What?'

'Five pounds, mademoiselle. I say no more.'

Six months ago Phoebe wouldn't have known what he meant. Her education had certainly come on in leaps and bounds. She raised an eyebrow, but regardless of the ethics of such a transaction, she was tempted.

'I don't have five pounds,' she said.

Guillaume peered beadily at her, sizing up her clothes, her earrings. His gaze settled on her watch.

'You're not having that,' she said.

'Then you are not having him.'

She ground her teeth, unable to reconcile her desire with her natural instincts to hang onto the watch, her good-luck charm. 'I can't.'

'I take it as ... how you say? Insurance? And you bring me five pounds.'

Phoebe unfastened the watch and placed it in his palm. 'Very well. I'll get your five pounds.'

She walked out, back into the cab. When she stepped into the enclosed space she could smell him, the scent of him lingering on her fingers. She hoped to God that Louisa wouldn't smell it too.

'I was about to give you up for lost,' said Louisa.

'Sorry.'

'Did you see him?'

'No. He wouldn't let me. I was arguing for ages, but he kept saying no.' She was amazed by the ease with which the lie tripped off her tongue.

'Damn. Well, never mind. We'll think of another way.' Louisa yawned and called to the cab driver to take them home. She slid her fingers under the back of her hat and scratched her head. 'I've got a bloody hairpin sticking in my head. It's driving me to distraction.'

For the first time Phoebe bit back a sharp retort. Louisa's concern about Garou seemed superficial, but then Louisa didn't have her own vested interest. Phoebe immediately felt guilty and worse for criticising Louisa.

There was no denying it, though. Louisa could be

superficial. Phoebe didn't know if it was her own infatuation talking but for the first time she was finding Louisa's previously charming triviality somewhat annoying. A couple of gentlemen were coming that evening and Phoebe knew that Louisa wanted to rush back and pick out the right dress for company. She had dressed to the nines just to take a cab to Monsieur Guillaume's. The charm of beauty was wearing thin now that Phoebe knew what effort went into creating the illusion – the skin creams, the corsets, the paints and perfumes. Seeing Garou made it worse. He was untamed, uncombed and unwashed, and still beautiful. His very presence made Louisa's extensive wardrobe, pots of unguent, pumice stones, tweezers and bottles of scent look quite ridiculous.

'Should I wear the red dress, do you think?' Louisa asked, on the ride home.

'It depends what they're coming *for*,' said Phoebe, darkly.

'Oh darling, don't be jealous. It's just a profession. They're coming for a reading. I thought it might be fun to give them something to look at.'

'A reading?' Phoebe thought of Louisa's tarot cards, bundled up and tied together with a hair ribbon. 'Their fortunes?'

'No. They like me to read books to them. Dirty books. *Chacun à son goût*, and all that.'

'Oh. Well, I was going to do some repairs to the red one,' Phoebe said. 'There's a rose come loose on the neckline.'

One of Louisa's sloppily sewn roses had somehow slipped Phoebe's attention, and she had stitched it onto the neckline, where it was now unravelling.

'I doubt it's going to bother *men*,' Louisa said with a laugh.

'It bothers me.'

'Sorry, darling. I quite forgot. I know you'd hate anyone to see your magnum opus in disrepair. I shall wear
something more modest. The contradiction should be
exciting enough in itself, don't you think?'

Phoebe didn't particularly care. Her mind was elsewhere. Having the red gown in her possession made her
insane decision more than just a moment of madness.
She had given away her watch and now she realised she
must get it back, and the only way to do so was to
deliver the five pounds, which she didn't have. She
wished she hadn't frittered money away on hair prepa-
rations and haberdashery, but she thought she might
sacrifice the watch if it meant she could have what she
desired, if she could have Garou.

And the red dress provided the way. She knew that. If
she wore it and slipped on a long overcoat over the top
then she would appear quite decently dressed but she
would be able to grant him access to her body. The
thought wasn't fully formed in her mind and she didn't
know that she dared, or that she should. It seemed a
terrible betrayal.

When she came to look back on that evening she
always felt as though circumstances conspired to send
her to Garou, as if everything beyond her control was
goading her in his direction. The 'gentlemen' in question
were a pair of noisy young toffs with voices like cut
glass and the sophistication of barrow boys. Louisa didn't
let Phoebe retire to her room to sew and kept her at
hand to pour champagne, which Phoebe resented.

Perhaps it had been for Louisa's protection that she
kept her there, because the men were rambunctious and
lewd, but Phoebe knew that Louisa would only have to
scream or ring a bell she kept specifically for that purpose and Mrs Dalton would come running. Mrs Dalton,

Louisa assured her, was an expert in dealing with men who'd had too much to drink and became overly familiar.

Phoebe was driven to the conclusion that Louisa had done this to taunt her and the more she resented Louisa, the more she knew she was going to do what still felt like madness. Besides, when the men did become overly familiar, Louisa did nothing to stop them. She was quite drunk and Phoebe was forced to feign interest in a book as one of the men lifted Louisa's skirts and fucked her on the chaise longue, while the other one looked on with interest, anticipating his turn.

'What about Little Miss Prim over there?' he asked, looking at Phoebe. 'What do you think, duckie? You and me should make it a foursome?'

Phoebe pointedly said nothing.

Louisa glanced up, her hair askew and her face flushed. 'Leave her alone,' she slurred. 'I'll do both of you. Don't be greedy.'

'Oh, it seems a waste.'

'Wait your bloody turn,' panted Louisa, lying back and stifling a yawn as the first man noisily climaxed inside her.

Phoebe got up and left. She had had enough. She stole into the dressing room and fumed, staring at the red gown and knowing now that she dared.

She and Mrs Dalton had to help Louisa to bed once the men had gone. Louisa was as drunk as a lord, a further confirmation in Phoebe's imagination that she wouldn't be handed such an opportunity if some higher or infernal power hadn't meant for her to use it. Louisa slept like the dead when she was drunk. She also snored, making it easy for Phoebe to keep an ear out for her while she pilfered the red gown.

It still seemed insane, even while Phoebe stood alone

in the dressing room staring at the gown and listening to Louisa's snores. Madness segued to a thrill she'd never experienced before when she slipped out of her clothes and into the dress. It was loose on her – it had been designed to be filled by Louisa's curves, after all – but the sense of wickedness at having her breasts almost bared and her legs showing through the front was undeniably delicious.

She took a long fitted overcoat from the cupboard and buttoned it tightly over the dress, concealing the worst indecencies of her own devising, slipped off her shoes and tiptoed downstairs. The key to the back door was on the Welsh dresser in the kitchen. She pocketed it, put her shoes back on and stepped out into the moonlit night.

14

It was only a short walk, really. The moon was full and seemed impossibly bright and, although it was no time for a woman to be out alone, Phoebe didn't so much fear being set upon as she feared some kindly stranger asking her if she was lost and needed directions home. She felt as though her intentions must have been written on her face.

The place was closed but Guillaume was still up, standing at the door with her watch in his hand and a knowing look in his eye.

'You'll have to keep it for now,' she said. 'I haven't got five pounds. I told you.'

He leered and opened the door. '*Amusez vous bien, mademoiselle.*'

'Go away,' she snapped. 'Leave. *Allez.* I won't have you watching.'

Just in case, she found an old liquorice wrapper in the pocket of her overcoat and crushed it into a ball, meaning to stuff it in the keyhole when she was on the right side of the door. The room was almost dark, lit by a single gas jet near the door.

Garou was still in the cage. She turned around to ask Guillaume what he meant by this but Guillaume shut the door on them both, and then she heard the sound of the key in the lock.

'Wait! What are you doing?'

There was a gabbled stream of French from behind the other side of the door and the sound of footsteps moving away rapidly. She was sure Monsieur Guillaume sounded afraid, although she couldn't be sure, and she didn't know what there was to be afraid of. It rattled her. She was alone in the room with Garou and she still wasn't sure of him. She had no fear of rape – it had been her intention to fuck him, after all – but what if he did strangle girls with his bare hands as she had feared?

'Well,' she said, crumpling the paper in her pocket tight between her fingers. 'Sod him.'

She pushed it into the lock, just to be on the safe side, and turned back to Garou.

He was curled up in the corner again, peering suspiciously at her as if he didn't recognise her in different clothes.

'It's me,' she said. '*C'est moi?*'

He looked sullen and crawled forwards a little way. He seemed subdued and she was disappointed. She didn't know what reception to expect but this hadn't been it. She moved closer to the side of the cage and put her hands to the bars, almost crying out in surprise when the door swung forwards at the least pressure. It had been open all along.

Phoebe opened the cage. 'Come out,' she said, beckoning to him. 'Come on. It's open. *Viens ici.*'

He shook his shaggy head and made a sound, a rusty disused sound that could have been speech. She was shocked, but she pressed him to repeat himself so that she might understand.

He was speaking. He was actually speaking. He pointed to himself, to the cage and croaked out something unintelligible. Straining her ears, she picked out the sounds he was making but couldn't organise them into a semblance of words. Shay ma? What was he saying?

'Shay ma,' he said again, waving his hands to encompass the cage in a gesture that was strangely eloquent and beautiful.

Phoebe frowned. '*Chez moi*?' she said, amazed when he nodded enthusiastically.

'You're afraid,' she said, wonderingly. He thought of that cage as home and was not being compelled to stay there. Why was he afraid to leave it and venture out? He was an oddity, there was no denying that, but he could learn to speak. He could be dressed, washed, taught to straighten his spine and unbend his knees and then he would look like an ordinary, albeit exceptionally handsome young man.

Visions of his rehabilitation danced through her mind for a moment before she looked back at him, naked and perfectly wild, and wondered if it would be a shame to do that to him. She had once seen an elephant dance at a circus and felt uneasy about joining in with the audience's laughter. The ringmaster's patter had introduced the elephant as the wise old man of the savannahs of Africa, a beast both noble and fearsome. And there he was, dancing, being laughed at, his old eyes inscrutable and nobody questioning if this intelligent animal enjoyed such treatment. It had struck her as cruel, and worse, unthinkingly so.

Cautiously, she entered the cage. He seemed to relax somewhat, even if his eyes were still as round as saucers. It seemed strange that he should be so timid all of a sudden. He'd been so bold that afternoon. She had held his prick in her hand and stroked it and let him push his finger into her mouth.

'I won't hurt you,' she said, unbuttoning her coat. It covered her from throat to hem and it took some fumbling to get all of the buttons unfastened. She struggled to bend and was gratified and relieved when he slunk across the floor, sat at her feet and began unfastening some of the lower buttons with fingers that seemed surprisingly dexterous. She hoped he hadn't done this before with some other woman. She was jealous at the mere notion of it.

She shrugged off the coat and placed it carefully on the floor. Something about his feral demeanour made her want to move slowly in his presence, so as not to startle him. As she moved she was extremely conscious of the air on her skin, on her bared shoulders. When she bent down she was sure the ruffled neck of the gown exposed her breasts completely. It was far too large for her.

Did she really and truly dare to do this thing? Offer herself up to this bestial man who didn't speak a word of English and barely spoke two of French? She stood in front of him, dressed from head to toe in scarlet, unsure of what she should do next. Touching him again seemed like a distant dream, even though she had held his prick in her hand that very afternoon, scenting him on her fingers for hours after she had reluctantly relinquished her grip.

The moon shone bright through the small barred window and she felt her knees weaken once more, as if remaining upright was becoming impractical and uncomfortable. She wondered if maybe she should get on all fours and come down to his level, make him more at ease. Her spine and hips seemed to ache sympathetically at the thought of it, almost like one of her monthly cramps which she could alleviate somewhat by getting onto her hands and knees and arching her back.

Garou peered up at her with inquisitive eyes. He reached up and touched her skirt, the first real contact there had been between them other than his unexpected help with her buttons. This was different. This was touching for the sake of touching and it made her breath slow and ragged. His fingers were long, brown and he barely grazed the velvet with his fingertips, as if he thought she were an apparition that might vanish if he tried to grasp at her.

Timidly he reached between the folds of her skirt, his fingers brushing the back of her knee. She had never realised how sensitive the skin was there and the shock of it made her stumble backwards so that she was leaning against the bars of the cage. Garou was startled once more and she had to nod and beckon to him to assure him that he hadn't hurt her. He slunk forwards again, as skittish as a wild wolf.

'It's all right,' she said, quietly. She shuffled her feet apart so that the dress divided and showed more of her legs, and he lifted his face to sniff at her thighs. Her head was reeling with fear and anticipation now – not fear of him, but fear of discovery. There was no longer any way she could pretend an innocent motive for her presence there if someone caught them. The dress in itself was brazen enough but with a naked man snuffing and smelling at her thighs – the scene spoke for itself, a thought that thrilled her to the core and made her mouth dry.

She closed her eyes, feeling his cheek brush against her thigh. His face was rough, unshaven, and when she felt his lips they were cracked, yet warm. His hands slid around the backs of her thighs and he drew her to him, gathering her legs in his arms as if he could somehow tug her out of her dress that way. She clutched the bars of the cage for support and bit her lip to hold back an involuntary cry as he pressed his face to her naked upper thighs. Some part of her still couldn't believe she was doing this, as if it were some fevered dream.

When she felt his tongue against her skin she tightened her grip on the bars and shuddered. He dragged his tongue over her like an animal rather than a human, licking not to taste but to caress and reassure. She knew it was only a matter of time before he ventured higher and braced herself as if for a blow.

The anticipated sensation was better than she could have imagined. His tongue seemed thicker, longer and rougher than Louisa's, less insinuating in its explorations, lapping at her because it was all he knew how to do. There was innocence in him even when performing the basest of acts.

She wanted so badly to touch his hair, to hold his head in place and encourage him to continue what he was doing, but the pleasure was so great that she was sure that if she loosed the bars with even one hand she would slide to the floor like a rag doll. He made the lowest of murmuring sounds, almost like the whimpering of pups and she could hear the faint liquid noise of his tongue on her wet flesh as he licked inexpertly, exquisitely.

He peered up at her and if he was gratified at the realisation that he was pleasing her he showed no sign of it. He scrambled unsteadily to his flat awkward feet and reached for her breasts. He was as hard and huge as he had been the last time and she would have felt more fear if her quim wasn't aching with a strange emptiness she had never understood until she met him. He caught her eyes for a moment, his big dark eyes giving no sign of what he was thinking but so filled with animal beauty that she couldn't see how anyone could resist their gaze. What struck her most were the little haloes of gold around the pupil and that their colour was always a shade lighter than she remembered.

He set upon her breasts as if they were animate creatures quite divorced from the rest of her, turning his full attention to them and staring at them as he pinched one nipple and then the other. He looked slightly surprised when she gasped.

She regained her footing enough to reach behind herself and try to unhook some of the fastenings of the dress. Fortunately it was easier than she expected; the dress was too large for her and she had not needed a corset underneath it. The hooks and eyes came loose and with it the bodice crumpled under her breasts, pulled down further by Garou's inquisitive hands. She managed to unhook another couple of fastenings and the gown slipped so that she was bared to the waist and it hung onto her hips only by the pressure of the bustle against the bars.

Knowing that there was no going back, she pushed him away and stood up straight. The dress fell off her and left her naked but for her sensible high-button walking boots. Garou stared and she stared back at him, as if he were also aware of what they were about to do.

Slowly, she sat down on the cold stone floor and then lay flat, unsure as to whether she should spread her legs or not. She began to feel afraid as he crawled over her on all fours and gazed down at her. He was so large. She didn't know if she could take it. She was sure she was mad enough to be locked up by now.

He leant over and nuzzled at her thighs with his face once more and she shivered. It hadn't been what she expected but if he liked to lick at her then she wouldn't argue. She could feel her legs parting as if of their own volition as his tongue slithered down between them. Her hips rose to meet his mouth and she couldn't help but cry out, a low keening sound that he was now too absorbed in what he was doing to mistake for pain.

She stretched out on the floor of the cage, as blissfully as if it had been a deep feather bed. His raspy tongue moved over the apex of her cunt and she gasped and curled her fingers around one of the bars. Her body felt stretched, straining towards consummation already. When she opened her eyes the moonlight bathed her face and she breathed deeply as if fancying she could inhale the silver into her soul. Somewhere she heard a clocktower chime. The witching hour, she thought.

She motioned to him, pulling him down on top of her and grasping his long smooth prick once again. It was time. He murmured faintly as he pushed against her, trying to gain entry and she moved her hips to help him. There was a dull pain as she felt herself stretch to accommodate him but after that she could feel nothing but pleasure as he began to thrust into her. She was surprised that it should be so easy after all of that. He moaned into her shoulder, the first really human sound she had ever heard him make and she shushed him, pressing her fingertips into his back. It felt so strange to be joined to him like this and yet completely wonderful. The back and forth slide of his prick inside her was delicious, so delicious she didn't care that her buttocks were getting scraped on the floor. She moved her hips with him, amazed to find how her body responded to him, sure that she could come.

She was too immersed in what they were doing to wonder more than vaguely if his back had always been that hairy. She could feel herself moving towards the peak of sensation and her body felt tense, limbs stretching and bending effortlessly in ways she had never imagined before. The moon's light seemed blinding now.

The first thing that hit her when her climax came was the smell. It was suddenly as if the world had turned into a sea of smells, as if every individual thing in the room, the metal of the cage bars, the velvet of the discarded dress, his hair, her cunt, everything had its own completely distinguishable smell and she wondered why she had never noticed it before. She arched under him and cried out, knowing somewhere in the back of her mind that she had never made a sound like that in her life before, that no *human* could have let out that howl.

He tumbled off her and she saw his eyes – the same eyes but without the colour, just black, and peering out of a face she knew from her dreams but knew wasn't his as she knew it. When she looked down at her hands they were neither where they were supposed to be nor *what* they were supposed to be. She didn't feel as surprised as she thought she should, didn't feel much except the desire to run, stretch her legs and run off out under the moon. She knew she could hear human voices shouting but the words made no sense in any language. She only knew that when the door opened a fragment that she must follow Garou's lead and escape.

She could make out the shape of a man and dimly recognised him, even though the colour of his bright coat had faded to grey. He made sounds that she might once have recognised as prayers, entreaties, but it merged into an irritating, noisy jabber that hurt her sensitive ears. When she snapped at the annoyance she smelt a sharp ammonaical smell as the man's bladder failed. Garou bristled, excited by the scent of his fear. He advanced, hackles raised and Phoebe followed, drawn by an entirely new impulse. It was like anger, lust and starvation all rolled into one. She could smell the man's flesh – not too well washed but warm, succulent nonetheless, with blood moving beneath the skin, dark toothsome muscle, creamy yellow fat as rich as butter.

There was a leap, a snarl and a scream between her and her quarry. No sooner had her mouth flooded with the rich coppery taste of blood than a light shone in her eyes. She heard a dismayed babble of voices, screams from the wounded man, but it was effortless for her and Garou to wheel around as one and run away. It wasn't like running in her dreams, stumbling on two feet, encumbered by clothes. The efficiency of her new limbs delighted her. This grey new London whirled past her ears as she ran like the wind.

There were ducks by a lake, roosting in their waterside nests. They made short work of the ones that didn't fly away in time. She watched the moon on the water while cracking bones with her teeth. They skulked and scared away a whore and her customer with their crunching and low growls over their coveted meal and Garou howled after them, as if he meant to laugh but his throat would produce nothing but this eerie serenade.

This new liberty was nothing short of dazzling. For the first time she didn't have to be afraid of the city at night. Everyone was afraid of her. Garou hung back but Phoebe took great delight in barrelling through the crowds in Covent Garden, watching the opera-goers in their finery scream and scatter. Some dim part of her mind remembered coming here and hearing the music and she gave her own version of the Queen of the Night's aria under the mock Greek columns – howling above the shrieks of terror.

15

When she opened her eyes it was daylight and she knew immediately that she wasn't in her bed, or even in Louisa's bed. She could smell hay and dung and straw scratched her painfully sensitive skin. Light filtered down through the rafters over her head and when she peered up to look at the motes of dust dancing in the sunlight the light seared her eyes and made her head hurt. She was horribly thirsty. She felt as though she had been drinking heavily the night before but she couldn't remember having touched a drop and every muscle in her body felt taut, stretched, protesting at some exertion.

She moved and collided with someone, another body, another naked body. Garou was sleeping beside her in the straw, curled up like a puppy. Suddenly it came flooding back to her and she realised what she'd done – she was naked and she had no idea where Louisa's dress was! She had probably left it at Guillaume's place where she had taken it off, but how had she come to be here? Had she run naked through the streets and been arrested and this was some cell in Newgate?

It was only when she heard a human voice that she was slightly reassured. Although the words were indistinct she recognised the sounds and tone. It was Peter, the groom, and she knew where she was. She was in the mews in one of the horse stalls, but there was no sign of the horses. Oh God, what had happened to the horses? Louisa would be heartbroken.

'Wake up,' she murmured, shaking Garou by a bare, brown shoulder.

He grumbled in his sleep then peered up from under his unkempt tangle of dark hair and smiled, oblivious to the mess that they were in. He pressed his cheek into her breasts and nuzzled at her, looking hurt and confused when she roughly pushed him away.

She could hear Peter's voice more clearly now and heard footsteps on the flagstones outside.

'I'm not bloody going in there, miss,' Peter was saying. 'You can fire me if you like – don't have to give me a character or nothin' but I ain't going in there again.'

'Well, give it to me then.' Louisa's voice. Oh God.

Phoebe knew there was nothing she could do. She knew she was going to be discovered like this and part of her wanted to be found. It was better than lying. She peered through a gap in the boards and saw Louisa enter the stable. She wore a dressing gown and her hair was lank around a face that was the colour of whitewash. She held a pistol and even from a distance it was obvious that her hand was trembling.

'Come out!' Louisa said, sounding braver than she looked. 'Come out at once or I shall have no alternative but to send for the police.'

That was a threat, coming from Louisa, and probably a hollow one. The police were the last people Louisa wanted sniffing around her home.

Garou scurried for cover behind the manger and Phoebe saw Louisa stiffen at the sound of his scufflings. 'I'll shoot!' Louisa said. 'Don't think I won't.'

'Louisa!' Phoebe called, her voice sounding rusty to her own ears. Her throat was sore.

'Phoebe?'

Louisa peered over the door of the stall. Her face was as pale as the moon, her lips white. There were dark shadows under her eyes and the light from above showed lines around them that Phoebe had never seen before. 'What the hell . . .?' Louisa murmured, her confusion swiftly giving way to rage. 'Who did this to you? Where is the bastard?'

'Put down the gun,' Phoebe croaked.

Louisa lowered the weapon, cautiously. 'What the fucking hell is going on here?' she asked, slowly. She reached again for the pistol as Garou stuck his head out from behind the manger and Phoebe leapt unthinkingly to her feet and stood naked before the barrel.

'Don't!'

'But he . . .'

'He didn't,' said Phoebe, softly.

She saw Louisa's nostrils flare slightly and a tremor run through her body. There was a horrible silence for a moment.

'I'm sorry,' Phoebe said.

Louisa shook her head. 'You bitch,' she whispered.

Phoebe began to cry, but Louisa ignored her. Instead Louisa called briskly for Peter to fetch blankets, to tell Mrs Dalton to draw a bath, two baths. Even in the depths of her misery it was clear that Louisa wasn't going to turn a friendless creature like Garou out of doors, even if he had been complicit in her betrayal. Phoebe began to sob all the harder at the realisation of how much she had hurt this good-hearted woman.

She found herself bundled upstairs, wrapped in a blanket. She wept uncontrollably as Mrs Dalton helped her into the bath, scrubbed her, washed her hair and muttered soothing platitudes – least said, soonest mended, it'll all come out in the wash. She could hear Louisa in the next room, shouting at Peter.

'Why didn't you go in there, you bloody coward? A man and a girl – how could you be afraid of *that*?'

'I'm tellin' you, miss,' Peter was shouting back, 'they weren't 'uman. Like bloody dogs or something. *Big* bloody dogs. They scared the bleedin' 'orses off, din't they?'

'How can people be big bloody dogs at night and human in the morning, you idiot? It's absurd. It's *impossible*! You'd have just stood back and whimpered if Miss Flood was being raped in there, would you?'

'Oh no, miss. She weren't . . . were she?'

'It'd be no fucking thanks to you if she were.'

'I'm no coward, miss, I swear. I'm not a bleedin' coward. But you din't see what I saw. Horrible, it was. Biggest dogs I ever seen in my life – I swear on me ma's grave, miss.'

'Oh go away. Go and see if anyone's found my horses yet.'

'Yes, miss.'

'Impossible,' Phoebe heard Louisa say in an angry undertone. 'Fucking ridiculous.'

'There now,' Mrs Dalton said, holding out a bath towel. 'That feels better, doesn't it, dearie? Nothing like washing it all off to clear your head.'

Phoebe wondered how many times the housekeeper had said such things to girls who were smarting or bruised from a night's abuse. Louisa had told her something of Mrs Dalton's history and Phoebe had never been able to look at her the same way since. She must have seen some things in her time – funny things and horrible things.

Wearily Phoebe consented to be dried and dressed, not relishing the thought of venturing out to face Louisa but knowing that she must. She felt terrible and she still didn't know if Louisa knew that the dress was missing. It was a subject she dreaded broaching.

For once she was grateful for the laces and bone

holding her in place, for the stiff starched petticoats that hid the tremble in her knees. Her cumbersome clothes felt as though they were the only things of substance, the only thing holding her up as she stepped, light on her legs, into the drawing room.

Louisa looked puffy eyed and sullen. She was sitting beside the hearth smoking a cigarette and by the looks of the scattered butts in the grate she had smoked a few more besides.

'Better?' she said, with brittle courtesy.

'Yes. Thank you.' Phoebe stood uncertainly in the middle of the room, wanting to sit but not daring to presume.

'Don't stand on bloody ceremony,' Louisa snapped, after an uncomfortable pause. 'You're not in the dock, woman.'

'I wish I was,' Phoebe said, sitting down heavily on the end of the chaise. 'I deserve it.'

Louisa turned her face away and sniffed, hard. 'Oh, please.'

'I'm sorry.'

Louisa swallowed and shook her head. 'Look, I know I asked too much of you to expect you not to be jealous of my men but –'

'No,' Phoebe interrupted. 'I know. It's different. I knew what you were from the beginning. You've been honest with me, always honest. And I haven't been honest with you, and I'm so sorry. You have no idea how sorry I am.'

There was another long uncomfortable silence and Louisa eventually asked, 'Why? Why did you do it? Why him?'

'I . . . I felt sorry for him.'

Louisa turned to look at her and raised a sardonic eyebrow. 'You felt sorry for him? *I* felt sorry for him too. I suppose my compassion didn't extend that far.'

'It's more than that,' said Phoebe, her head aching abominably with unshed tears. 'It's me. I didn't tell you. I never told you. I'm mad. I must be.'

'Mad?' Louisa snorted. 'Oh, well, I'll give you credit for originality. I've never heard that one before.'

'I am!' protested Phoebe, her voice becoming shriller. 'Think about it, Louisa! I can't be sane. No sane woman's going to go running around the city at night with no clothes on, is she?'

'No,' Louisa agreed. 'Not even I'd do that. Why did you do it?'

'That's the point! I barely remember! I remember being at Monsieur Guillaume's and getting into the cage and then ... I remember some things but they were like dreams.'

'Spare me the details,' Louisa said, disdainfully, holding up a hand.

'More like nightmares, dreams ... oh God.' Phoebe clutched her head. 'I don't know. I've been having these dreams ever since I can remember and it was like that – running and things.'

'It's the "and things" I'm not interested in knowing too much about, thank you,' Louisa said, going to the window and pushing it open to let out the cigarette smoke.

The noise of the street drifted up into the room, the straw-muffled clop of hooves, the hiss of carriage wheels. A newspaper boy was shouting indistinctly. A normal morning, only Phoebe felt as though nothing would ever be normal again.

Louisa pushed the window wider and leant her forehead against the pane. The paperboy's voice became more distinct as he passed under the balcony. 'Extra, extra! Read all about it! Wolves Loose In The City!'

Phoebe felt her stomach take a lurch and a strange

sensation overtake her, as though her dreams were tumbling out of her head and into her waking life. She pinched herself just to make sure.

Just as she did so Louisa turned away from the window and stared at her, stared with all her might and main as if she had never seen Phoebe before in her life.

'No,' Louisa said, more to herself than anyone else. 'That's . . .'

'I know,' said Phoebe, quietly, although she knew it was far from impossible. It had to be real since everything else was real.

'Do you remember?' asked Louisa.

'Not much,' Phoebe admitted. 'What . . . happened to the horses?'

'Bolted. I expect you gave them a fright. Wouldn't be the first time, would it?'

'I'm sorry. I hope they're all right.'

Louisa shook her head and sighed. She looked exhausted and half mad. 'And to think I laughed about it – well, anyone would, wouldn't they? When Charlie mentioned it I thought it was just him being Charlie – him being a papist with all the accompanying bloody superstitions.'

'Why?' Phoebe said, defensively. 'What did he say about me?'

'He said there were some women who were like wolves, who *were* wolves. Were wolves. Werewolves. Something like that.' Louisa couldn't help but giggle at her own pun. 'But of course I said that was insane. He said he'd run into one in Italy. The artist's missus, no less.'

Phoebe stared at her. 'Hoyland?'

'Yes.'

'Louisa, don't you remember? The newspaper from Paris? They said he was attacked by wild animals.'

'It's absurd,' Louisa said, still determined not to believe it. 'If his wife wanted to kill him then naturally she'd make it look as though he were attacked by wild animals, which is probably what she did, because nobody's seen hide nor hair of her since he was killed.'

'You don't understand,' said Phoebe, quietly. 'It makes sense. To me, anyway.'

'I'm glad it does to someone.' Louisa's tone was frosty, reminding Phoebe of her mistake.

At that moment Mrs Dalton ushered Garou into the room. He was washed and combed and walking upright, albeit with a slightly hunched, bent-kneed gait. He was dressed in pyjamas and a dressing gown and someone had tried to take a comb to his matted hair. It stuck up around his face, thick and unshiny. In the silk dressing gown he looked like a prince from the *Thousand And One Nights*, with his dark complexion and dark eyes; a prince who had been under some terrible enchantment.

'Hello,' Louisa said, stiffly. 'I hope you're feeling better.'

He swallowed and stared uncomprehendingly at them both.

'Try French,' Phoebe whispered. 'I don't think he speaks any English.'

Louisa folded her arms. 'I wasn't saying it to make conversation, darling. Trust me,' she said, bitterly. 'What are we going to do with him?'

'I don't know.'

'Tea?' Louisa said, sounding so lost that Phoebe had to hurry out onto the balcony to hide her amusement. She knew it was not the time to be laughing.

She leant on the rails and caught her breath and then she saw a man step out from behind a bush across the street. He wore a red neckerchief and lifted his hat to her.

'You!' she said, aloud, as recognition dawned.

He waved. 'Iassou, Miss Flood!' he called. 'I gather you had an interesting night.'

'What do you know about that?' she shouted, forgetting her manners in her sudden anger. Had he been spying on her all this time?

'My apologies, Miss Flood.'

'What's going on?' asked Louisa, hurrying out onto the balcony. 'Phoebe? Do you know this man?'

'I met him once,' said Phoebe. 'Once. Maybe six or seven months ago.'

'I have something for the young lady, *Kyria*,' Mr Spiriakis said, waving a hand in which he was clutching something. 'If you will permit me . . .'

Louisa pulled a face. 'I don't think it's my business to refuse permission for anything,' she said, archly. 'Phoebe does as she pleases.' She glanced over her shoulder. 'Show the gentleman in, Mrs Dalton.'

Phoebe went back inside, no longer inclined to laugh. Garou stared at her with big uncomprehending eyes and she wondered if he had any conception of the fix they were in. Something strange and possibly sinister had happened last night with their coupling and she wondered if he had any clearer idea than she had. Even if he had, he couldn't tell her, and that knowledge frustrated her further.

He looked so confused and so perfectly innocent that she wished she could touch him, embrace him, drag him off to bed and back to something he understood, but she knew that would be in bad taste given Louisa's feelings.

'I must say,' Louisa said, stepping back through the French windows, 'you *can't* believe this, Phoebe. It's too bloody absurd for words.'

'I know.'

'It would be easier just to admit you were a false little tart than concoct some nonsense about werewolves.'

Phoebe swallowed hard. 'Please. I'm sorry. I didn't ... I didn't mean you to think I was some kind of innocent swept up in things beyond my control. I knew what I was doing last night. Or at least I did when I went there.'

Louisa's nostrils flared slightly. She folded her arms over her bosom and looked as judgemental as if she hadn't been stinking drunk and cavorting with those two men the night before.

'I was angry,' Phoebe admitted. 'And jealous.'

'It's my *job*, you stupid bitch,' said Louisa, coldly.

'It doesn't make it any easier,' Phoebe found herself replying, with more venom than she intended.

Garou looked extremely uncomfortable but he was spared any further confrontation when Mrs Dalton ushered in Mr Spiriakis. He bobbed an odd little bow to Louisa and apologised for the intrusion, then turned to Phoebe.

'Your watch, Miss Flood,' he said, handing it to her. It was wrapped in a scrap of blood-stained cloth and Phoebe must have gone paler than she knew because even Louisa grabbed her arm, fearful that she might faint.

'Blood?' Phoebe whispered, her voice a thin croak in her own ears.

'You were lucky,' said Mr Spiriakis. 'He will suffer no lasting damage, but I worried it would come to this.'

'Who?'

'The Frenchman. He will be all right, but we knew when we saw the moon and heard you cry that your time had come.'

'What the hell are you talking about?' asked Louisa. 'The Frenchman? You mean Monsieur Guillaume? And what time?'

'*Kyria*,' said Mr Spiriakis, with a somewhat impatient wave of his hand. Phoebe had never noticed before how hairy the backs of his hands were. '*Kyria*, you cannot understand. Our people have been on this earth since the flood. We are everywhere, and nowhere. With some it never comes to this, but with others – like –' he smiled wryly at his own pun '– this Flood ... well, it happens that she is drawn to her own kind.'

'Werewolves?' asked Louisa, incredulously.

Mr Spiriakis wrinkled his nose. 'Please. We don't like that term.'

'Call it what you like, dearie,' snapped Louisa. 'Where are my bloody horses?'

'They are safe, I'm sure. Horses are intelligent animals. Sensitive. They know when to remove themselves.'

'If we're not werewolves,' said Phoebe. 'Then what are we?'

'We have better names,' said Mr Spiriakis. 'But that is not important now. You must get out of London, out of this country, if you can. Go somewhere big, with less people. I hear America is good.'

'America?' echoed Phoebe, incredulously. 'Why would I want to go to America?'

'What you want is not what you can have,' he said, shrugging. 'You cannot be in London, not now that you have found him. If you had met any other man it would be no problem. You would have lived harmlessly, like your mother.'

Phoebe frowned. 'What do you know about my mother?'

Mr Spiriakis sighed. 'Your mother was one of us. It's where you get it from. The same as his mother. They are what we call Potentials. It never comes out unless they find a male like him and then ...' He threw back his head and let out a chillingly lupine howl.

Phoebe sat down heavily. 'I still don't understand. This is ... silly. Things like that don't happen.'

He raised an eyebrow and shook his head slowly. 'But they do, Miss Flood. You know they do. You have experienced it for yourself. You did last night, didn't you?'

'*Elle a vu le loup*,' Louisa murmured.

'Quite so, *Kyria*,' said Mr Spiriakis. 'She can never go back. She is dangerous now.'

16

There was a whiff of autumn in the air but the sun shone brightly. From her kitchen Phoebe could see the mountains, see the colours turning on the trees. She had been warned about the winter in these parts but she had been busy sewing patchwork quilts, some from scraps of cloth and other, more macabre quilts pieced together from the pelts of rabbits. At first Garou had just torn them inexpertly to shreds but he had become handy with the knife and now he could make a few cuts here and there and pull off the skin as easily as if it had been a fur jacket. He didn't need a snare to catch rabbits. He knew how to wait, motionless, and then reached out and snapped their necks with his bare hands – a gruesome process that impressed her nonetheless and kept the cooking pot full.

People had warned her, of course. 'There are bears out West, miss. Grizzlies. No place for a lady.' She'd yet to encounter a bear but she thought she could handle a bear if it tangled with her on one of her nights out in the mountains. It was just as well she was no lady. She didn't think any 'fallen woman' had ever suffered such ostracism or such consquences for the loss of her virtue. Pregnancy was one thing, shape-shifting quite another, especially when the shape in question wasn't especially friendly.

But it wasn't bad. It was a good life. If she worried that one day she would find Garou's lack of conversation and social graces annoying or boring then she didn't show it, or hadn't reached that conclusion just yet. She believed herself to be deeply in love with him and it wasn't difficult to imagine whenever she watched him walking naked to the spring for a bath. His body was as lean and brown as ever, only more muscled from the exertions of life in the unfinished wilderness of Colorado.

She had grown muscular herself. Garou was dexterous only in the bedroom or when dealing death to supper. When it came to practical things like hammering in nails, stretching ropes to make a bedframe or cutting wood he was frighteningly clumsy and she was reluctant to even let him do the log pile for fear he'd lop off a toe. She did a lot of it herself and had become brown, hard and spare. Her hands were rough and ruined and she would sometimes look at them and laugh at what London ladies would make of her half-moons now. She didn't care. She loved her new body and the liberty to stray naked out of doors on hot days, to sprawl in the long grass with Garou and do whatever they pleased to one another.

Today she hiked down the mountain to the nearest post office. She wore hard, solid boots, tied her hair under a scarf and gloried in the short simple skirts that the pioneer women preferred out of practicality. Everything was simple here, except for the business of surviving. That was hard, but people made the best of it.

The postmaster made no secret of his confusion as to why she was here. 'I dunno why you'd go and leave London, Miz Flood,' he said. 'Seems to me it must be dull up here in the Rockies when you're used to the big city.'

'The city's not used to me,' she said, wryly, and took the mail from him.

She had expected the letter but it still came as a shock. She took it out into the sunlight to read it and perched on the edge of the horse trough.

My dearest Phoebe,

I hope that this letter finds you in good health and I hope that enquiry dispenses with all the polite salutations nonsense and I can talk frankly to you as I hope you would do so with me.

I'm afraid I've rather missed you. I didn't want to miss you at all. I wished for a time that I'd never clapped eyes on you, but there – that's just spite talking. Spite and jealousy. I admit, I'm horribly jealous. I'd do anything to be out there with you instead of him, but I daresay you'll write back and tell me that I'd be so bored that one day I'd roam off into the forest with a shotgun and never come back.

I hope that you're not bored, but I doubt it. You're in your element, after all. I know (and I *do* know, darling; I'm much more observant than you might suspect) that you lapped up all the glitter and champagne and cab rides in London much the same as any young woman would, but I know it meant very little to you, didn't it? I suspected then and know now that you were different. There was always a look in your eyes that I could never quite pin down and for a time I thought that it might have been desire, desire for me.

You can't imagine how hard I laughed when Charlie first voiced his suspicions about you. I would never have entertained the possibility in a million years. I thought he'd just cracked, at last. You know his mother is quite mad, don't you? Did I ever tell you that? Nobody suspects a thing – she's terribly good at pulling herself together when the occasion requires, but when she has one of her 'heads' she retreats to her room and I often heard the servants muttering about how she screamed and talked to herself. Naturally I thought that Charlie had gone the same way when he came back from Naples.

He hasn't come out of the ordeal unscathed. He's not so much as touched a woman since he returned and turns to Will for comfort. Will is in love with him, the poor fool, but I don't think Charlie returns his feelings in the way that he'd like. Charlie is dreadfully afraid of scandal, the coward. It's not as if he's heir to any great fortune anyway, but he fears being taken for an effeminate, even though he lets Will bugger him almost nightly.

Will and I have resolved the situation anyway, for the sake of appearances. We work together so often we thought that we might as well and so the first Saturday in June (May is dreadfully unlucky for weddings, particularly sham ones) we tied the knot and I am now a respectable married woman and there's nothing peculiar to be inferred about my husband's commendable and indeed, *manly* intimacy with his bride's favourite cousin.

I daresay you're shocked at me putting my head on the block like that, but don't be. It makes excellent business sense. A charming young married couple are so much less threatening to buyers than an upstart tart or a suspiciously effete young pen-pusher. Besides, it's not like any of those lords or baronets I used to service would ever make an honest woman of me. They all had their own honest women tucked up at the family seat, popping out heirs and spares. At least that's one thing Will is never going to trouble me with. In fact it will just add an extra dash of affecting pathos to our relationship, don't you think? Such a delightful couple, so sad that they remain childless. Ha! If only they knew!

Please don't be angry with me. It's simply a business arrangement, and I find myself getting tired so often these days. My monthlies have been an absolute fright and I get furious so easily. I'm troubled by strange dreams, but I think it's just because of you. I dream about you very often. Sometimes you're a woman, sometimes you're a she-wolf coming to devour me and I'm strangely unafraid of the prospect. Perhaps it's because I never minded you devouring me in your own way when you were here.

But there, I'm being silly and sentimental, and I promised myself that I wouldn't. I was never a sentimental tart before I met you and however dear to me you are I refuse to allow you to turn me soft. It's just not in my nature.

I miss you quite dreadfully. I hope that you're safe and well. I'd pray if I was so inclined, but you know I'm not, so I'll settle for hoping.

Yours
Always,
Louisa.

Visit the Black Lace website at
www.black-lace-books.com

FIND OUT THE LATEST INFORMATION AND TAKE
ADVANTAGE OF OUR FANTASTIC FREE BOOK OFFER!
ALSO VISIT THE SITE FOR . . .

- All Black Lace titles currently available
  and how to order online
- Great new offers
- Writers' guidelines
- Author interviews
- An erotica newsletter
- Features
- Cool links

**BLACK LACE – THE LEADING IMPRINT
OF WOMEN'S SEXY FICTION**

**TAKING YOUR EROTIC READING
PLEASURE TO NEW HORIZONS**

LOOK OUT FOR THE ALL-NEW BLACK LACE BOOKS – AVAILABLE NOW!

All books priced £7.99 in the UK. Please note publication dates apply to the UK only. For other territories, please contact your retailer.

MÉNAGE
Emma Holly
ISBN 978 0 352 34118 1

Bookstore owner Kate comes home from work one day to find her two flatmates in bed . . . together. Joe – a sensitive composer – is mortified. Sean – an irrepressible bad boy – asks her to join in. Kate's been fantasising about her hunky new houseshares since they moved in, but she was convinced they were both gay. Realising that pleasure is a multi-faceted thing, she sets her cares aside and embarks on a ménage à trois with the wild duo. Kate wants nothing more than to keep both her admirers happy, but inevitably things become complicated, especially at work. Kate has told her colleagues that Joe and Sean are gay but the gossip begins when she's caught snogging one of them in her lunch hour! To add to this, one of Kate's more conservative suitors is showing interest again, but she's hooked on the different kind of loving that she enjoys with her boys – even though she knows it cannot last. Or can it?

COOKING UP A STORM
Emma Holly
ISBN 978 0 352 34114 3

The Coates Inn restaurant in Cape Cod is about to go out of business
when its striking owner, Abby, jumps at a stranger's offer of help – both
in her kitchen and her bedroom. Storm, a handsome chef, claims to have
a secret weapon: an aphrodisiac menu that her patrons won't be able to
resist. It certainly works on Abby – who gives in to the passions she has
denied herself for years.

   But can this playboy chef really be Abby's hero if her body means
more to him than her heart, and his initial plan was to steal the
restaurant from under her nose? Storm soon turns the restaurant
around, but Abby's insatiable desires have taken over her life. She's never
known a guy into crazy sex like him before, and she wants to spend
every spare moment getting as much intense erotic pleasure as she can.
Meanwhile, her best friend Marissa becomes suspicious of the new
wonder-boy in the kitchen. Before things get really out of control,
someone has to assume responsibility. But can Abby tear herself away
from the object of her lustful attention long enough to see what's really
going on?

Coming in April 2007

WING OF MADNESS
Mae Nixon
ISBN 978 0 352 34099 3

As a university academic, Claire has always sought safety in facts and information. But then she meets Jim and he becomes her guide on a sensual journey with no limits except their own imagination – and Claire's has always been overactive. She learns to submit to a man totally, to be his to use for pleasure or sensual punishment. Together they begin to explore the dark, forbidden places inside her and she quickly learns how little she really knows about her own erotic nature. The only thing she knows with absolute certainty is that she never wants it to stop . . .

THE TOP OF HER GAME
Emma Holly
ISBN 978 0 352 34116 7

It's not only Julia's professional acumen that has men quaking in their shoes – she also has a taste for keeping men in line after office hours. With an impressive collection of whips and high heels to her name, she sure has some kinky ways of showing affection. But Julia's been searching all her life for a man who won't be tamed too quickly – and when she meets rugged dude rancher Zach on a business get-together in Montana, she thinks she might have found him.

He may be a simple countryman, but he's not about to take any nonsense from uppity city women like Julia. Zach's full of surprises: where she thinks he's tough, he turns out to be gentle; she's confident she's got this particular cowboy broken in, he turns the tables on her. Has she locked horns with an animal too wild even for her? When it comes to sex, Zach doesn't go for half measures. Underneath the big sky of Montana, has the steely Ms Mueller finally met her match?

Coming in May 2007

BRIGHT FIRE
Maya Hess
ISBN 978 0 352 34104 4

Jenna Bright's light aircraft crash lands en-route to Scotland, hurtling her out of her hectic modern life as a courier pilot and back in time over two thousand years. Leaving behind her fiancé Mick, who's more interested in bedding Jenna's friends than planning his wedding, Jenna faces iron-age Britain and is revered as a goddess by the Celtic villagers she encounters.

Having no choice but to adapt while trying to find a way home, Jenna encounters mystery, magic and a sexual hunger equalled only by the powerful urge to survive. Caught in an erotic tangle between Brogan and Cathan, two of the village's most powerful men, Jenna finally glimpses a way home but, having never felt so sexually free and adored by so many, she's not sure she's quite ready to go back to her old life.

VELVET GLOVE
Emma Holly
ISBN 978 0 352 34115 0

Audrey Popkin realises she has bitten off more than she can chew when she gets embroiled with icy-cool banker, Sterling Foster. His ideas about how to have fun are more bizarre than any English Literature graduate should have to put up with! One morning she packs her bags and walks out of his luxury Florida apartment, heading back to Washington DC in search of a more regular deal with a more regular guy. But, for a girl like Audrey, this is not as easy as it sounds.

When Patrick Dugan, the charismatic owner of an old-world bar with a talent for mixing the smoothest cocktails, fixes Audrey in his sights, some strange alliances are about to be formed. Within a week Audrey talks her way into a job at Patrick's bar and a room in the apartment he shares with a drag queen jazz singer called Basil – who has a great line in platinum wigs. Audrey soon realises that Patrick is not all he seems. Why is he pretending to be gay? And what is he covering up for his father, a pillar of the local community? Audrey is so besotted with the enigmatic barman that she doesn't realise they are connected by a mutual adversary – a steely, cold-hearted son of a bitch who will take them all down if he doesn't get his little plaything back.

Black Lace Booklist

Information is correct at time of printing. To avoid disappointment, check availability before ordering. Go to www.black-lace-books.com. All books are priced £7.99 unless another price is given.

BLACK LACE BOOKS WITH A CONTEMPORARY SETTING

☐ ALWAYS THE BRIDEGROOM Tesni Morgan	ISBN 978 0 352 33855 6	£6.99
☐ THE ANGELS' SHARE Maya Hess	ISBN 978 0 352 34043 6	
☐ ARIA APPASSIONATA Julie Hastings	ISBN 978 0 352 33056 7	£6.99
☐ ASKING FOR TROUBLE Kristina Lloyd	ISBN 978 0 352 33362 9	
☐ BEDDING THE BURGLAR Gabrielle Marcola	ISBN 978 0 352 33911 9	
☐ BLACK LIPSTICK KISSES Monica Belle	ISBN 978 0 352 33885 3	£6.99
☐ BONDED Fleur Reynolds	ISBN 978 0 352 33192 2	£6.99
☐ THE BOSS Monica Belle	ISBN 978 0 352 34088 7	
☐ BOUND IN BLUE Monica Belle	ISBN 978 0 352 34012 2	
☐ CAMPAIGN HEAT Gabrielle Marcola	ISBN 978 0 352 33941 6	
☐ CAT SCRATCH FEVER Sophie Mouette	ISBN 978 0 352 34021 4	
☐ CIRCUS EXCITE Nikki Magennis	ISBN 978 0 352 34033 7	
☐ CLUB CRÈME Primula Bond	ISBN 978 0 352 33907 2	£6.99
☐ COMING ROUND THE MOUNTAIN Tabitha Flyte	ISBN 978 0 352 33873 0	£6.99
☐ CONFESSIONAL Judith Roycroft	ISBN 978 0 352 33421 3	
☐ CONTINUUM Portia Da Costa	ISBN 978 0 352 33120 5	
☐ COOKING UP A STORM Emma Holly	ISBN 978 0 352 34114 3	
☐ DANGEROUS CONSEQUENCES Pamela Rochford	ISBN 978 0 352 33185 4	
☐ DARK DESIGNS Madelynne Ellis	ISBN 978 0 352 34075 7	
☐ THE DEVIL INSIDE Portia Da Costa	ISBN 978 0 352 32993 6	
☐ EDEN'S FLESH Robyn Russell	ISBN 978 0 352 33923 2	£6.99
☐ ENTERTAINING MR STONE Portia Da Costa	ISBN 978 0 352 34029 0	
☐ EQUAL OPPORTUNITIES Mathilde Madden	ISBN 978 0 352 34070 2	
☐ GOING DEEP Kimberly Dean	ISBN 978 0 352 33876 1	£6.99
☐ GOING TOO FAR Laura Hamilton	ISBN 978 0 352 33657 6	£6.99
☐ GONE WILD Maria Eppie	ISBN 978 0 352 33670 5	

❏ BARBARIAN PRIZE Deanna Ashford	ISBN 978 0 352 34017 7	
❏ DANCE OF OBSESSION Olivia Christie	ISBN 978 0 352 33101 4	
❏ DARKER THAN LOVE Kristina Lloyd	ISBN 978 0 352 33279 0	
❏ ELENA'S DESTINY Lisette Allen	ISBN 978 0 352 33218 9	
❏ FRENCH MANNERS Olivia Christie	ISBN 978 0 352 33214 1	
❏ LORD WRAXALL'S FANCY Anna Lieff Saxby	ISBN 978 0 352 33080 2	
❏ NICOLE'S REVENGE Lisette Allen	ISBN 978 0 352 32984 4	
❏ THE SENSES BEJEWELLED Cleo Cordell	ISBN 978 0 352 32904 2	£6.99
❏ THE SOCIETY OF SIN Sian Lacey Taylder	ISBN 978 0 352 34080 1	
❏ UNDRESSING THE DEVIL Angel Strand	ISBN 978 0 352 33938 6	
❏ WHITE ROSE ENSNARED Juliet Hastings	ISBN 978 0 352 33052 9	£6.99

BLACK LACE BOOKS WITH A PARANORMAL THEME

❏ BURNING BRIGHT Janine Ashbless	ISBN 978 0 352 34085 6	
❏ CRUEL ENCHANTMENT Janine Ashbless	ISBN 978 0 352 33483 1	
❏ FLOOD Anna Clare	ISBN 978 0 352 34094 8	
❏ GOTHIC BLUE Portia Da Costa	ISBN 978 0 352 33075 8	
❏ THE PRIDE Edie Bingham	ISBN 978 0 352 33997 3	

BLACK LACE ANTHOLOGIES

❏ MORE WICKED WORDS Various	ISBN 978 0 352 33487 9	£6.99
❏ WICKED WORDS 3 Various	ISBN 978 0 352 33522 7	£6.99
❏ WICKED WORDS 4 Various	ISBN 978 0 352 33603 3	£6.99
❏ WICKED WORDS 5 Various	ISBN 978 0 352 33642 2	£6.99
❏ WICKED WORDS 6 Various	ISBN 978 0 352 33690 3	£6.99
❏ WICKED WORDS 7 Various	ISBN 978 0 352 33743 6	£6.99
❏ WICKED WORDS 8 Various	ISBN 978 0 352 33787 0	£6.99
❏ WICKED WORDS 9 Various	ISBN 978 0 352 33860 0	
❏ WICKED WORDS 10 Various	ISBN 978 0 352 33893 8	
❏ THE BEST OF BLACK LACE 2 Various	ISBN 978 0 352 33718 4	
❏ WICKED WORDS: SEX IN THE OFFICE Various	ISBN 978 0 352 33944 7	
❏ WICKED WORDS: SEX AT THE SPORTS CLUB Various	ISBN 978 0 352 33991 1	
❏ WICKED WORDS: SEX ON HOLIDAY Various	ISBN 978 0 352 33961 4	
❏ WICKED WORDS: SEX IN UNIFORM Various	ISBN 978 0 352 34002 3	
❏ WICKED WORDS: SEX IN THE KITCHEN Various	ISBN 978 0 352 34018 4	

To find out the latest information about Black Lace titles, check out the website: www.black-lace-books.com or send for a booklist with complete synopses by writing to:

Black Lace Booklist, Virgin Books Ltd
Thames Wharf Studios
Rainville Road
London W6 9HA

Please include an SAE of decent size. Please note only British stamps are valid.

Our privacy policy
We will not disclose information you supply us to any other parties. We will not disclose any information which identifies you personally to any person without your express consent.

From time to time we may send out information about Black Lace books and special offers. Please tick here if you do <u>not</u> wish to receive Black Lace information.   ☐

Please send me the books I have ticked above.

Name ....

Address ....

....

....

....

Post Code ....

Send to: Virgin Books Cash Sales, Thames Wharf Studios,
Rainville Road, London W6 9HA.

US customers: for prices and details of how to order
books for delivery by mail, call 888-330-8477.

Please enclose a cheque or postal order, made payable
to Virgin Books Ltd, to the value of the books you have
ordered plus postage and packing costs as follows:

UK and BFPO – £1.00 for the first book, 50p for each
subsequent book.

Overseas (including Republic of Ireland) – £2.00 for
the first book, £1.00 for each subsequent book.

If you would prefer to pay by VISA, ACCESS/MASTERCARD,
DINERS CLUB, AMEX or SWITCH, please write your card
number and expiry date here:

....

Signature ....

Please allow up to 28 days for delivery.